CALLED LUCY

by Pierre Accoce and Pierre Quet

TRANSLATED BY A. M. SHERIDAN SMITH

Coward-McCann, Inc., New York

Illustrations follow page 126

Foreword to the American Edition

GREATER than Sorge? Greater than Cicero? These are only some of the cryptic claims made about the late Rudolf Roessler—a man called Lucy. Allen Dulles, in *The Craft of Intelligence*, remarks: *"The Soviets developed a fantastic source located in Switzerland, a certain Rudolf Roessler (code-name 'Lucy'). By means which have not been ascertained to this day, Roessler in Switzerland was able to get intelligence from the German High Command in Berlin on a continuous basis, often less than twenty-four hours after its daily decisions concerning the Eastern Front were made. . . ."*

Alexander Foote, himself a member of the Lucy ring, said in his book, *Handbook for Spies: "Lucy held in his hands the threads that led to the three high commands of the German forces. . . . The effect of his communications on the strategy of the Red Army and on the defeat of the Wehrmacht was incalculable."*

Ronald Seth, a British Intelligence agent, says in his book, *Unmasked: "Rudolf Roessler must be ranked among the great spies of all time."*

Even in a review of our own book (the French edition)

under the heading "Greater Than Sorge," the (London) *Times Literary Supplement* remarks: *"Of all the espionage networks active during the Second World War, the one which has received the most respectful admiration from professionals is the one operated from Lucerne between 1939 and 1943 by Rudolf Roessler, code name 'Lucy.' Neither Sorge nor Cicero, to quote the best known examples, can match his achievements."*

Who was this man called Lucy? Why, despite these fragmentary references, is so little known about him? How did we happen to pick up his trail? Like almost everything involved with this mysterious man, his tracks were well hidden—we stumbled across them almost by accident—and what we have attempted here is the first complete presentation of the greatest untold espionage story of World War II.

It is strange when a book changes subject in midstream. But this is what happened to ours. When we set out to write it, our subject was to be "Switzerland, 1939-1945." Hundreds of volumes had been published about the Second World War, but we were particularly struck by one gap. Very little seemed to have been written on the neutral countries; yet they too, in their own way, lived through the war. Their war did not take place on the battlefield, but in secret, through diplomatic pressure, unofficial agreements and exchanges of information.

Of all the European neutrals—Spain, Portugal, Sweden and Switzerland—it seemed to us that Switzerland offered the most interesting field for study. How had the five years of war affected the country? How did the Swiss feed and clothe themselves? What had been their economic and defense policies? Their relations with the French Resistance—and the Germans? These were some of the problems with which we were concerned. Now they are no more than the background to the book that we have, in fact, written.

As it now stands, and because of Rudolf Roessler, this is a story of espionage and resistance. When we first came across this aspect of our material on Switzerland our reaction was to put it aside. No, we were not going to end up writing another spy story. Naturally, we assumed that the Swiss Confederation—a neutral country surrounded on all sides by the Axis but maintaining relations with the Allies—must have been a prime battlefield for spies of every nationality. We knew that this tiny area contained more German agents per square yard than any other part of Europe. But who would have dreamed that Switzerland—jeopardizing her neutrality—would permit one of the most astounding anti-Nazi espionage networks of the war to operate on her territory? Yet the discovery would not leave us alone. It led us irresistibly from the frontiers of the Swiss Confederation to the heart of the German and Soviet High Commands.

Almost invariably, whenever we broached the subject of Roessler, we were met with evasiveness, silence, sometimes hostile refusal—and we knew we had run into the heart of the mystery surrounding the man called Lucy. For the deeper we dug, the more we began to sense that Roessler had not remained one of the most enigmatic figures of World War II purely by chance—history seemed to have *conspired* to keep him obscure.

In short, those best qualified to vouch for his invaluable contributions dared not admit they had any part of Roessler. Switzerland, for example. Determined at all costs to protect her "neutrality," would the Swiss, even after the war, announce to the world that they had sheltered a master spy on their home grounds—permitting him to conduct his operations in return for first look at his reports? Would Stalin, who gained so much vital information from Roessler, be willing to acknowledge that his vaunted reputation for military strategy stemmed largely from the communiqués of an obscure German émigré? On the other hand, Germany was, and still appears to be, equally protective about revealing a leak in the very heart of the High Command, a conspiracy of anti-Nazi "traitors" who were siphoning off top secrets and feeding them directly to the enemy.

This "conspiracy of silence" obtains, even with the Allied governments involved. The British, who, once Hitler was contained on the Russian front, received the brunt of Lucy's reports, claim to have placed little value on them. Then why did a British general declare upon Roessler's death that the man was worth "a dozen atom bombs"? What of the Americans' official silence on Lucy? Allen Dulles in his new book, *The Secret Surrender,* states: "What went on between Swiss Brigadier Colonel Roger Masson, head of Swiss Intelligence, and S.S. Brigadeführer Walter Schellenberg, head of the Nazi Secret Service [who both played such a part in the Roessler affair] I do not know to this day." Yet of a forthcoming official German history of World War II, the London *Sunday Telegraph* remarks that the volume dealing with German opposition in general and Roessler in particular "will, no doubt, be studied closely and with interest by the British Secret Service and the surviving members of the *American Office of Strategic Services.*"

Then there is the matter of Roessler's behavior, which was most unorthodox for the average "spy." Roessler was willing to supply his information on one condition—that the identity of his sources remain secret. As a result, for a long time his intelligence was discounted: how could it be assessed without knowing who was supplying it, where it was coming from? Only after repeated attempts and a long series of rebuffs did he manage to establish the value of his contacts, and this he

achieved only because of the uncanny accuracy of his information. Even then his motivation was suspect. Some chalked him
off as an *agent provocateur*, others as a German plant, still
others as a Russian spy; Paul Carrell states that Stalin prior to
the German invasion considered him a Western plant; everything, in other words, but the one theory that satisfied all the
facts and fitted the pieces together—and which we think is
one of the important disclosures of our book—that Roessler
was simply and clearly a deeply dedicated anti-Nazi. In short,
this man who posed as a Swiss bookseller and publisher was
the "spiritual conscience" of ten top German generals dedicated to Hitler's destruction who used Roessler as the instrument for transmitting secret intelligence directly to the Allies.
And what secrets they were!

A continuous flood of dispatches poured forth steadily from
Roessler for over *four years*, dispatches that totaled 12,000
typed pages, the equivalent of 40 average-size books. Here are
only some of the high-level disclosures attributed to Lucy:

The demilitarization of the Rhineland, the seizure of Austria,
the invasion of Poland precipitating World War II, the first
hint of the Nazis' "final solution" for the Jews, the invasion of
Holland, the invasion of Belgium, the invasions of northeastern
France and Luxembourg, the invasion of Denmark, the invasion of Norway, the first mention of the V-1 and V-2 rockets,
progress reports on German jet plane development.

And, transcending even those astonishing revelations: advance warnings and complete battle plans of Operation Barbarossa—Hitler's second-front attack on his former ally Russia!
All this was followed by almost daily communiqués giving detailed military operations, breakdowns of men and matériel;
often the Russians were provided with German plans in less
than twelve hours. (In one instance, in an assault on Lomzha,

the German commander overran the Russian position and found a copy of his own attack orders.)

Colonel Friedrich Hossbach, staff officer and Wehrmacht delegate to Hitler from 1934-38, had spoken in *Zwischen Wehrmacht und Hitler* of "those who had betrayed secrets concerning military operations and sabotaged our military strength." Paul Carell noted in *Opération Barbarossa:* "Hitler's secrets were strewn all over the Kremlin table. Berlin was naturally bowled over to learn how accurately the Soviet agent in Switzerland was informing Moscow, and the Germans tried to discover the source. Who could have been so up to date concerning the plans of the German High Command? And become familiar with them within a day or so? The Nazis never found out. And even today no one knows."

Roessler went to his grave without revealing the names of his sources to anyone—neither to the Swiss, the Russians nor the other Allied powers. Schellenberg, assigned by Heydrich to track them down, had been obsessed by the question of their identities; and more than twenty years later we found ourselves in the same position. We began very simply by going to the Swiss Embassy in Paris, where we explained our mission to the cultural attaché, M. Bischoff, an obliging man who agreed to obtain the necessary introductions for us in Switzerland. From that moment on, our inquiry in Switzerland was conducted on two levels: first, we interviewed Swiss businessmen, journalists and officials who had survived the war; second, we sought out the key man who had interested Schellenberg, Brigadier Colonel Roger Masson, wartime head of Swiss Intelligence, with whom M. Bischoff had put us in touch through the air attaché at the Swiss Embassy in Paris. Seventy years of age, affable and cordial, Masson told us what he had told Schellenberg: nothing. It was about eight months before we realized that although he talked freely—and at great length—about his wartime service, each time we touched on Rudolf Roessler, Masson entirely evaded our questions. But—and this proved to be enough—one day when he had had a bit too much wine, he did reveal that the head of the spy ring in Berlin was a general in charge of transportation. By closely studying the organizational charts of the Oberkommando of the Wehrmacht, we were able to give this general a name.

In the meantime, having determined that the Roessler affair was obviously of enormous importance and that the Swiss, like the Allies, were suspiciously reticent on the subject, we resolved to alter our method of investigation—to abandon the Swiss officials and attempt to arrive at the truth about Rudolf Roessler by other means. We then got in touch with highly placed members of the French secret service, who had lived through the war in the resistance or in espionage and who knew a great deal about the Roessler affair. Contacts like these were extraordinarily difficult to establish, and it was only due to the backing of the office of the President of the French Republic, where we had close colleagues, that we made them at all. When we proposed the German general's name, they indeed confirmed our guess. (Our technique with our contacts in the British secret service, with whom we also had good relations, was identical. They never volunteered information, only replied to our questions. Often we had to wait weeks, sometimes months, before getting satisfaction on a particular point, but by and large they did not evade us.) It was thanks to these contacts that we were able to identify, beyond any doubt, the ten "traitors"—a spy ring at the heart of the OKW in Berlin, so secret that it had managed to survive all of Hitler's successive purges, including the wholesale reprisals taken after the unmasking of the July plot of 1944.

Parallel to our interviews with the secret services, we had direct contact with surviving members of the Lucy Ring. The Swiss officials were not helpful, and it was only by checking and cross-checking information that we succeeded in obtaining their addresses. At our first meeting, Roessler's colleagues, who still operate his publishing house, the Vita Nova Verlag, in Lucerne, were very wary. Joseph Stocker, manager of the Vita Nova bookshop, was visibly distraught when he learned that we intended to write a book about Roessler. "Who are you? What are your credentials?" he demanded. "Rudolf Roessler was a saint—do you hear?—a saint. After the war we were besieged by representatives of the secret services of every country. We've had enough!" When he discovered that we were only journalists, working for a publishing house and sympathetic to Roessler, he grew calmer and telephoned Xavier Schnieper, one of Roessler's close friends during the war. Schnieper set up the first of many meetings we had with him. It was he who led us to Roessler's grave and provided, in the months that followed, the principal facts on the Lucy Ring's method of operation. However, unaware that we had already learned their identities, he told us that Roessler had entrusted the names of his sources in Berlin to only one person, his son, who had been killed two years earlier in an automobile accident.

Later, we met Tamara Duebendorfer and her husband, Jean Louis Vigier, one of France's greatest living mathematicians. Tamara is the daughter of Rachel Duebendorfer, who, with Alexander Rado and Paul Boetcher, was a member of the Communist intelligence ring to which Roessler turned when he desperately needed a means of sending vital intelligence out of Switzerland to Moscow. Through Tamara, who now lives in

Paris and has broken with the Party, we learned that her mother and Boetcher are today living in Leipzig, where Boetcher is editor in chief of the *Leipziger Zeitung* and Rachel is mentally disturbed, perhaps even insane.

We also interviewed Edmond Hamel, one of the three radio operators who transmitted to Moscow the intelligence from Roessler that Rado gave him after having it coded by Rachel Duebendorfer. Today Hamel has a radio shop on the rue de Carrouges in Geneva. He told us that during the most important campaigns of the war in the East, he often broadcasted for entire nights, from midnight to eight o'clock in the morning. Hamel is a voluble little man who lives entirely in his past, without ever having understood precisely what it was he was broadcasting or exactly how vital it was to the Russian victory in the East.

Finally, we located Roessler's wife, Olga, living in Augsburg with her sister, who, ironically enough, is married to a former Nazi. Mrs. Roessler lives in wretched circumstances, since the German government gave her no reparation for the destruction of their home at Templehof, near Berlin; she is sustained only by the memory of her husband. An immensely cultivated woman, she has had to endure a good deal of unpleasantness at the hands of local merchants ("Here is the wife of the traitor") since the publication of our book. Of all the hundreds of people we interviewed on the trail of the man called Lucy, Olga Roessler was—understandably enough—the most reserved.

Supplied with all this information—information enabling us to reconstruct the activities of the Lucy Ring in great detail— we got in touch once more with Brigadier Colonel Masson. This time, we explained the full scope of our book. Now he immediately understood that the wartime role of his country, as portrayed in our book, was to be different from its official version. Masson abruptly closed his files and announced that he had nothing further to tell us.

Confirmation of the Swiss government's official position was quickly forthcoming. The day after our final interview with Masson, we telephoned Colonel Rosset, chief of the Sureté of the Canton of Vaud who was, during the war, an important member of the counterespionage service. "I know your scheme," he told us, "and I have nothing to say to you. I understand that you met yesterday with Brigadier Colonel Masson, but I tell you today that the Swiss authorities will no longer cooperate with you." In fact, they did continue to cooperate, but they kept us under close surveillance on each of our many trips into Switzerland. Strange solicitude; they even investigated our private lives to see if they could find any pretext whatsoever to prevent us from entering Swiss territory. As a high official in the Swiss police told one of our colleagues who inquired about the official attitude toward us: "No, no, you can tell your friends that they can always come to Switzerland; they are always welcome. Besides, we have found nothing with which to charge them: they pay their taxes, they have never been in prison, and they are not homosexuals.

Our investigations concluded and the activities of the Lucy Ring fully revealed at last, we realized that we could not disclose the names of Roessler's sources to the public: Germany lost millions of soldiers on the Eastern Front, and vengeance-crazed men are still to be feared. Nothing could happen to the officers themselves, for all of them are dead; but their families might conceivably be in serious danger.

Today we are more than glad that we observed such prudence. Shortly after the publication of our book in France, a furor broke out in Germany. The neo-Nazi party, whose success in the last elections in Hamburg and Bavaria surprised political observers, had seized upon the affair, demanding that light be shed on it and the names of the "traitors" be revealed. A journalist for *Die Welt* has already named several who he thinks belonged to that incredible plot, doubtless the only conspiracy that struggled against Nazism from the beginning of the conflict until the very end. And in the columns of the *Times Literary Supplement*, several months before our book was to be published in England, a spirited debate broke out concerning individual generals, even though we tried to disguise full names.

"It looks as though the explanation of Roessler's 'fantastic' success is found at last," remarked the *Times Literary Supplement* after our book did appear in England. Although we devoted two and a half years to intensive research, interviewed more than 150 people (some of them more than ten times) and traveled more than 30,000 miles in our pursuit of the man called Lucy, it is also true that even we cannot deny the "fantastic" nature of some of our findings. How else would one describe the relentless cat-and-mouse game played by Schellenberg and Masson; the sophisticated triangulation and "radiogoniometric" devices used by the Germans *and the Swiss* to pinpoint the transmitting stations of the Lucy Ring (known in Switzerland as the Viking Line); the day Lucy's code was broken because a German expert happened to remember the name of the hero in one of Jack London's novels; Roessler's staggering Christmas present to Stalin—one of the greatest intelligence coups in history—the complete plans of Operation Barbarossa (the Nazi invasion of Russia), only nine copies of which were in existence—a "present" that took Roessler's network over twelve hours to decode and forty-eight hours to transmit; Schellenberg's diabolic plan to mount a full-scale "invasion" of Switzerland—just to confirm the reality of Roessler. And the pathetic ending to the career of probably the world's greatest spy— captured and jailed in the postwar years for leaking "intelligence" available to anyone in an ordinary bookstore.

Over the years, bits and pieces of the "fantastic" jigsaw puzzle of Rudolf Roessler have cropped up, but now for the first time we have assembled all the pieces in a single book. Here as best we can, we have attempted to present in some semblance of coherence and continuity the logical chain of events that led this obscure political journalist and World War I officer into the role of master spy of World War II.

Gathering these facts was a major effort; rarely has a man's life been so surrounded with obscurity and contradiction. Disagreements still arise over such commonplace facts as his birthplace and religion (some news reports describe him as Catholic). As with so many other key figures in the story, who have either died or vanished, Roessler himself is dead. He died in Switzerland in 1958, too impoverished to have made provision for his funeral, the costs of which had to be borne by an anonymous donor. Schellenberg and Guisan are dead. Rado, chief of Russian Intelligence (the Center) in Switzerland, now lives behind the Iron Curtain (although many newspaper accounts have reported him executed). Foote, who has written about what he knows of Roessler—he met him in person only once—lived in England (where he was variously reported working for British Intelligence and living the life of a simple clerk) until his death in 1958.

The story we were finally able to track down was so complex, it ranged over such a broad sweep of time and geography that, to give it the greatest possible unity, we have presented it almost as a narrative, even colloquially in some instances, while always carefully adhering to the facts as we knew them.

Only in this way, we felt, could we incorporate all our research, all the important side issues that cast vital new light on this fantastic story.

This, then, is our reconstruction of the man who was described by a British general as "having contributed more to our victory in Europe than could have a dozen atom bombs." A man who may have cost Hitler World War II. Certainly and unquestionably one of the master spies of all time.

Rudolf Roessler—a man called Lucy.

PIERRE ACCOCE
PIERRE QUET

A MAN CALLED LUCY

1

THIS resistance story differs from all others in some important respects: it is entirely lacking in conventional romance, no *femme fatales*. The few women who do move into its periphery and out again are indistinguishable from the men they work with. There are no extraordinary raids, carried out by invincible supermen. It is a story of resistance and espionage in the raw.

The few strategists who know of this remarkable affair have been asking themselves since the end of the war: without the intervention of the men who made up the Lucy Ring, would Hitler have failed to take Moscow? Or Stalingrad? Might he not have won the war? No one, in fact, was better placed than they to have a decisive influence on the outcome of battles or on the eventual fate of whole armies. For these men, a mere handful of Germans, high-ranking officers, attached to army headquarters, were members of the Oberkommando of the Wehrmacht.

Their motive for what undeniably constituted a major act of treason was a potent one. These patriotic German soldiers abhorred Nazism and hated the Führer.

All the other plots against Hitler, now so well known, failed utterly—and for one fundamental reason. Their instigators were hesitant men, terrified of their own decisions, aging soldiers hypnotized by the Nazi phenomenon.

A case in point was the bomb plot of July 20, 1944. General Friedrich Fromm and General Otto Herfurth, past masters in the art of not compromising themselves, turned against their fellow-conspirators the day before, hoping to avoid the fury they were helping to unleash. It was Fromm who arrested Hoepner, Olbricht, Stauffenberg, Haeften and Mertz. He drove the elderly General Beck to suicide. He organized a court-martial, "in the name of Hitler," and in the headlights of a military car, in the courtyard of the OKW headquarters in the Beudlerstrasse, Berlin, had the arrested officers shot on the spot. But this double betrayal spared neither Herfurth nor Fromm. The first was hanged at Ploetzensee prison. The second avoided the scaffold, but was shot on March 19, 1945.

In the affair with which we are concerned here, there was no ostentation—just a slow, infinitely painstaking determination and effectiveness. These officers of the Oberkommando of the Wehrmacht were fighting not only Hitler but also his mystique, the mystique of the swastika. They knew that their double struggle, waged with all the strength at their command, would inevitably bring about the defeat of Germany, their Germany. They would continue to work together until Germany lay in ruins around them, until the last vestiges of the Nazi monster had been eradicated. They would then take leave of one another and not meet again. They would no longer have a nation of their own, but at least they would have exorcised its demon.

None of them expected glory. In their eyes, it was a family affair—dirty linen to be washed in private. This is why it took twenty years before the truth came out. For as soon as their work was done, these Germans retreated at once into anonymity

—a judicious precaution. Anonymity alone preserved them from the ever-active Nazi survivors of the holocaust, among them the mysterious General Reinhard Gehlen, now head of the West German secret service.

The work of these men, which was to become the most fascinating resistance and espionage affair of the Second World War, began many years before the war itself, as early, in fact, as Easter Sunday, April 17, 1922.

Only the month before, Joseph Stalin, the new General Secretary of the Soviet Communist Party, had assumed the leadership of the USSR: it was his task to carry out the plans laid down by Lenin. At Rapallo, an ancient watering place on the Genoese Gulf of the Italian Riviera, on that same April 17, Germany and the Soviet Republic signed a treaty, reestablishing diplomatic relations between the two countries. Nicolai Krestinski, an ex-lawyer, would represent the Soviets in Berlin. The distinguished Count Brockdorff-Rantzau would go to Moscow as the ambassador of the frail Weimar Republic, presided over by Friedrich Ebert.

Germany had just lost the Great War. A serious crisis threatened the country. Inflation galloped ahead as the Reichsbank printed bank notes with an ever-larger format and an ever-increasing number of zeros. The dollar was finally worth 4,200 milliard marks, until Dr. Jans Luther, the Finance Minister, and Dr. Hjalmar Schacht, the President of the Reichsbank, succeeded in 1924 in stabilizing the German currency. Throughout the country, the "reparations" demanded by the Allies caused bitterness and protest.

The USSR, cut off from the world since the creation of its Communist regime, was hardly better off. It refused to acknowledge the obligations of Imperial Russia or the debts of Tsar Nicolas II. Its economy was suffocating. For the West, after trying unsuccessfully to overthrow the regime by military intervention, now intended to strangle it with a naval blockade.

At Rapallo a defeated and resentful Germany and a precarious USSR recognized each other as equals. They decided to grant one another priority in all commercial transactions. America and Europe might ridicule this union of the blind and the halt, this "alliance of poor devils," as Paul Carell called it in his *Operation Barbarossa*. Yet Rapallo broke the diplomatic and economic isolation of Europe's down-and-out countries. Their transactions were to develop and help set them on their feet. The Soviet Union would buy machines from German firms. Their engineers and business representatives would travel continuously between Moscow and Berlin. German technicians would get good jobs in Soviet mines and electrical installations. Gradually, the Allies would learn that this pact was not as foolhardy as they had thought. But they would have shuddered indeed had they discovered what was actually going on between Germany and Russia.

Since Rapallo had enabled the two countries to break the quarantine imposed on them by other nations, they resolved to apply its spirit and letter to more serious matters—the military blockade, as far as the USSR was concerned, and the prohibitions of the Treaty of Versailles in the case of Germany. The Red Army lacked troops and method. No military school would agree to provide it with the necessary training. Germany had neither tanks nor heavy guns, neither an air force nor a navy. Its tiny army, limited to 100,000 men, was unable to train properly. Meanwhile, in Moscow, Karl Radek was conceiving a coalition that would surreptitiously blow open the locked doors of the West:

"Place the experience of German officers at the disposal of the new Soviet army; and help rebuild the completely demolished Russian war machine. In exchange, the Soviet Union will manufacture the arms forbidden the Reichswehr, and the Reichswehr will then use them to train on Russian soil."

Radek was a journalist on *Izvestia*. He was a brilliant expartriate, born in Poland, and regarded by Leon Trotsky as his closest colleague. Newly appointed the director of Soviet propaganda, he was already calling for "the struggle of the Comintern against the Treaty of Versailles and against the capitalist offensive."

In Moscow, supporters of Stalin were spreading the rumor that Radek's brilliant scheme had been suggested to him by Colonel Nicolai, head of the Reichswehr intelligence service and a great friend of Trotsky. Both Trotsky and Radek were strongly suspected of deviationism. But such political differences were not, at the moment, of the greatest importance. What mattered was that the Red Army should obtain as soon as possible the units it disastrously lacked. So, in Berlin, the Soviet ambassador, Nicolai Krestinski, made discreet approaches to General Hans von Seeckt, the head of the Reichswehr, and to Otto Gessler, the German Defense Minister. A flow of secret agreements resulted.

Each year, until 1930, a third of the annual budget of the Reichswehr, plus 120 million "stablized" marks, went into a strange cartel: the *Gesellschaft zur Förderung gewerblichen Unternehmen,* the Industrial Enterprises Development Corporation. From its two offices, one in Berlin and a second, more important one in Moscow, it dealt directly with the Soviet government and had a number of subcontracting branches throughout the Soviet Union. Junker planes were produced at

Fili and Samara, on the border of Central Siberia; shells at Tula and Slatoust; poison gas at Krasnogvardeisk; submarines and even a battleship in the shipyards of Leningrad.

Moreover, three large training bases were prepared for the use of the German army. Two of these, at Lipetsk, and Voronezh were intended for the air force. The third, at Kazan, on the middle reaches of the Volga, was for the tank corps. It was there that the "black" Reichswehr carried out its exercises—20,000 strong in all, chosen from among the best combatants of the Great War to be the future officers and noncommissioned officers of the Wehrmacht. Before leaving for Russia, each of these soldiers had his name "erased" from the army lists. On his return, he would quite simply be reinstated—a cunning camouflage.

It was a fantastic undertaking. Prototypes of planes and tanks, developed in Germany's secret workshops, went, in parts, to the USSR, via the free port of Stettin. They were unloaded in Leningrad, assembled and tested; finally, they were mass-produced in Soviet factories. The first "Jabos" fighter-bombers, the prototype of the "Stukas" and the future Focke-Wulf were all developed on the banks of the Don and used in Red Army exercises.

It was also from Stettin that the troops of the "black" Reichswehr set off for Russia. And to Stettin, in hermetically sealed zinc containers, were brought the remains of those German soldiers killed in the rigorous training exercises. This remarkable organization was the work of General Kurt von Schleicher. Without Lipetsk, Hermann Goering would never have been able to muster all the élite pilots that were to transform the Luftwaffe into such a formidable force. Without Kazan, the armored divisions of Heinz Guderian, Erich Hoepner and

Hermann Hoth would never have acquired the attack that was to make them the spearhead of the Wehrmacht.

On the other hand, the young Soviet soldiers, selected to become commanding officers, and the political commissars, chosen for the same reasons, trained side by side with the cadets of the Reichswehr. Side by side they learned the art of war by studying the theories of men like Moltke, Clausewitz and Ludendorff. The governments of the two countries pursued different political aims, but, in the field, their soldiers were on excellent terms.

General von Seeckt, embittered by the Treaty of Versailles, which he labeled a calamity, cherished a plan of revenge: to strike Poland. With this country, an outpost of France in eastern Europe, one of the important pillars of that detested peace would collapse. But to achieve it, he needed the help of the Russians.

Von Seeckt's scheme, and the strongly anti-Western spirit that motivated it, delighted the head of the Red Army, Marshal Mikael Tukhachevsky, and its potential high command, Generals Yakir, Kork, Uborevich and Feldman, who were later to fall with him in Stalin's purges. Tukhachevsky believed von Seeckt and was unreservedly in favor of his plan, because Poland was an embarrassment to Russia too, and also because his high command, who professed an almost servile admiration for German militarism, considered that an alliance between Germany and the Western powers was to be prevented at all costs. A new armed intervention of this kind would place Russia in mortal danger.

It is easy to understand why no Russian or German military leader could conceive the possibility, let alone the plan, of a Germano-Soviet war before Hitler came to power. Such a conflict would have been regarded as fratricide between two high commands that had grown up together.

One man was to make an objective inquiry into pro-Russian feeling in the German army, among the Junker caste and the officer corps, after the First World War—Walter Schellenberg. In 1937, Reinhard Heydrich, head of the Sicherheits-dienst, the SS Security Service, or SD, whom Schellenberg was to replace five years later, gave him the job of making a study of past relations between the Reichswehr and the Red Army.

"These relations were marked," Schellenberg wrote, "by what I shall call the *spirit of Tauroggen*. I am referring to the alliance directed against Napoleon in 1812, between the Prussian general, Yorck von Wartenburg, and the Russian army, signed in the village of Tauroggen in East Prussia despite the express orders of the king of Prussia. It is interesting to note that the Prussian military resistance to Napoleon had been prepared (by Baron von Stein and Clausewitz) in Russia, where they had found refuge under the protection of the Tsar. Co-operation with Russia was of vital importance for the implementation of Bismarck's foreign policy. The treaty of Rapallo marked a return to this policy."

The spirit of Tauroggen—this was the spirit motivating that group of officers who, at the heart of the Oberkommando of the Wehrmacht, were to work for the destruction of Hitler and Nazism. There were eleven of them in all. They were Bavarians and Protestants: all from families in which, traditionally, only two careers could be considered, the civil service and the army.

Their names are known to very few. To make them public would, even today, bring the opprobrium of the new Germany upon their families, even, perhaps, expose them to serious reprisals. There must be many people in West Germany who believe that these men who hampered the operations of the Wehrmacht—out of hatred for Nazism—stabbed the German combatants in the back, causing incalculable losses of both men and materials. This is why we shall reveal only the initials of these enemies of the "Brown" revolution, confirming only the identity of their leader—Rudolf Roessler—because he devoted his entire life to the struggle against the Nazi mystique.

Nothing predisposed Rudolf Roessler to conspiracy—or to treason, as some would have it—any more than it did his ten companions. Helmuth S., Hermann F., Rudolf G., Fritz T. and Georg T. were to become generals. O. became a colonel and K. a major. The last three, S., A. and O., reached the rank of captain.

Although he had not chosen, like the other ten, to become a career officer, Rudolf Roessler came from the same background, the same social class. His was one of those conventional, middle-class German families, hostile to any spirit of adventure; to them, order means bread and disorder famine. The Roesslers came from Kaufbeuren, a former imperial free city, medieval in atmosphere, but then one of Bavaria's industrial centers, situated on the Wertach, with a population of 23,000. The father, a local dignitary and a senior civil servant in the Ministry of Waters and Forests, brought his children up in the Protestant faith. Rudolf's elder brother studied law and became a public prosecutor; his sister became a teacher at the Gymnasium in Augsburg, also in Bavaria.

Rudolf Roessler first met his ten companions at the front during the First World War and they became close friends. The other ten were from one of those military academies where young cadets were turned into loyal and efficient officers and where individualists soon learned conformity—where, too, a good grounding in literature and philosophy was provided. Admiring his extensive knowledge and his artistic tastes, they readily adopted this "civilian," who had volunteered at the age of seventeen. Roessler was to become their intellectual leader and their contact with real life. He was to show them horizons wider than those of the barrack walls.

Then came defeat—a time of doubt and despair. The German army was broken up, humiliated, and fell into the hands of soldiers' commitees. Institutions seemed to collapse around them. The Weimar Republic tottered between the thrusts of the extreme right and the extreme left. *Coups d'état* followed one after another, violent and short-lived. In Berlin the Red Week alone caused 1,200 deaths between March 4 and 13, 1919. In Munich, the headquarters of the Communist Party went up in flames. The fall of the mark ruined the middle classes, while gigantic trusts, like that of Hugo Stinnes, were being established.

A new right-wing movement, much more extreme than any that had appeared so far, was born in Bavaria: National Socialism. At its head were some extremely dubious characters— Dietrich Eckart, a journalist; an ex-sergeant major, Max Amann; two other soldiers, Rudolf Hess, an ex-lieutenant, and Ernst Roehm, an ex-captain, flanked an ex-corporal, a soapbox orator named Adolf Hitler. Most of Hitler's support came from the workers, for his fanaticism only alarmed the middle classes. Five years of fear and chaos followed, until the death in 1925 of the President, Friedrich Ebert, and his succession by the reassuring figure of Marshal Paul von Hindenburg, the very symbol of tradition. The various right-wing groups united behind him. Meanwhile, Hitler was building up his forces.

Rudolf Roessler was a small, thin, quiet man, but his eyes were bright, intelligent and his expression mobile. He wore thin-

rimmed glasses. Violence horrified him, and after leaving the
army, he had become a pacifist, while still retaining his right-
wing opinions. But he no longer hoped that society could be re-
formed without revolutionary methods. The rise of Nazism,
which he had carefully observed and analyzed, terrified him.
Germany was asleep, enveloped in a false sense of security—
after all, hadn't the Allies evacuated the Ruhr? And wasn't pros-
perity returning by leaps and bounds? Roessler decided that
at all costs he must try and awaken his fellow-countrymen to the
danger within. He joined the Augsburg *Post Zeitung* as a journalist and became the scourge of Nazism. Meeting his army
friends more frequently than ever before, he took part with
them in the great processions organized by the *Stahlhelm*, the
"Steel Helmet." He tried to communicate to them his fear of
the "Brown" revolution, but they gently ridiculed his appre-
hensions.

They were members of the Reichswehr. When, in 1920, General von Seeckt tried to save the Weimar Republic by depriving
the army of all political influence, they signed on for twelve
years which allowed them to be among the "Hundred Thousand." Didn't the Reichswehr—that haven of peace and discipline—harbor enough enemies of disorder? The Nazis were
powerless. They had been crushed in 1923.

Had Roessler forgotten? While he had been fighting the
Brownshirts with his pen, they had fought them in the street.
They had been among the troops who had encircled Roehm,
Chief of the Sturmabteilung (the S.A., or Storm Section of the
Party) in the War Ministry, in the Schoenfeldstrasse in Munich,
at the time of Hitler's abortive putsch in November. The Nazi
Party was dissolved, then made legal again, and now, they in-
sisted, it was dying out. At the last election, it had received less
than a million votes: 12 seats out of 491 in the Reichstag.

They urged Roessler not to worry. Hitler's insane ideas would not catch on. They confided that, although General von Seeckt had forbidden his soldiers to participate in elections, they had other, far more effective ways of working for the revival of Germany's great past. One after another, they were to leave for Russia, for Lipetsk and Kazan, where they would train with weapons that the Reichswehr were "forbidden" to possess.

This prospect of a national revival did not quiet Rudolf Roessler's fears. While not severing his ties with his army friends, he took refuge in the study of theology and other subjects. He became a friend of Nikolai Berdyaev, the Russian philosopher of freedom, a critic of rationalism, who was deeply concerned for the spiritual condition of modern man. He also met Karl Barth, the Swiss theologian, then professor at the University of Münster, in Westphalia.

Finally, Roessler became secretary of the *Bühnenvolksbund*, an organization devoted to the development of the theater, and director of the magazine, *Das National Theater*, in Berlin. Meanwhile, his ten military friends had all obtained good positions at the Reichswehr's headquarters. And it was through them that Roessler's intellectual influence reached its peak, when he was invited to join the very select *Herrenklub*, in the Vosstrasse in Berlin. Up until the crisis that overtook the Reichswehr in 1930, Rudolf Roessler was to give no fewer than two thousand lectures there.

With the Wall Street crash, the Weimar Republic stood once again on the verge of ruin. Its economy, based on American loans and on exports, collapsed. Unemployment mounted. The army received its first great setback.

On September 20, 1930, the ten friends of "R.R.," as they called Roessler among themselves, finally woke up. They had been deaf to his innumerable warnings, but suddenly, on that

day, the ground collapsed from beneath them. There was to be
an important trial before the Leipzig Supreme Court: three lieutenants from the garrison at Ulm, Wilhelm Scheringer, Wendt
and Hans Ludin, were accused of spreading Nazi propaganda
within the Reichswehr. Membership in Hitler's party was
enough to exclude any prospective soldier from membership in
the "Hundred Thousand." This had been decided by General
von Seeckt. His edict also included civilians working in the ar-
senals and military stores. There were to be no Fascists in the
army. Yet, despite this, the officer corps, particularly its younger
elements, had become contaminated. But Scheringer, Wendt
and Ludin were also accused of a much more serious crime:
high treason. They had tried to persuade their fellow soldiers
not to open fire on Hitler's supporters in the event of an armed
uprising.

General Wilhelm Groener, the Defense Minister, wanted to
have the lieutenants brought before a simple court-martial, in
order to avoid unsavory publicity. But Scheringer had secretly
alerted the *Völkischer Beobachter*, the Nazi newspaper. Everything would take place in the open, and the trial would reveal
how far the gangrene had already advanced.

Adolf Hitler, summoned as a witness for the defense, could
hardly have hoped for a better public platform. He had long
been waiting for an opportunity to dissipate the mistrust the
Reichswehr instinctively felt toward him. He would captivate
the army with his favorite tactic, the lie. The fate of the three
young lieutenants was of little concern to him compared with
his larger aim—securing the support of the officer corps. He
would simply disown his three disciples, in order to reassure
the others.

"These three young men were quite wrong," he declared, "to
believe that we would ever contemplate armed rebellion. We

will use only constitutional means to gain power. I will never fight the army. Quite the contrary. When the government of our country is in my hands—which will be in a matter of months— I shall regard you, gentlemen, as the essential nucleus from which the great army of the German people will emerge."

Lost among the crowd of military spectators, Roessler's friends were struck with terror at the hypnotic power of this street politician's arguments, while around them their colleagues were swiftly seduced by Hitler's reassurances.

In that troubled time, most of the soldiers of the Reichswehr lacked both confidence and a sense of purpose. Many were beginning to wonder whether this National Socialism, which was regarded as a danger, and which claimed to be capable of assuming the destiny of the nation, might not after all be what the German people needed to restore their country's former greatness—and to shake off the humiliating shackles imposed on them by the Treaty of Versailles. As if he guessed the hopes of his audience, Hitler went on:

"Germany is bound hand and foot by the peace treaties. We National Socialists do not regard these treaties as having the force of law. They were imposed upon us. We cannot allow that our sons, who are innocent, remain under this yoke. If we protest these treaties, with every means at our disposal, we will find ourselves on the road to revolution."

Hitler declaimed his speech, one hand on his heart, the other brandished with clenched fist. It had its effect. A cold shudder passed through the courtroom, followed by tumultuous applause. The minutes of the trial leave no doubt of this. Looking back, it seems inconceivable that the Leipzig judges could have tolerated such an outburst. But the event must be seen in its historical context. Perhaps they too were moved by Hitler's speech. Most of the audience on that occasion were deeply impressed and felt suddenly well-disposed toward a political movement that declared itself ready, according to its leader, to support the army, instead of sapping its strength as they had feared. Hitler restrained his delight. He had taken the Reichswehr in completely. They would pay for it later, en masse.

The sentences passed on the three condemned lieutenants, eighteen months each, satisfied no one. For those who sympathized with Hitler, they were too heavy; for the others, far too light. If the judges had acted with greater severity, respecting the rules and discipline of the Reichswehr, they would have done much to revive the army's confidence. It would no doubt have recovered quickly enough from the shock it had experienced while listening to Hitler. The hesitancy of the Leipzig judges completely demoralized the army. It was hopelessly divided by the activities of the ever more numerous and arrogant supporters of Hitler. Even General von Seeckt himself, though later deprived of his functions, was temporarily a Hitler backer and insisted that his sister vote for the ex-corporal rather than for Marshal Hindenburg.

On the evening of September 20, 1930, Roessler and his small circle sized up the situation. They now felt certain that, exasperated by the weaknesses of the Weimar Republic and with nothing in their bellies, the German people were willing to embark on an era of madness. They would make the worst possible choice, Nazism, the negation of German culture. They would give their support to men who had no coherent or rational philosophy and who would act as merciless butchers. Hitler had said as much during the Leipzig trial. It had slipped out during his interrogation by the president of the tribunal:

"I can assure you that when the National Socialist Movement is victorious, there will be a national socialist court of justice. Our revolution will take its revenge and heads will fall!"

No reasonable man could lend his support to these future masters of Germany, thought Roessler's friends. On the contrary, he should fight ruthlessly against them.

Little time remained for them to prepare their secret resistance, to work out their plans in detail. Events were rushing ahead. Thirty-four months after the Leipzig trial, on July 14, 1933, the Nazi Party, now completely in power in Germany, issued a decree:

"The National Socialist Party of German Workers is the only legal political party in Germany. Whoever tries to preserve or found any other political party will be condemned to a maximum sentence of three years' hard labor or from six months to three years in prison, unless the crime is punishable by more serious penalities under the terms of other laws."

Hitler had triumphed, destroying all legal opposition. A month later, in August, 1933, Rudolf Roessler met a young Swiss citizen in Berlin: Xavier Schnieper. Schnieper was twenty-three years old, the son of an important magistrate in the canton of Lucerne. Because of his left-wing ideas he was regarded as the black sheep of the family. He was studying for his doctorate in philosophy and was passionately concerned over the upheavals that he foresaw in Europe. Anyone, he maintained, could see what would happen merely by analyzing the Nazis' rise to power. And there was no better vantage point than Berlin. It was there that he became friendly with the director of the revue *Das National Theater*, which was rather too right-wing for his tastes. But he liked Rudolf Roessler himself, that fiercely independent man who was forever repeating Luther's words, "I am standing and cannot do otherwise."

Schnieper soon realized, however, from his frequent conversations with Roessler, that he was capable of far more than writing articles for a theater revue. Of how much, he did not yet know. But it was he who suggested to Roessler that he go and settle in Switzerland, where he would be safe. Roessler did not hesitate. With his wife, Olga, and only ten marks in his pocket—the most one was allowed to take out of Germany at that time—he boarded the train for Lucerne. What did money matter? Peace of mind would make their exile less bitter.

When all the officers of the army high command were compelled shortly afterwards to take the oath of allegiance to the Führer, before General Werner von Fritsch, in the great hall of the Reichswehr Ministry in Berlin, Roessler's ten friends did not reveal themselves. But at the same time, silently, they each made another promise: to do everything in their power to defeat Hitler and Nazism. Germany was entering its dark night of madness. Yet a delicate thread linked the ten officers to the free world, to light. At the end of this thread was their friend Rudolf. Some six hundred miles away, he waited, ready to be of use.

2

FROM 1934 on, Rudolf and Olga Roessler lived in a small flat in Wesemlin, a suburb of Lucerne, two and a half miles from the city center. Every morning, punctually at seven-thirty, Roessler would arrive at a small publishing house situated among the winding streets of the old town. The Vita Nova Verlag, of which he was the manager until his death in 1958, was founded by a group of his Swiss friends. Its offices at 36 Fluhmattstrasse no longer exist, but Roessler's colleagues still live in Lucerne today.

Day after day, with obstinate patience, Roessler devoted himself to his task. In article after article, pamphlet after pamphlet, he laid bare the ravages that Nazism was inflicting on Germany. The "ammunition" for his writings came, of course, from Berlin. Almost every day, he received a letter from one of his German friends, in which confidential intelligence was concealed in apparently innocent gossip. Sometimes, too, one of the ten would come and visit Roessler in Lucerne.

Thanks to them, Roessler "announced" in his pamphlets a month in advance the Wehrmacht's intended occupation on March 7, 1936, of the demilitarized zone of the Rhineland. He exposed the events leading up to the fall of General von Fritsch and the seizure of Austria. But above all he published political analyses in which he revealed the true nature of the new, aggressive, prosperous Germany that so impressed the Western democracies.

Roessler and his ten friends could not accept as their own this new Germany that arrested thousands of Catholic priests and Protestant pastors, that disbanded the Christian youth movements and forbade the publication of any works of a spiritual nature, that burned tens of thousands of books "poisoning the roots of German thought," that controlled every sphere of the country's cultural life, that excluded the Jews from artistic activity and destroyed 6,500 works of art which the Nazis regarded as decadent. They attacked the Nazification of education, the falsification of history and the degeneration of the sciences. They hated this regime that banned non-Nazi newspapers, turned journalists into mouthpieces for the Propaganda Ministry and exercised strict control over the film industry. They bitterly criticized a Germany that returned to a feudalized system of agriculture in which the peasant was confined to his piece of land and his work rigorously controlled; that reduced the industrial worker to the level of a serf, controlled the movement of labor and increased income tax; that had Nazified its entire civil service and juridical profession; that had set up the dreadful People's Courts and had opened fifty concentration camps since 1934.

Swiss readers might well be astonished by the revelations of this inexhaustible anti-Fascist who signed himself R. A. Hermes. Why Hermes? Hermes was the son of Zeus, but much more to the point, he was the messenger of the gods; the choice of name was no accident. From about the middle of 1939 onward, Roessler's role as messenger was suddenly to take on quite different proportions—so different and so vital that his previous literary work was to seem of comparatively small moment. On May 23, in Berlin, an event took place that was to have profound historical significance.

That day the Führer called a meeting of his army chiefs at the Chancellery. Hitler seemed nervous. The day before he had signed the Steel Pact inextricably linking the fate of Italy and Germany. Opposite him sat fourteen officers, including Goering and General Erhard Milch for the Luftwaffe, Admiral Erich Raeder and Rear-Admiral Otto Schniewind for the Kriegsmarine and Wilhelm Keitel, Walter von Brauchitsch and Franz Halder for the Wehrmacht.

Hitler wasted no time in discussion. As William L. Shirer remarks in *The Rise and Fall of the Third Reich*, none of those officers left the Chancellery on May 23, without a very clear idea of what the summer held in store.

"No more victories can be won without bloodshed," Hitler declared, according to the notes of the meeting made by Lieutenant-Colonel Schmundt. "We must expand to the East, in order to guarantee our food supplies and also to resolve the problem of the Baltic States. There is no other course to be taken in Europe. If we are forced by fate to come to grips with the West, the possession of a vast territory in the East will be an incalculable advantage. There can be no question of sparing Poland. We shall attack her at the first favorable opportunity. War will break out.

"If Great Britain and France support Poland, then they too must be attacked. Dutch and Belgian air bases must be occupied militarily. Declarations of neutrality cannot be respected. We must make a lightning attack on Holland. Our aim must be the establishment on Dutch territory of a defense line going right up to the Zuyder Zee. The war with Britain and France will be a fight to the death. The idea that we shall be able to avoid this is a dangerous one. It will no longer be a matter of being right or wrong, but whether or not there are to be eighty million Germans."

The fourteen officers sat hypnotized. Not one dared to interrupt Hitler's analysis. In 1937, the Führer had suggested similar plans of aggression to his military chiefs. Werner von Blomberg and von Fritsch had protested, on the grounds that Germany lacked the forces necessary to win a European war. But von Blomberg and von Fritsch were no longer there. This time Hitler was not making suggestions, he was giving orders. He digressed on the subject of Britain and the character of the British people. This was what haunted him—the British lion. He repeated himself, as though trying to convince himself of the rightness of his decision. Finally, the Führer ordered his officers to pay particular attention to the outlines he would give them of a strategic plan that they were to work out in greater detail:

"The objective must be to deal the enemy a crushing and absolutely decisive blow at the outset. No consideration of right or wrong, or of treaties, must interfere with the plan's execution. We must prepare both for a long war and for a surprise attack. Any possible intervention by Britain on the Continent must be stopped immediately. The army must occupy the positions essential to the navy and to the Luftwaffe. If we succeed in occupying Holland and Belgium, together with France, we shall have the bases for a victorious war against Britain. Taking off from the west of France the Luftwaffe will be able to exert a strict blockade against Britain. And the blockade will be completed by our submarines.

"The decisive condition for success is secrecy. I shall reveal my objectives neither to Italy nor to Japan. And I regret to say that I cannot entirely trust my High Command. Our plans must not be communicated to them. Form a small commission within the OKW, whose task it will be to draw up the military details of the plan."

Perhaps Hitler was already suspicious. German agents in Switzerland sifted every word that was published concerning German problems. Naturally, they had read the writings of the mysterious Hermes. Yet his reports did not constitute a betrayal of defense secrets. The Führer's apprehension could be due to nothing more than his instinctive mistrust. However, his fears were fully justified.

On May 30, two Germans in civilian dress got out of the train at Lucerne; Generals Fritz T. and Rudolf G., the leaders of the small conspiracy in Berlin. They had come from the Reich. Rudolf Roessler took the precaution of receiving them at his home at Wesemlin; the Vita Nova Verlag might be watched by German spies.

Rudolf G. began: "War will break out in a matter of weeks, three months at the latest. Hitler decided on it on the twenty-third of this month."

"Are you sure?" asked Roessler.

"Positive. The Führer had never entirely trusted the Ober-kommando of the Wehrmacht. He wants the job of drawing up the Wehrmacht's plans of attack to be confined to a small commission. Brauchitsch and Halder have just asked us to join it."

Rudolf G. continued, emphatically:

"Nazi Germany must not win this war."

"Has she any chance of winning it?" Roessler asked.

"Who knows? Thomas, the economic chief of the OKW, has just produced his estimates. In four years, the Wehrmacht has expanded from seven to fifty-one divisions. The Luftwaffe has twenty-one squadrons and 270,000 highly trained men. Not enough, of course, to take on all of Europe." He then revealed

Hitler's intention to try and break the conflict up into manageable pieces, beginning with Poland. This would give him time to continue the military buildup before attacking the West. German industry was expanding at a colossal rate, working entirely for the army. If it were not beaten at once, he cautioned, the Wehrmacht would become a terribly powerful instrument. Hitler was taking a chance, convinced that Britain and France would not stand in his way.

"The break has come," murmured Roessler.

"We shall win," Rudolf G. went on excitedly. "We shall bleed this Germany that we have disowned to its death, so that our Germany may be reborn. You know why we joined the Wehrmacht when it superseded the Reichswehr: we were waiting for an opportunity. Brauchitsch and Halder have given it to us."

He reviewed the reasons for their optimism—the vital importance of their posts in Operations, Logistics, Transport, Military Economy and Communications, and, most important, their own appointment to the small commission. Try as they might, the Nazis could not do without experts. They had to admit that at least the Reichswehr knew how to train soldiers. Rudolf G. assured Roessler that they would send him all intelligence of any importance to use as he saw fit. "Give it away or sell it, as you wish—and to whom you wish. But preferably to the staunchest enemies of Nazism."

Roessler regarded the two generals in silence. At last, he said:

"You understand where this will lead you. Once we have begun, there'll be no turning back. You realize this?"

It was Rudolf G. who replied:

"Of course. Don't forget, we've always considered you our conscience. Now we need you more than ever before. We shall not be able to see or even to write to each other. So Fritz will explain to you how we shall communicate from now on."

General Fritz T. had been able to get a small trunk through customs at Basle. It was a great risk, of course, but it was the only way—time was running out. The trunk contained radio-telegraphic equipment: a shortwave transmitter-receiver, one of the latest models issued only to the Wehrmacht. Fritz T. had taken it from the stores of the broadcasting department, in the form of spare parts. It had been an easy matter to get hold of the instructions for assembling the set and to reconcile the inventory records to disguise the theft. Did Roessler have a friend in Switzerland whom he could trust, who could put the equipment together and who knew enough Morse code to act as operator?

Roessler knew someone who fit the description exactly—a German émigré called Christian Schneider, working for the International Labor Office in Geneva. But he would simply ask Schneider to assemble the set and teach him how to operate it. Roessler would do the transmitting himself. The fewer people involved in a conspiracy, the better.

Fritz T. agreed. He turned the equipment over to Roessler, with the codes and lists of wavelengths that would be used. Roessler's friends had laid their plans meticulously. Eight of them, simply by virtue of their posts, were at the very source of intelligence concerning the Wehrmacht's movements. Each transmission of news concerning the army would be preceded by the word *Werther*—simply because the first two letters of the title of Goethe's work are also those of Wehrmacht. The other two conspirators, high-ranking officers in the Luftwaffe, would communicate any intelligence concerning the air force, but it would pass through the same channel as the other. This news would be announced by a different signal, *Olga*—the name of Roessler's wife.

How could the Oberkommando of the Wehrmacht allow

such an important and continuous "leak" to be so easily set up and remain undetected? Many observers have remarked that as the war continued, the OKW became more like a public meeting than a powerful and disciplined command center. By taking over on February 4, 1938, the posts of supreme commander of the Wehrmacht, War Minister and commander-in-chief of the Wehrmacht, Hitler intended to concentrate all his forces in his own hands. As a result, he created a Frankenstein.

In 1925, under the iron rule of General Hans von Seeckt, the Reichswehr command comprised no more than 220 high-ranking officers—assisted, of course, by a large contingent of civil servants. By 1933, this number had doubled. In 1939, the Wehrmacht High Command seemed as if it had been possessed by an absolutely irresistible tendency to expand. There were now 2,000 officers of all ranks and 7,000 civil servants. This swelling of the numbers at the OKW was to continue at a rapidly increasing rate until, in 1940, there were double the number of army officers wearing the purple stripe down their trousers.

Each of the commanding officers appointed by the Führer brought his own retinue with him, which he duly added to that of his predecessor—and which, in turn, he left to his successor when he moved on. There were strata of every loyalty and shade of opinion. A superficial examination of the OKW quickly reveals who von Seeckt's men were, then von Blomberg's and von Fritsch's—then those of Beck, von Brauchitsch, Halder, Zeitzler, Guderian and Krebs. In addition, there were the favorites of the moment, appointed by Wilhelm Keitel, Alfred Jodl or Hitler himself as a simple demonstration of faith in Nazism. This mass of officers was jammed into the offices on the Tirpitz embankment, the Wilhelmstrasse, the Bendlerstrasse and in Maybach camp at Zossen, at the gates of Berlin. The cleverest among them succeeded in getting appointed to the Führer's own headquarters, which followed Hitler wherever he went.

The OKW swarmed with fiercely competitive cliques and festered with repressed jealousy and rancor. The great thing was to avoid any serious responsibility and therefore any chance of making an irremediable mistake, which would be enough to get one sent to active service on the front. And the entire organization was under constant surveillance by agents of the Gestapo.

Outside this world of intrigue and violent internal convulsions were a number of technicians, more interested in improving the Wehrmacht's efficiency than in attending parades and receptions. Among them were Roessler's ten friends. The surrounding anarchy, produced by an overconcentration of power, acted as a perfect screen for their activities. It was easy enough for them to obtain the strategic plans and the details of the Wehrmacht's movements because they were among the men who produced them. They were then transmitted to Rudolf Roessler from the official broadcasting center of the OKW itself.

Inside this building were two huge halls that buzzed incessantly night and day with the noise from nearly a hundred transmitter-receivers. On one side was a long row of small offices housing the coding technicians, who held the keys to the OKW dispatches. The wireless operators knew nothing, but simply transmitted, uncomprehendingly, the long series of cabalistic letters they were given, taking note of the times and wavelengths indicated in the margin of every message. In the same way, they would record, without the slightest idea of their meaning, the floods of mysterious dots and dashes they received.

Fritz T. was one of the assistants of General Erich Fellgiebel, the head of the Communications department, with practically the entire center under his direct control. There were a number of wireless operators he could depend on—among them two sergeants who had good reason to be grateful to him. Nothing ever surprised them, and they never asked questions. In turn, they transmitted the messages of *Werther* and *Olga,* without any awareness of what or to whom they were communicating— Fritz T. having coded everything beforehand and Roessler being for them merely one correspondent among many others, known only as RAHS, his call number.

Fritz T. did everything possible to reduce the chances of discovery. He insisted that his transmission should never last longer than a half-hour except in extraordinary circumstances. The longer dispatches were to be broken up and spread over several days if necessary. Roessler was never to call either of the two sergeants. In the event of an unexpected silence on Roessler's part, *Werther* and *Olga* would know that something had happened and would not try to contact him. It would be up to Roessler to reestablish contact, which he would do by sending out his signal, RAHS, for several days in succession at midnight. His friends in Berlin were then to reestablish contact. The plan had its risks, of course, but it was one with a very good chance of success. However, if the break came from Berlin, Roessler could do nothing more than pray for the safety of his friends. A prolonged silence would mean that the Gestapo had arrested everyone.

The machine could now be turned on. They had only to await the Führer's decisions to feed into it. Each one would be turned against him and contribute to his ultimate, irrevocable fall. He would thus destroy himself. This simple, meticulous plan could not fail. Of course, its results would not be evident at once; there would be no sudden, spectacular reversals. But in time they would do their work.

Only one problem remained—and it was no minor one. How

and to whom was the mass of intelligence that would soon begin to flow be given? This was up to Roessler. For a long time, he considered his options. Make the rounds of the Allied embassies, his wares under his arm? No one would take him seriously. He would be dismissed as an *agent provocateur*. There was only one answer—Switzerland. She had generously taken him in in 1933. If she thought fit, she would distribute the information to the nations concerned. Roessler dared not admit to himself that he would be offering his hostess a poisoned present. For if she did as he wished, she would be jeopardizing her neutrality.

A few days after his two co-conspirators had returned to Berlin, Roessler arranged to meet Xavier Schnieper. The young Swiss had become a close friend. However, Roessler was careful not to entrust him with the whole truth of what he was doing: the most devoted friend does not reveal what he does not know. He told Schnieper quite simply that an absolutely reliable source had informed him that war would break out shortly. Moreover, through his contacts in Berlin, he would be in possession of exceptional and continuing intelligence, which he would like to communicate to the Allies.

There was a simple motive for this "indiscretion." Roessler knew that since the spring of that year Xavier Schnieper had been serving, as a soldier, in a branch of the secret service, directed by Brigadier Roger Masson, head of Swiss Intelligence. It had been Schnieper himself who had confided in him. He had been recruited on account of his journalistic work and also because he knew Germany well. He had often been asked if he knew anyone who might be useful to the service. Would Roessler allow him to propose his name? The German émigré accepted with alacrity. So Schnieper introduced him to Major Hans Hausamann and his colleagues.

Hausamann owned a large photographic shop near the Zürich

railway station. Before the war he had had the reputation of belonging to the extreme right. And yet there could have been few Swiss more hostile to Nazism than he was. Well before 1939, sensing the need to provide his country with secret eyes and ears, he had developed through his business a series of personal contacts throughout Europe, from Italy to Finland, which might if necessary be transformed into an intelligence service. Brigadier Masson had been delighted to discover this private network and quickly mobilized Hausamann, leaving him, of course, a considerable amount of autonomy. Moreover, he set Hausamann up with his own staff in the Villa Stutz, at Kastanienbaum, about five miles south of Lucerne, on a tip of land that protrudes far into the Lake. This center was christened Bureau Ha.

If an up-to-date analysis of the political situation in Germany was required, the Bureau Ha supplied it. If observation of German diplomats in Switzerland or protection of Swiss diplomats in Germany was needed, the Bureau was called in. And it was the Bureau Ha that sent Swiss agents into Germany.

Other branches of Masson's service also sent spies into the Third Reich—usually dressed as privates or noncommissioned officers of the Wehrmacht and supplied with splendidly forged papers made in Berne, which allowed them into almost any garrison in Germany. Occasionally, these spies had extremely unfortunate experiences on their return to Switzerland—like the spy who managed to steal in Germany a *panzerfaust*, or bazooka, with its shell. On his return, he was arrested at the Col des Roches by Corporal Chevallier, of the Swiss customs, who would not let him enter the country because he did not have an import license for his weapon! This produced a fine scandal that the customs service had great difficulty in hushing up. But customarily this kind of exploit was handled by the Bureau Ha. In the event of some unfortunate incident, it was easier to disown them, since they were semiclandestine in any case.

Xavier Schnieper introduced his friend Roessler as an accomplished military specialist and praised his highly placed contacts in Germany. Without waiting for an answer, Roessler laid down his sole, but essential, condition: he must never be questioned as to the sources of his information. While this was highly unorthodox, Major Hausamann agreed. He knew too much about this kind of contact to insist. He would content himself with judging the recruit by his work. He was not to be disappointed.

The Berlin-Lucerne intelligence service worked very well indeed. Suddenly on the night of Wednesday, August 23, 1939, the transmitter-receiver given to Roessler by Fritz T. began to crackle. That morning, the chief of the Oberkommando of the Wehrmacht had held an extraordinary meeting. General Halder had told them of the order given the night before by the Führer. "D Day against Poland fixed for Saturday 26."

In fact, after a last, desperate diplomatic maneuver by Britain and France, it was not until dawn of September 1 that the troops of the Wehrmacht crossed the Polish frontier en masse and converged on Warsaw from the north, south and west. On September 2, 1939, war was declared. *Werther* and *Olga* began their work of destroying the regime that had been intended to last for a thousand years.

3

SWITZERLAND: a population of under 5 million and an area of 15,944 square miles, one quarter of it uninhabitable rock and ice. A calm, reserved, hard-working people, rearing the finest cows in the world and producing probably its best Gruyère cheese and finest watches. But their most precious asset was their neutrality—not just any kind of neutrality.

The *Journal de Genève* for Wednesday, August 30, 1939, claimed that the "voluntary" neutrality of Belgium and the "independent" neutrality of Holland were not juridically the same thing as the Confederation's "total" neutrality, Switzerland being *more* neutral than the other neutral countries.

Switzerland believed that she had secretly done everything possible to keep herself outside the bonfire that Hitler was preparing for Europe. At the end of August, 1939, she appeared in her most traditional role. A week before the war's outbreak, two symbolic events occurred—events with which Switzerland was delighted to identify and which occupied the front pages of her newspapers. On Monday, August 21, the 33rd World Peace Conference was solemnly opened in Zürich. All Europe, except Germany, Italy and Spain, was represented. The next day, the

International Red Cross, that owed so much to Switzerland, celebrated its 75th anniversary in Geneva.

In this stormy, rainy holiday month—at Basle the firemen were called out seven hundred times on Monday the 21st to pump out flooded cellars—all the hotels were full. Never had there been so many British and French tourists. The national exhibition in Zürich was enjoying an immense success; on Sunday, August 20, the seven millionth visitor passed through its turnstiles. Everything helped to hide the specter at the feast. Two movie houses, however, offered programs that reflected the oncoming drama. In Geneva, the Cinebref announced "Danzig, the only newsreel taken in the Free City." And in Lausanne, the Moderne-Cinema was presenting a documentary on "The Maginot Line, the most amazing defensive creation of modern times." But box-office receipts were far greater at the Rex, with Fernandel in *Raphaël le Tatoué*, and at the A.B.C., with Raimu in *Monsieur Bretonneau*.

However, on Thursday, August 24, 1939, the Federal Council took a secret census of Swiss industry—an action of the greatest importance, since it was intended to provide the essential basis for Switzerland's commercial policy, particularly for its war economy. The same day, just as secretly, the Swiss postal department, with the agreement of the Federal police, seized hundreds of letters intended for Germany. They contained anti-Nazi propaganda of British origin. On the eve of war, the Confederation could not afford to give Hitler the slightest pretext to question Swiss neutrality.

An indication that the war was not far off occurred the following day, Friday, August 25. The United Kingdom's ambassador in Berne warned all British subjects wishing to leave Switzerland to do so that same night, since it appeared that the normal services of the international railways were about to be suspended.

The next day, August 26, the Federal Council held an extraordinary meeting in Berne. The German Minister there had just confirmed that the Reich would respect Switzerland's neutrality in the event of war. Giuseppe Motta, head of the Political Department, emphasized that this in no way released Switzerland from her own obligation to take all necessary measures to ensure that her neutrality be preserved. It was no more than the other neutrals, Belgium, the Netherlands, and Luxembourg, had done after receiving similar assurances from Germany. Herr Minger, head of the Military Department, insisted on the fact that Switzerland must be ready to defend her frontiers at the first sign of danger. All the Federal councillors were therefore requested to remain in Berne, so that they might be consulted immediately in any emergency.

They did not have to wait long. At 3 P.M. on Monday, August 28, the councillors filed once more into the Federal Palace. At the same time a significant event took place at Chiasso, a town on the Italian frontier, near Lake Como. Sixty-two Polish Jews, who had come to attend the Zionist Conference in Geneva, were on their way home, via Italy—thus avoiding Austria or Germany. Insulted and stoned by Italian fascists, they stood huddled together in the Chiasso customs office, awaiting the return of their representative who had gone to ask for the help of the Swiss authorities of the canton of the Ticino.

At 5 A.M. the next day, Switzerland mobilized its frontier troops. By press and radio, Herr Philippe Etter, the President of the Confederation, instructed all men who had a red form in their army books, to go directly to the assigned meeting places. He asked the rest of the population to keep calm.

"Do not panic. I would particularly ask you to refrain from spreading false rumors, from making unnecessary food purchases and from sudden withdrawals of money from the banks. All steps have been taken to guarantee adequate food supplies and the free circulation of money. Tomorrow, Wednesday, August 30, at 5 P.M., the Federal Assembly will elect a general. I repeat: all necessary steps have been taken."

What stuck in the minds of most of the President's listeners were the words, "The Federal Assembly will elect a general." This was sure proof that war was imminent. For the Swiss army possesses no general in peacetime and each soldier keeps his rifle, ammunition and other equipment at home. According to Article 89, Chapter 3, of the Constitution, the Assembly entrusts the command of this army to an officer elected for the purpose only when the Confederation's neutrality is threatened. There had been General Guillaume Dufour in 1859, at the time of the war between Italy and Austria; General Herzog in 1870; General Ulrich Wille in 1914. The fourth Swiss general was to be Henri Guisan. Switzerland had been expecting the outbreak of war for so long that Colonel Guisan had known for some months that he would be offered the post.

On Wednesday, August 30, Guisan, a very young-looking sixty-five, was duly elected general with 204 votes, against 21 for his opponent, Colonel Borel. There were two abstentions— those of the Communist councillors, Bodeman and Humbert. Guisan took the oath of allegiance to the Confederation, swearing to defend, with the troops under his command, the honor, independence and neutrality of his country.

It was the same oath that Ulrich Wille had taken in 1914. There the resemblance between the two men ends; Wille was an extremely cautious man, whereas Guisan did not hesitate to gamble if he considered that it was for his country's good. Under Wille, Switzerland had been pro-German. In 1939, under Guisan's guidance, Switzerland was to play, as best it could, the Allies' game. Wille was cold and forbidding. Henri Guisan was to become the most popular citizen in the Confederation.

The day before the general mobilization, Giuseppe Motta, head of the Political Department, had received in turn the representatives of the future belligerents. They all assured him that the Confederation's territory and neutrality would be respected. Signor Tamaro, the Italian ambassador, had even told him that Italy's transalpine ports and roads would be open for Swiss traffic. All that was needed was for the two governments to settle the "details" of such an agreement. Motta thanked the ambassador for what seemed a very generous offer. But, secretly, it gave him no pleasure at all. It could not be as simple as Signor Tamaro made out. Switzerland was entering a time of compromise, of overt commitments and secret agreements.

On Saturday, September 2, the day of the mobilization, armored trucks toured the Swiss banks. Their safes were emptied and the contents taken to a virtual Ali Baba's cave in the middle of the Alps. Switzerland was quick to protect one of its chief assets—the fortunes of others.

At dawn, that same Saturday, 400,000 men took up their positions around the country's frontiers. On the orders of the Federal Council, Henri Guisan had had to set up his headquarters in the Bellevue Hotel in Berne—to be nearer the Federal Palace. It was there, on the third floor, that General Wille had housed his headquarters in 1914. Wille may have felt at home there. Certainly Guisan did not. He insisted on moving. He went first to Spiez, then to Gumligen, then to Interlaken and finally to Jegenstorf.

The Swiss upper class, which always tended to be pro-German, was quick to claim that Guisan traveled around far more than was necessary, that too many little girls came to bring him flowers and murmur compliments, that he tended to court popularity to the detriment of his military duties. It was even pointed out that he had totally eclipsed the President of the Confederation in the people's affections. But it was not to the office, but to the man that the Swiss were drawn. The Swiss felt vaguely that Guisan was doing more for the defense of their country than any of his predecessors and that they were safe in his hands. But Guisan did not always stop to receive the crowd's acclamations; his time was severely limited. For, contrary to what some believed, he never stopped working on behalf of his army and slept no more than five hours a night.

When he took charge of Switzerland's defense, Guisan commanded a terribly vulnerable army, which, he is said to have remarked, could not have held out longer than a week against attack: 600 rounds of ammunition per man, 44 antiaircraft guns, 835 antitank guns, 121 reconnaissance planes and 86 fighters, most of them obsolete. He resolved to change all that. He would entrench the Swiss army in fortresses, dug out of the Alps, and block the mountain passes and tunnels. Stocks of food and ammunition would be organized. He was determined to build up an army that could stave off an aggressor for two years. This would act, if not as a guarantee, at least as a front, to his country's often quoted "total" neutrality.

Secretly, Henri Guisan carried his plans much further. He was well aware that a German émigré of exceptional value had settled in Lucerne and had offered his services to Major Hans Hausamann's Bureau Ha, in which he took a particular interest. Guisan felt that before long such a collaboration might present very serious problems of conscience. But he decided, at least temporarily, to ignore them and stifle his scruples. For him, too, it was absolutely vital that Nazi Germany should lose the war.

4

MOST espionage cases are based upon a single, often quite crucial, but nonetheless isolated event of short duration. The masterstroke of Richard Sorge, for example, was the acquisition of intelligence proving that Japan would not attack the Soviet Union. It enabled Stalin to leave Siberia virtually undefended and to throw his best divisions against Hitler without fear of attack from the east. The enormous value of Rudolf Roessler and his ten collaborators of the Lucy Ring, or Viking Line, as the Swiss named them, was based on a body of intelligence just as sensational as that of Richard Sorge, but which lasted for more than *five years*.

The quantity of intelligence communicated by these German resisters to the Swiss—quite apart from the information they supplied later to others, in even larger quantities—amounts to twelve thousand closely typed pages, the equivalent of about forty average-length books.

Almost every day, Roessler arrived at the Villa Stutz, at Kastanienbaum, with a pile of documents in his briefcase. From the time he was engaged by the Swiss, military experts were able, with the information supplied by *Werther* and *Olga*, to reconstruct the movements and strategy of the Wehrmacht in the greatest detail. It may not be an overstatement to say that these eleven men, ten of whom remained unknown to Brigadier Masson, were largely responsible for the reputation of the Swiss secret service.

Masson had been faced with a serious problem of conscience when he learned that an agent as well informed as Roessler had offered his services to Switzerland. In the wealth of information Roessler promised it was obvious that very little would be of direct concern to Switzerland, a very minor objective for German expansionism. On the other hand, it was just as obvious that western Europe would be attacked. But Masson could not compromise the Confederation's future by officially warning the diplomatic representatives of these countries whenever he received intelligence concerning them. Yet his sympathy for the Allies obliged him to try to discover some effective means of helping them without involving Switzerland, at least overtly.

It was Hans Hausamann who found a temporary solution— one that was to last until 1944. Quite by chance a foreigner, said to be the Canadian uncle of Hausamann's wife and whom they nicknamed "Uncle Tom," was at the Villa Stutz when Roessler arrived with intelligence that would be of great service to the Allies. This man, in fact, was Czech, a Colonel Thomas Sedlacek and he volunteered to act as contact with the Allied governments.

Soon after the opening of the Wehrmacht's campaign in Poland, Roessler had become a fairly accomplished wireless operator, having absorbed in three months the lessons of his friend Christian Schneider. Schneider asked no questions. He claimed to be a Communist, and although he did not share Roessler's ideas, he knew that it was not to help the Nazis that he had obtained the transmitter.

The first news received by Roessler concerned the Nazi terror in Poland. On September 23, 1939, he arrived at the Villa Stutz overcome with emotion, bringing with him a copy of a plan that Heydrich had issued to the Army High Command two days before:

"The Third Reich will not rebuild Poland. As soon as the conquest has been completed, the aristocracy and the clergy must be exterminated. The people must be kept at a very low standard of living. They will provide cheap slaves. The Jews will be grouped into the towns where they will remain easily accessible. The *final solution*," Heydrich stated, "will take some time to be worked out and must be kept strictly secret."

For the officers of the Wehrmacht—and for those Swiss who learned of this message—there could be no doubt as to the meaning of the phrase "final solution." It meant extermination. These orders, inspired directly by the Führer were to be carried out by Hans Frank, who had been appointed Governor General of Poland.

"It is a difficult matter," he was later to admit, "to shoot or poison three and a half million Polish Jews, but we will be able to take the necessary steps to bring about their annihilation."

Frank's words were to prove true enough.

Colonel Sedlacek was at the Villa Stutz when Roessler sent news that the Wehrmacht was preparing to attack Holland, Belgium and northeastern France. It was October 13, 1939. Three days earlier, Hitler had called a meeting of his generals. He was furious because Halder and Brauchitsch had declared that it would take several months to repair the damage done to the tank units by the Polish campaign. The Führer had raged, banging his fist on his desk in the Chancellery.

"Time is on the enemy's side!" he was reported to have roared. "Preparations must be speeded up for an offensive through Luxembourg, Belgium and Holland. We must do the worst possible damage to the French army and gain as much ground as possible. I am asking the commanders-in-chief to supply me with detailed reports of their plans immediately. A war of position, as in 1914-18, must be avoided. The armored divisions will be used for the crucial thrusts. The attack on Holland and Belgium will take place on November 12."

"Uncle Tom" went at once to inform the British Embassy. The Dutch and the Belgians were also warned. On November 7, Roessler announced that the offensive had been postponed. The conflict between Hitler and his generals had not been resolved. During the autumn and winter of 1939-40, there were to be fourteen such decisions and postponements. Each time, Rudolf Roessler contacted the Swiss, and the Allies were informed.

On November 23, 1939, the Führer again summoned his generals to the Chancellery. This time, in addition to the offensive to the West, with which he was principally concerned, Hitler mentioned the possibility of a war on two fronts—a nightmare for any military leader. For the first time he spoke of an attack on Russia, despite the treaty binding Germany to the Soviet Union. To justify expansion onto a second front, he attributed his own motives to the Soviet Union, disguising his personal objectives.

"Treaties," he declared, "are respected as long as they serve a particular interest. Russia will respect ours only as long as she considers it to her advantage . . . She still has very far-reaching aims, notably the strengthening of her position in the Baltic. The moment seems to be a judicious one."

This new intelligence from Roessler deeply disturbed the Swiss. Helping the western Allies flattered their dignity, their instinctive solidarity with a world like their own. But this was

another case entirely. Despite their previous hospitality to a few
of the Russian revolutionary leaders, they distrusted the Communist regime. Worse still, the Soviet Union was not yet at war
with Nazi Germany—she could even be regarded as her accomplice, since the gasoline used by the Wehrmacht in Poland
came from Baku and the corn consumed by these same German
soldiers came from the Ukraine. To offer help to the Russians
would constitute a betrayal.

After some reflection, the Swiss decided to postpone any decision. So the Bureau Ha simply tabled Roessler's message—
and Roessler went along with them. At this stage, he was still
full of confidence, not realizing that the West would take no account of the exceptional value of his information.

A flood of communications followed. *Werther* and *Olga* omit-
ted none of the Führer's plans and their application by the
OKW. In January, 1940, and throughout February, as Hitler
moved on to the preparations for the invasion of Norway, the
Bureau Ha was kept informed. From February 26 onward, Masson's men had complete details of the coming invasion.

On March 1, Hitler addressed a directive to his generals
concerning the future occupation of Denmark—an operation
that was to be linked to General Nikolaus von Falkenhorst's invasion of Norway. Both operations, claimed Hitler, would prevent Britain's getting a foothold in Scandinavia and the Baltic.
They would also guarantee Sweden's ore resources, which had
been put at Germany's disposal. On March 8, the Bureau Ha
received the main contents of this directive.

Well before the Wehrmacht could put their plans against
Scandinavia into practice, Denmark and Norway had been
alerted by the Swiss. Nonetheless, both countries were "surprised." On the evening of April 8, the King of Denmark went to
the Royal Theater, despite his knowledge that a German

troopship had been torpedoed by a Polish submarine south of Norway and that a fleet of the Kriegsmarine was making for its ports. That day, the Norwegian cabinet, too, seemed strangely inactive, even after several ships had been sighted moving toward the coast.

On March 30, 1940, and again on April 3, 1940, Colonel J. G. Sas, Dutch military attaché in Berlin, was warned by the Swiss military attaché of the fate awaiting Denmark. Curiously enough, Colonel Hans Oster, an adjutant of Admiral Wilhelm Canaris, the head of the Abwehr (the counter intelligence department of the OKW) who was on close personal terms with Sas, also warned him of the danger. Sas immediately informed Captain Kjölsen, the Danish naval attaché. But the Danish government failed to act, even though the information was confirmed by two sources.

On March 25, 1940, on the basis of information from the Bureau Ha, the Norwegian government was also alerted to the threat of invasion through its legation in Berne. The Swiss agent emphasized the extreme reliability of the intelligence—but to no avail. He, too, was completely ignored. Again, another source —this time the Swedish military attaché in Berlin—confirmed the news on April 5, in vain. The German plan, *Weserübung*, succeeded perfectly.

This tragic episode was typical of the curious attitude of the European high commands and the democratic governments of the period. Unaccustomed to the participation of intelligence services in the conduct of battles, they reacted with instinctive mistrust. Neither Belgium, Holland nor France was to escape disaster. Like Denmark and Norway they were given ample warning from secret agents, but refused to listen.

Astonished, but in no way discouraged by the indecision of the Danish and Norwegian leaders who had played so well into Hitler's hands, Rudolf Roessler persevered, as a flood of alarming intelligence reached him from Maybach camp.

He had long known that Belgium, the Netherlands and France were next on the list for attack. The final version of the "yellow plan" against the West, devised by General Fritz Erich von Manstein, appeared on February 27, 1940. On March 10, 1940, General Delvoie, the Belgian military attaché in Paris, on orders from his government, which had been warned by Roessler's hosts, the Swiss, passed the main outlines of the plan on to the French High Command.

Von Manstein's "yellow plan" involved an offensive on the Meuse, between Charleville and Sedan, and a breakthrough across the Ardennes, while the main body of the Wehrmacht was to hold down the mass of French, Belgian and British forces to the west, on the Belgian frontier. The panzers of General Hoth and General Guderian would make the intended attack on the Sedan Gap, then describe a gigantic curve in the direction of the lower Somme, with the intention of reaching the sea, thus trapping most of the Allied army. General Georg Thomas had provided for only three weeks' supplies of ammunition and fuel.

So, on March 10, 1940, the French High Command was in possession of the full details of the plan.

On May 1, Roessler received a brief message from *Werther*: "Attack 10 May in the Sedan Gap. Yellow plan still holds. Fifty divisions massed along the Belgian and Dutch frontiers. Guderian and Hoth ready to charge on Sedan."

On the same May 1, 1940, the French military attaché in Berne, secretly alerted by Colonel Sedlacek, telegraphed at once to Paris:

"German attack will probably take place 10 May. It will be directed against Sedan."

It was to be hoped that this time the Allied high commands

would not be taken by surprise, as those of Denmark and Norway had been, but would be ready for the Wehrmacht, with the necessary equipment already in position to confront the oncoming 136 German divisions. This was all the more to be expected, since, on the same day, General Gauché, head of the Deuxième Bureau and Colonel Rivet, head of the Cinquième Bureau, never stopped sending to the French government and high command the numerous confirmations they had received from Switzerland—on May 4, 6 and 8, among other dates.

On May 10, at dawn, the Wehrmacht attacked. And still no one was prepared to defend the point where it made its main thrust—at the exact location indicated by *Werther*—and on May 13, Sedan fell. Three days later, Guderian's tanks were rolling, sixty-two miles to the west of Sedan, across open countryside, with no opposition in sight. On May 24, the Allies were encircled, "the gigantic curve" was complete. The whole operation had been conducted with perfect rigor, for German land forces were not noted for their powers of improvisation. The three armies, the Belgian, British and French, endured a terrific bombardment, within a small triangle of ground. The only hope of escape, for some, was by sea, from Dunkirk.

Strategists may argue at leisure about the development of this campaign of 1939-40, comparing figures and hypothetical tactics. But they will find no valid explanation for this tragic fact: the French and British high commands made no use of the extraordinary intelligence that had been communicated to them, always well in advance, to turn events to their advantage.

As a result, these high commands were in large part responsible for the defeat of 1940. They cannot seek to evade their share of the responsibility, nor will they ever be able to exculpate themselves fully from the accusations that can be leveled against them for their failure at that time. Largely through their fault, Europe fell under German occupation and millions of human beings were sacrificed to the madness of the Nazis.

At Lucerne, the collapse of the Allies, due to great extent to the military high commands' failure to believe in the secret struggle being waged in their support, stupefied Roessler. Astonishment was followed by bitterness. From his home at Wesemlin, where his transmitter-receiver was hidden, he alerted his friends: they were to stop sending documents and limit themselves to weekly interchanges. It was pointless for *Werther* and *Olga* to expose themselves to danger when no one took the slightest notice of their warnings.

General Guisan, too, was now undergoing a certain amount of anxiety. Although the military leader of a neutral country, he, like Roessler, had been trying to help the Allies. Convinced of an early Allied victory, he had even been imprudent enough, though with the assent of the political bureau of the Federal Council, to sign a secret military convention, well before the Wehrmacht had invaded Europe, with General Maurice Gamelin of France—an agreement which might be used against the Confederation if it were ever to fall into German hands. Guisan and Gamelin had agreed that the Confederation could ask for the help of French troops, and even allow them access to their territory, if their strategic needs required it.

Anxiety over the compromising agreement now prompted Guisan to conceive of the necessity for a line of national defense. It was more than ever necessary to maintain the Berlin-Lucerne contact that Masson and Hausamann regarded so highly and of which they were so proud. In the event of Hitler's deciding to invade Swiss territory, Guisan would know about it sufficiently well in advance to organize his last desperate resistance.

For the Swiss general had never underestimated the importance of the secret service. It might even be said that it formed one of the basic components of his strategy. Masson himself, or one of his assistants, attended every meeting of the High Command—which was the case in remarkably few other countries. Now, ignorant of the existence of the temporary interruption in activity between Roessler and the Bureau Ha, Masson instructed Xavier Schnieper to ask his German friend to come to the Villa Stutz at once.

Hausamann managed to find the right words for the occasion:

"Switzerland is in danger," he told Roessler, "and the Nazis are drunk with victory, but the war is not yet over. A resistance movement has begun in Norway and before long a similar movement will begin in France. On June 18, General de Gaulle made an appeal from London. Great Britain will not surrender. We must continue our work. It is your duty to do so. The Confederation opened its frontiers to you when misfortune struck your country. You, in turn, should help them in the trials that lie ahead."

Only too happy to serve, Roessler immediately alerted his friends in Berlin. They would not give up. The struggle would be begun again.

5

FROM June, 1940, onward, Roessler had been giving top priority to any intelligence received from Berlin that might be of value to Switzerland. In mid-July, 1940, a tense situation existed on the western frontier, between Saint-Louis and Gex. Masson's own agents had discovered six German divisions, two of mountain troops, encamped near the border and ready to attack. They also mentioned border patrols, the laying of telephone cable and German espionage activity around Swiss installations in the area. Were these preparations for a surprise attack? Roessler asked Berlin. On July 18, less than twenty-four hours after his request, he received a full reply. There was nothing to fear for the moment. The OKW was too preoccupied with the problems presented by a possible invasion of Britain—the "Otarie plan"—to give time to Switzerland.

Reassured for the present and wishing to make full use of Roessler's services, the Swiss now asked him whether in addition to his present work, he would take on another job. They wanted him to sift and evaluate the mass of intelligence they received. Most of the business of their secret service consisted simply in amassing data. But the data had then to be interpreted, assigned its relative importance and fitted into a total synthesis. Roessler was perfectly suited to such a job. Moreover, his nationality and intellectual training rendered him particularly able to predict how a fellow-German would react or tackle a particular problem. Roessler agreed.

Nevertheless, he in no way neglected the mission he was carrying out for *Werther* and *Olga*. On August 3, 1940, Roessler relayed a vitally important message to the Swiss center at Lucerne. On July 31, Hitler had informed his High Command of his irrevocable decision to attack Russia. His statement on that occasion shows that his own plans of aggression had long been ready:

"I am convinced that Britain's determination to continue the struggle is based upon the expected support of the USSR. Strange things are taking place on the other side of the Channel. Yesterday, the British were faltering. Now they are on their feet once again. It is enough that Russia, anxious on account of our conquests in the West, should let it be understood that she would not view with favor any further development of German power, for the British to cling like drowning men to the hope of a complete reversal of the situation within a few months. If we crush Russia, Britain's last hope will fade with her. And Germany will become the mistress of Europe, including the Balkans. Russia must be liquidated. The attack will take place in the spring of 1941.

"We shall launch two offensives at once—one in the south, in the direction of Kiev and the Dnieper, the other in the north, through the Baltic States, toward Moscow. There the two armies will link up. Then, if necessary, a special operation will be mounted to secure the Baku oil fields. One hundred and twenty divisions will be allocated to this front. Sixty will be enough in the West. The offensive will last five months and begin in March 1941. . . ."

This information was a great consolation to the Swiss, for if war broke out between Germany and Russia, the Reich would have no troops left to invade the Confederation. But, at the same time, the information was a source of embarrassment. Not knowing how to handle it, the Swiss were prepared to keep it to themselves.

"But one day, you will have to decide to communicate this news to the Russians," Roessler told Hausamann. "You know very well that we are bound to receive more and more of this sort of intelligence. I must remember that my objective, and that of the men I represent, remains the death of Nazism. We are ready to help whoever will do most to achieve that end, whatever their nationality."

"Germany and Russia are not at war yet," Major Hausamann said. "And nothing indicates that the Russians have turned against Hitler and his Nazis. In any case, we shall never communicate with them."

"Am I to understand that *I* shall be allowed to warn them?"

Hausamann was clever enough not to reply.

From that August of 1940, while continuing to supply the Swiss with intelligence on the movements of German troops within the Reich, and analyzing it, Roessler was studying ways of warning the Russians. Time was running short. An avalanche of data, pouring out of the OKW headquarters in Berlin, revealed in ever greater detail that preparations for the invasion of the Soviet Union were proceeding steadily.

On December 5, 1940, Generals Halder and Brauchitsch submitted to the Führer the "Otto plan," the details of the attack worked out by the High Command. Moscow, it suggested, was not an important objective. The Red Army would be pushed back into the Pripet Marshes from the north and the south, there to be encircled and destroyed. Rumania and Finland would share in the spoils—and the two attacks would be launched from these countries. They would also supply support troops for the Wehrmacht. At the head of the Finnish troops, General Eduard Dietl's mountain troops would advance on Petsamo in Lapland and occupy the Arctic ports. This division would have to be transferred from Narvik, in Norway, to Finland through Sweden, which had just agreed to this.

Hitler accepted the "Otto plan" enthusiastically. Putting some finishing touches to it, he renamed it "Operation Barbarossa" and read it out to his generals on December 18, 1940. The preliminaries of the operation were to be completed by May 15, 1941. This perfect plan was to remain unaltered. To preserve the maximum possible secrecy, Hitler ordered that only nine copies be made of it. One was distributed to each of the armed forces: the Wehrmacht, the Luftwaffe and the Kriegsmarine. The other six were to remain at OKW headquarters.

A week later, just after Christmas, Roessler received the longest message so far, in eight installments spread over a period of forty-eight hours that took twelve hours to decipher. It was a real bombshell—nothing less than a complete copy of "Operation Barbarossa." Confronted with this document, Roessler was troubled, imagining the difficulties his friends must encounter daily. Even if they were able to see important plans in the normal course of their work, it was also necessary to get hold of them, secretly. They were obviously taking ever greater risks. And he did not know what to do with the results.

He had tried unsuccessfully to find a way of warning the Russians through a third party. There remained only one solution—one he had so far rejected because it would compel him to deal with the Communists—his friend Christian Schneider, the man who had helped him assemble his transmitter-receiver and taught him Morse. Roessler knew Schneider's opinions only too well, having argued against them on the occasion of the signing of the German-Soviet pact. He invited his fellow-countryman to lunch. During the meal, in a Lucerne restaurant, the Unter der Egg, on the banks of the Reuss, not far from his office, he asked Schneider point-blank:

"Do you know how I could talk to the Russians? I have vital intelligence in my hands that could be of the greatest use to the Soviet Union. If they want to pay for it, they can do so later, as I shall have much more. I am quite willing to collaborate—though I don't care for the word—for nothing."

Schneider pondered for a time.

"If you don't make them pay you," he said at last, "they'll take you for an *agent provocateur*. I know them. Is it really important intelligence?"

Roessler resolved to be frank.

"The Germans intend to invade Russia."

"Are you sure of your source?" Schneider asked incredulously.

"Absolutely." And Roessler reminded him of the wireless set. He told Schneider he had friends in Germany who could hardly be better placed. Then he laid down his one condition—the Russians must never try to discover their identity.

Schneider rose and murmured doubtfully:

"That would certainly be the most difficult thing for Moscow to accept."

Two weeks later, Schneider called at the Vita Nova Verlag in Lucerne. The anonymity clause had not helped matters. The Russians still knew nothing about the matter. But in Geneva there was a Soviet intelligence cell, for which Schneider worked.

Without mentioning him by name, he had spoken of Roessler to the group's leader, who did not seem very impressed. He was willing to pass the intelligence along, but could not answer for the reactions of the MGB—the Center, as it was known familiarly to Soviet spies—the Ministry of State Security in Moscow that directed the activities of all the "delegations" abroad. For security reasons, Roessler would never meet Schneider's group leader, nor even know his name. Similarly, Geneva would know nothing of Roessler.

Between Geneva and Lucerne there would be two "go-betweens," two people who would pass on Roessler's information. If the Swiss—or the Germans—arrested them, neither the cell in Geneva, nor Roessler, should suffer. For these intermediaries always carried a capsule containing cyanide, which they would swallow if the situation grew serious enough.

The first go-between would be Schneider himself and the second would be a friend of his, Rachel Duebendorfer. If anything happened to him, she would take his place as first intermediary. Like Schneider, Rachel was employed by the International Labor Office. She lived in Geneva, with her daughter Tamara. Although of Balkan origin, she had a Swiss passport; just before the war she had gone through a "white" marriage with a Swiss. This was a fairly common practice at the time, one that had been highly profitable to a number of Swiss citizens who had sold their names—and the security that they brought with them. In fact, Rachel was living with her lover, Paul Boetcher, an ex-German minister—also an émigré and a Communist.

"Is everything clear, then?" Schneider asked. "You give me your intelligence, I pass it on to Rachel, who takes it to Geneva. Two more things. If Moscow accepts your cooperation, you will be paid. And, you must change your name. We all have aliases. I'm 'Taylor,' Rachel Duebendorfer is 'Sissi.' You will be known as 'Lucy.'"

Thus, in the spring of 1941, Rudolf Roessler, a liberal, Protestant German, from a respectable, conservative, upper-middle-class Bavarian background, a man who, despite his emigration, had retained the class-consciousness of his caste, became, out of hatred of Nazism, a Soviet secret agent. He did so with the blessing of the Bureau Ha and Masson, who agreed on condition that he continue to work for Switzerland and supply intelligence that would be useful to the western Allies.

Fate, which played so great a role throughout this extraordinary affair, was soon to appear once more in a strangely ironic way. Roessler, though frail in appearance, had boundless vitality and slept no more than three hours a night. In spite of all his various secret activities, he managed to continue with his writing—as always, under his pen name, R. A. Hermes. At the beginning of 1941, he published a remarkable analysis of the strategy of the Wehrmacht, *Die Kriegsschauplätze und die Bedingungen der Kriegsführung* (Theaters of War and the Conditions for Their Conduct)—a work of ninety close printed pages. As illustrations for this little book, he needed twelve specially drawn maps showing the various movements of the German army.

So he called on the services of the best geographical firm in Switzerland, the Géo-Presse in Geneva. Its director came to Lucerne to discuss Roessler's sketches with him in person. Roessler was never to know that he had opposite him the most important Soviet spy in the world. Nor did he realize that this thickset businessman, who spoke six languages and was so adept at translating his ideas into concrete form, was the head of the Russian spy network in Switzerland, Alexander Rado, his new boss.

6

MORE than any of the traditional "covers" used by spies, it was his natural gaiety that protected Alexander Radolfi, known as "Rado" to his friends. It was far more difficult to imagine this happy extrovert engaged in plotting and spying, than to picture him pursuing a girl or savoring a good meal. Yet Rado was a master-spy, a colonel of the Red Army born in Hungary but trained in a very special school, Sekhjodnya, the training center of the Soviet espionage service, just outside Moscow. Prior to that, Rado had worked for the Comintern, fomenting revolutions throughout Europe—in his own country, in Czechoslovakia, Poland, and in Germany, where he met his wife Helene. In 1936, the MGB appointed him resident-director in Switzerland.

Contrary to the term's definition, a resident never lived in the territory for which he was responsible. He would operate from a neighboring country, whose laws he was careful not to contravene; his agents did the actual espionage work in the country concerned. He alone was in possession of the pre-arranged codes and performed the transmission of news to the MGB in Moscow. Living in the shelter of Geneva, Alexander Rado's responsibility was Germany.

Yet in 1939, shortly before the outbreak of war, he had barely begun his work. He had received strict instructions to build up a large network before attempting any important operations— and to protect it by means of the usual go-betweens. If possible, the sources of information should not be connected with the Communist Party: in the event of a catastrophe such people should be disowned. On the other hand, the go-betweens and the wireless operators—vital elements to an espionage organization—should belong to the Party. If they were sufficiently well-conditioned, they would be capable when captured of committing suicide if there was a danger that they might be forced to talk.

Finally, Moscow instructed Rado that his network must always be ready to produce information, but until the order to do so was received, he was to lie low and avoid the slightest suspicion. His "front" was excellent—head of a respected cartographical firm, the Géo-Presse, specializing in the manufacture of globes and other maps required by the press and the general public.

This decision to keep Rado's network in a state of watchful inactivity was in fact a tactical ruse. It was to serve as a reserve base and would operate only if absolutely necessary. At that time, the USSR had no shortage of espionage centers in Germany. About twenty resident-directors, assisted by 300 agents, were dotted around the country.

The wisdom of the MGB's decision to use Rado's network only as a last resort was to be demonstrated two years later, when the Abwehr and the SD were to wipe out almost to a man the mass of Russian spies operating on German territory. One after another they were captured. A few of them went over to the German side. The rest were shot.

But in 1939, no one expected such a situation. Alexander

Rado could take his time in establishing his network. In any case, a small Soviet cell was already operating from Switzerland against Germany. Since 1936, it had been directed by a woman known as "Sonia." Her real name was Ursula Schultz. Like her husband Alfred, "Sonia" was German. She had joined the Communist Party with the same fervor with which others enter holy orders. To serve the cause was her only aim. For a long time all went well with the Schultzes. They were spying together in China when the MGB purged its secret service of numerous suspected Trotskyites. The Swiss post fell vacant and Ursula was sent to fill it. Shortly afterward, Alfred Schultz, at a loss without his wife, was arrested in Shanghai and had been in captivity ever since.

"Sonia," was a tall, slim, attractive young woman of about thirty-five. She was not unintelligent, but had lost something of her original faith. She had been deeply shaken by the German-Russian pact. How could these Soviet diplomats enjoy such cordial relations with the Nazis in the open, while the two countries were secretly locked in ruthless struggle?

She lived with her two children and a housekeeper in a large, rented villa at Caux, a health resort overlooking Montreux. A monthly salary of 1,000 Swiss francs (about $230) enabled her to live in comfort. For some time she had been showing signs of a dangerous boredom. She had even set up the long aerial of her transmitter-receiver in her garden, while carelessly concealing the set itself in a biscuit tin in her dining room. She broadcast only once every two weeks and had only a few agents in Germany who supplied her at irregular intervals with very minor information.

Rado was more active. Foresight had always been one of his virtues, and although he had not yet begun to operate, he had assembled by 1939 about fifty sources of intelligence—primarily on Germany, but also on other countries. Among them was a Lithuanian Jew, "Isaac," who also worked for the International Labor Office and who supplied information on the League of Nations. "Isaac" was doubled by a Frenchman, "Brandt." "May" and "Anna" were concerned with the rearmament of Italy. "Lili of the Vatican" was a diplomat to the Holy See; Rado had thought that the Soviet government might one day be grateful for his knowledge of the official and unofficial positions of the Church.

Rado's best source—until Roessler was taken on—was a certain very talented spy named Otto Pünter. "Pakbo," as he was nicknamed, had set up his own small organization, which he called *Rot*. It operated in South Germany and was composed of Germans hostile to Nazism. Incomparably less well placed, and also less effective, than Roessler's friends, the members of *Rot* occasionally supplied military intelligence, but specialized in economic information.

Otto Pünter was a Swiss ex-journalist who had belonged to the Swiss Social Democratic Party. He had been fighting Fascism for a long time. During the Spanish Civil War he had been in Italy, supplying Spanish Republicans with intelligence concerning the transportation of arms, by sea, to General Franco. He had begun his espionage career on July 10, 1930, when he took part in the famous flight over Milan, conceived by the Italian Randolfo Pacciardi, when thousands of anti-Mussolini tracts were dropped over the city. Such a past had attracted Alexander Rado. Having discovered the Pünter's address in Switzerland, through an indiscretion on the part of the Swiss Communist Party, Rado approached and hired him.

The General Secretary of the Swiss Party, Léon Nicole, and his son, Pierre, had helped Rado in the recruitment of his go-betweens. All were members of the Party, as Moscow wished.

Most of them, like Christian Schneider and Rachel Duebendorfer, worked for the International Labor Office. The Nicoles
had introduced Rado to three agents in Geneva: Margareta
Bolli, an unmarried woman who lived at 8 bis rue Henri Mussard, and Edmond and Olga Hamel, who lived at 192 route de
Florissant. Margareta Bolli and Edmond Hamel became the network's wireless operators. Rado saw a great deal of his agents—
particularly the young and pretty Margareta, who became his
mistress. But none of them knew where Rado lived. He always
made several intricate detours before returning home to 113
rue de Lausanne, the long road stretching from the Gare de Cornavin, in Geneva, to the Parc Mon Repos, overlooking Lake Leman.

This, then, was the situation in this powerful, "inactive" organization, when it was suddenly galvanized by Rudolf Roessler. But before continuing the story, one last character must be
introduced, one who was to become as important as Rado himself. Thanks to him, the Center first began to take serious notice
of Roessler. He was an Englishman named Alexander Foote.

Foote's life had been a chaotic one—he seemed fated to become a secret agent. He belonged to that category of human
beings who are perpetually unsatisfied. They love money, but
abhor work. Possessed by a lust for power, they are paralyzed by
timidity. They rage constantly at their own failure, but do nothing to escape it. The profession of espionage provides them
with that escape, since it satisfies all their needs, and they
choose it as soon as the opportunity arises. Foote did just this,
without a moment's hesitation or reflection.

He was born in 1905, into a comfortable middle-class family,
was given a good education, but was incapable of benefiting
from it. Failure seemed to dog his footsteps from the beginning.
In two years, he passed from being manager of a small business,

to being in charge of a garage, chief salesman in a shop, only to end up unemployed. Little more was needed to thrust him into the arms of the Communist Party. The Spanish Civil War had just begun—there, at last, was a cause worth defending.

In December, 1936, Alexander Foote found himself near Madrid in the British battalion of the International Brigade. The Political Commissar of his unit, Douglas Springhall, soon noticed his intelligence, his meticulous sense of order and his great manual dexterity. Springhall was to be his Pygmalion; he turned Foote into a spy.

In September, 1938, Foote managed to flee from the dying Spanish Republic at the wheel of a Red Cross truck, which he brought back with him to Britain. Through the influence of Springhall, he was invited to attend the British Communist Party Conference in Birmingham. Foote had nothing to do at the Conference and was thoroughly bored. In fact, this had been no more than an excuse to get him out of Spain. When Foote presented himself at Party headquarters in King Street, in London, some days later, a surprise awaited him. Instead of being returned to the front, he was offered a special post, for which Douglas Springhall had warmly recommended him. It meant working for the Soviet Union as a secret agent in Europe.

Springhall had not misjudged him: Foote accepted immediately and was sent directly to St. John's Wood, to the headquarters of the resident-director in London. The initial formalities quickly performed, he was given his instructions. He was to go to Geneva. On October 10, 1938, he would be outside the General Post Office in the rue du Mont-Blanc, wearing a white scarf round his neck and holding a leather belt in his right hand. At noon, a woman would approach and ask him the time. In a string bag on her arm, there would be a green parcel, in her hand an orange. She would be his contact.

The woman was none other than "Sonia," the experienced Ursula Schultz. She was a little surprised by the choice of the recruit; this completely inexperienced Englishman would have a great deal to learn. She gave him 2,000 Swiss francs (about $450) and sent him to Munich, advising him to study German, act like a tourist—and keep his eyes and ears open. Three months later, on January 10, 1939, Foote met "Sonia" again— in front of the Post Office in Lausanne. She immediately noticed that the Englishman had considerably improved his German, that he was not a spendthrift, since the money had been sufficient for his needs and, more important, that he was a good listener. He had discovered that, when in Munich, Hitler always lunched at the same restaurant, the Osteria Bavaria, near the Karlsplatz. Foote's imagination kindled, and he suggested that he organize an attempt on Hitler's life. "Sonia" cooled his ardor and told him to go on observing and learning. This time, she sent him back to Munich with $900. He was not to return before May or June, and she would get in touch with him. One of her agents in Germany would visit him in April and give him more money.

Foote recognized this agent on sight. He was one of his friends from the International Brigade, William Philips, now engaged by the Russians to study the production of one of the factories of the I. G. Farben group, at Frankfurt. In August, 1939, Ursula Schultz urgently summoned her two British spies to Vevey. The Center had warned her that war was about to break out. And as there would be no new work for them for the time being, they were to learn radiotelegraphy. So Bill Philips and Foote moved into a modest boardinghouse in Montreux.

Every day, they went up to Caux and practiced on Ursula's transmitter-receiver. By January, 1940, Foote had become competent enough to communicate with the Center on Ursula's behalf—which suited her perfectly well. She felt more and more bored by her job—and had suddenly fallen in love with William Philips.

Seven months later, in August, 1940, the MGB posted Alexander Foote to Rado's headquarters in Geneva for long enough to teach Margareta Bolli and Edmond Hamel how to use the transmitter-receivers. Each of them had just been supplied with the latest models. Bolli had hidden her set at her home in the rue Henri Mussard, in the Eaux-Vives district. Hamel had no difficulty in concealing his—in his radio shop, near the Parc Alfred Bertrand. Hamel had previously studied radio-engineering in Paris. Yet, curiously, he was to prove the least gifted of the three as a Morse operator. The Center decided that Foote would act as wireless operator. Rado would communicate all urgent intelligence to him—Hamel and Bolli would deal with more routine dispatches. Foote was not to remain in Geneva, but would go to Lausanne, to avoid being rounded up by the Swiss authorities. His signal would be NDA and his call-sign FRX. "Sonia" and Philips resigned from the service and, in November, 1940, were given permission to settle in Britain. On December 20 they left for London, via Lisbon.

Meanwhile, Foote had found a flat, at 20 chemin de Longeraie, on the top floor of a large building. Any visitors would have to pass through two heavy, well-locked doors to get into the flat itself, thus providing Foote an entrance resembling a submarine's flooding-chamber. He was delighted with this ideal strategic arrangement. If intruders broke into his retreat, he would have ample time while they forced the second door, to sabotage his transmitter-receiver set and to destroy his files and codes.

Foote's first concern on moving in was to find a radio mechanic who would be willing to install an aerial, running entirely around his flat—an indispensable requirement if he were to correspond with Moscow successfully. Foote convinced the electrician who carried out the installation that he was an eccentric English millionaire, trapped in Switzerland by the outbreak of the war, who wished to be able to hear the BBC broadcasts with perfect clarity.

The care Foote took over his "cover" reveals that in a very short time he had transformed himself from an amateur spy into an experienced agent. In fact, Foote's dramatic talents were such that he was accepted at face value by the entire colony of retired British army officers and civil servants living in Lausanne, at Ouchy. They saw nothing unusual in the fact that a capricious bachelor should show an obvious reluctance to invite them to his home or that the rhythm of his life should be unique: he rose late, did little during the day and wrote, it seemed, well into the night.

This mask also confounded the aliens department of the Swiss police, which came to make inquiries shortly after Foote moved in. He put on a masterly performance for the benefit of the two deferential police inspectors, offering them the best whiskey and showing them bank statements that left no doubt as to his private means—"Sonia" had entrusted him with the funds of the Center before leaving for England. Of course, he realized that he was really breaking the law concerning foreigners in the Confederation. He knew, he assured them, that he ought to reside in one of the hostels or camps that had been put at their disposal, but he hated crowds and had wanted a place of his own. However, he had no desire to cause embarrassment to his hosts and was quite ready to follow them if they insisted. The ruse succeeded splendidly. The inspectors agreed to allow him to occupy the flat, on condition that he paid six months' rent in advance and that he came every two weeks to the police station to sign the aliens' register.

Every two weeks Foote also went to Geneva—this time on orders from Moscow—to meet Alexander Rado, in his offices at the Géo-Presse. The MGB had also fixed the times for his transmissions: twice a week, on Wednesday and Saturday evenings.

So, in the first week of January, 1941, Foote launched his appeals:

NDA. FRX . . . NDA. FRX . . . NDA. FRX . . .

Moscow did not reply. Foote did not even know if he was being heard, but he persevered. Suddenly, on Wednesday, March 12, 1941, at 1:30 A.M., Foote received a very clear reply: NDA. OK. QSR5 . . . NDA. OK. QSR5 . . .

A volley of series of five letters and five figures, concealing the agreed code, followed. The dexterity of the Moscow operator was so great that Foote was unable to keep up and asked him to begin again. The message was an important one. Following a series of reverses, most of the networks in Germany had been wiped out, and the MGB was suspicious of the little information that continued to arrive from the survivors. It was vital for the Soviet Union that the Rado network should begin operations.

On the night of March 15, 1941, Alexander Foote had hardly a moment's sleep. Rado had given him an enormous quantity of news for Moscow. There was information from "Pakbo," "Lili of the Vatican" and "Isaac." But it was completely eclipsed by the extraordinary revelations of Lucy—Rudolf Roessler.

On February 20, 1941, said Lucy, the Germans had massed

650,000 men in Rumania, near the Ukraine border. On the night of February 28, other German divisions crossed the Danube and took up positions in Bulgaria, following a secret agreement made three weeks before between List, the special envoy of the OKW and the High Command in Sofia. These troops were intended by Hitler to occupy Greece, in the event of the Allies' deciding to open a front above Salonika, as in 1914, in order to upset "Operation Barbarossa." There followed a long report on Hitler's plans for the invasion of Russia.

On March 19, the Center's sharp reply came as a disappointment to Rado. How could this resident-director imagine that Moscow would accept information from someone of whom they knew no more than a code name, and who, moreover, required, as a condition of his cooperation, complete secrecy concerning his sources? The dispatches communicated by this Lucy would be sensational—if true. They were so detailed that they could almost have come from the OKW itself. Lucy should not be trusted. He was probably an *agent provocateur.*

7

DURING those first few months of 1941, Roessler must have been sorely tempted to give up completely. It may well be that his obstinacy and determination played a principal part in making this resistance story so remarkable.

Through his ten friends in the headquarters of the Oberkommando of the Wehrmacht, Roessler was to know, before the rest of the world, the details of Hitler's every decision, from 1939 up until the end of April, 1945. Since the chiefs of staff to whom Hitler delivered his orders seldom remained in contact with the Führer for long, being replaced in their jobs after a matter of months, or sometimes even weeks, Roessler was in a unique position. For he had continuous knowledge of events that were to convulse the world, and was well aware of the importance of each piece of intelligence that passed through his hands. It was this knowledge, this sense of being at the center of world events, that must have sustained him in those early days of disillusionment and impotence, when first the Allies, then the Russians refused him credence.

Most men, as La Bruyère remarked, are more capable of a single great effort than of long perseverance in the pursuit of

their aims. But Roessler was different. He persevered—certain
that in the end he would overcome the Russians' mistrust. So,
on March 27, 1941, despite the rebuff he had been given a week
before, he contacted Christian Schneider. He had just received
news of the greatest importance. Hitler had decided to delay
"Operation Barbarossa" for another four weeks. It had origi-
nally been set for May 15, 1941. If the Russians listened this
time, they would have ample time to prepare themselves.

Roessler then went to the Villa Stutz to inform the Swiss
and to explain the reason for the delay. Twenty-four hours before, a popular uprising, supported by a majority of the army,
had overthrown Prince Paul, the regent of Yugoslavia, and a
Nazi sympathizer. The young heir to the throne, Peter II, had
been declared king. General Dušan Simović immediately proposed a nonaggression pact with Germany. But the people had
openly shown their hostility to the Führer by insulting his ambassador in Belgrade. Hitler was furious at being "defied" by a
minor nation and decided to take wholesale reprisals. He immediately issued his Directive No. 25, addressed to the opera-
tional headquarters of the OKW.

"The military *coup d'état* in Yugoslavia has altered the political situation in the Balkans. Despite her professions of loyalty, Yugoslavia must be regarded from now on as an enemy
of Germany and be brought to heel as soon as possible. I therefore intend to invade her as well as Greece and wipe out their
armies. Operations will begin at dawn on 6 April 1941. As a result 'Operation Barbarossa' will have to be delayed by four
weeks."

Roessler insisted that the Allies should be warned in time of
this new upheaval in that part of Europe. He was a shrewd
enough strategist to realize that the loss of these territories
would constitute a serious blow to Britain. On the other

hand, he was greatly relieved at the postponement of the invasion of Russia.

"This is a serious strategic error," he told the Bureau Ha, in his analysis of the situation. "A month's delay could ultimately prevent the Wehrmacht from achieving its objective, for it will be moving at the height of the terrible Russian winter. This error should favor the free world. And all this to satisfy Nazi pride."

From that day, Thursday, March 27, onward, Roessler was in daily contact with his sources in Berlin. Each time, Roessler informed Christian Schneider, then the Swiss at Kastanienbaum. The Swiss never seemed to mind this order of precedence; what mattered to them was that they be kept informed. In Rado's organization, on the other hand, there was increasing consternation over what they were to do with Lucy's information.

On Saturday March 29, despite the orders from the Center to ignore this dangerous source, Rado asked Foote to warn Moscow that evening that the mysterious "Operation Barbarossa" had been postponed for four weeks. The MGB's answer on Wednesday, April 2, was a short, sharp condemnation:

"Stop listening to this nonsense."

Alexander Rado did not insist further. Each of the reports transmitted by "Taylor" got no further than his office. On April 25 a violent argument erupted between the head of the network and his go-between, Schneider having guessed from Rado's lack of interest that Roessler's messages were no longer leaving Geneva.

"We cannot go on dealing with your German friend so long as he persists in concealing the sources of his information."

"He will never reveal them."

"How do you know that he isn't trying to use us?"

"You are making a serious mistake, comrade. It's madness, treason. The Nazis are about to invade the Soviet Union. And if they win the war because Moscow didn't know all there was to know of their plans, then you will be partly responsible."

"The Center has given instructions that they wish to hear nothing more of your Lucy."

"Send them the news anyway. It's your duty. I can't give you any convincing proof. But I can answer for him. He's as much an anti-Nazi as you or I."

"It's no use insisting. I'm not sending anything."

"Have you at least read the latest messages? The 17th German armored division, which was in central Poland, is now encamped in the Chelm forests within gunshot of Russian territory. What's it doing there? General Heinrich von Stülpnagel's 17th army is advancing toward the Ukrainian border. What's it going to do there? Did you know that the Skoda works in Czechoslovakia has been ordered by Berlin to stop taking orders for arms from the Soviet Union? Why?"

"It's no use. I refuse to send all this."

Schneider walked out, slamming the door of the Géo-Presse offices. The next day, he took the train for Lucerne to meet Roessler at the Vita Nova Verlag. He briefly explained Rado's attitude, trying rather clumsily to rationalize Moscow's decision. Roessler said that he understood. No one was willing to face up to the truth. But he would not give up.

"Unfortunately, my dear Schneider, events will prove that we were right to persevere. Moscow will listen to us then."

Throughout May, 1941, the Russians heard no more from Lucy. But he was far from idle. Day after day he had communicated to Christian Schneider, then to the Swiss, the movements of the Wehrmacht toward the Soviet frontiers—the group of armies under General Wilhelm von Leeb in the north, with

twenty-one infantry divisions and six armored divisions; Field
Marshal Gerd von Rundstedt's troops in the south, with seventeen infantry divisions, four mountain divisions, four divisions
of mobile infantry and five armored divisions; and a formidable
force under Field Marshal Fedor von Bock in the center, with
thirty infantry and fifteen armored divisions. Over a front of
almost 1,000 miles, three million men, 750,000 horses, 600,000
cars, 7,200 guns, 3,000 tanks and 1,800 planes were awaiting
"D" day, at "H" hour.

Roessler had enumerated everything in detail. It was an extraordinary piece of work. He had also described the state of
mind of the troops concentrated at Tilsit, Insterburg, Zichenau,
Chelm, Bialystok, Przemysl and Jassy. Above all, he had particularly emphasized the invasion plans assigned to this enormous war machine. Von Leeb's mission was to cross the Memel,
wipe out the Russian troops throughout the Baltic states and
move on to Leningrad. His spearhead would be General Hoepner's armored divisions. Von Bock's objectives were first Smolensk, then Moscow—with two groups of armored troops commanded by the best generals in the Wehrmacht, Guderian and
Hoth. Von Rundstedt would make a breakthrough between the
Pripet Marshes and the Carpathians, invade the Ukraine and,
if possible, reach Kiev. The strategy devised by the Oberkommando of the Wehrmacht seemed perfectly clear. A great effort
would be made in the center, across a marshy region crossed
by a great many rivers, where it would be least expected. The
Russian front would be broken and the Russian armies encircled in a number of pockets. In the same movement all the great
vital centers would be occupied.

Throughout that May and the first week of June, 1941, Alexander Rado had trouble sleeping; he read and reread the intelligence from Lucy. Perhaps the Center was wrong after all.

Why not trust Lucy? He couldn't get Christian Schneider's words out of his mind. "You will be partly responsible." The Kremlin had never had any difficulty in finding a scapegoat when things went wrong.

Curiously enough, Alexander Foote offered the same reasoning when the two men met some days later, on Thursday, June 12, 1941. The night before, Schneider had come to see Rado. They had scarcely been on speaking terms since the night of their argument. He had simply placed a piece of paper on Rado's desk. Rado could hardly believe his eyes when he read the message written on it:

"General attack on territories occupied by Russians dawn of Sunday 22 June: 3:15 A.M."

When Schneider had satisfied himself that Rado had taken in the message, he turned on his heels and went out without a word. All night Rado suffered the agony of indecision. On the morning of Thursday, June 12, unable to bear it any longer, he telephoned Foote—something he had never done before. Sounding deeply upset, he asked the Englishman to come at once to Geneva. Having insisted that Rado should meet him at the Gare de Cornavin at noon, Foote cursed and hung up.

The two spies walked silently down the rue du Mont-Blanc to the bridge that closes Lake Leman at the point where the Rhône continues on its way into France. They then turned left, stopping at a distance from the casino, in front of the landing stages, which in peacetime were used by pleasure boats. There, on a bench overlooking the Lake, Rado handed Foote the message.

"What are you going to do?" Foote asked.

After a long silence, Rado murmured:

"What can I do? You know how skeptical the Center was about Lucy's information. Perhaps the information isn't true."

Foote made no secret of his annoyance:

"So you've brought me all the way here just to tell me that you haven't made up your mind yet. If I were you, I'd send the information all the same. It would then be up to the Center to accept responsibility. Who knows, you might later be accused of criminal negligence. I wouldn't like to be in your shoes then."

The prospect of what lay ahead if this were the case suddenly forced Rado's hand. He gave Foote the message.

"Send it at the next normal transmitting time, the day after tomorrow. Come back to my office with me and I'll give you a dossier I've got in my safe—all the information sent in by Lucy for the past month. Ask the Center to give you three or four extra transmitting times—you'll need them to send that lot out. Never mind if they don't like it. At least we'll have done our duty."

So on June 14, then on 16, 17 and 18, 1941, Alexander Foote kept at his transmitter. The only answer he got was, "Understood. Over." When he had finished burning all the papers and all his code jottings, Foote collapsed onto his bed, exhausted. He slept for the next twenty-four hours. He would have liked to have kept a copy of all this exceptional intelligence for his own later use, but the orders of the MGB were that everything must be destroyed.

This time, the Russians showed no suspicion of Lucy's information. So many other sources confirmed the date of the invasion that they would have been mad not to believe the rest, which was infinitely more important. In fact, the date, June 22, had been confirmed by Richard Sorge, the best Soviet agent in the Far East. Moreover, Cordell Hull and Sumner Welles, the American Secretary and Under-Secretary of State, had just warned Constantin Umansky, the Soviet ambassador in Washington, that they had received word from their legations in

Europe of a planned invasion of Russia by the Germans. Finally, the date had also been confirmed by Churchill, who had got wind of it through his espionage network in Germany.

The MGB was in a turmoil of doubt. The arguments were reviewed time and time again. Had Stalin perhaps been wrong to base everything on the nonaggression pact signed with Hitler? If so, he was making a terrible mistake in not alerting the four and a half million soldiers of the Red Army at the frontier. The Army High Command had long been recommending this. Moreover, there were other facts—apart from intelligence that had come from espionage sources—that indicated that something was going on beyond the western frontier.

In the past two months, twenty-four German reconnaissance planes had flown well into Soviet territory, and one of them had crashed. Top-quality cameras had been found in the wreckage, with film that left no doubt that their sole mission had been to photograph Soviet military installations. Moreover, for the past three months, German firms that should have fulfilled the terms of the economic contract signed on January 10, had stopped sending their goods to the USSR. Yet the Russians continued to prove their good faith by increasing their supplies of cereals, gasoline, ferrous and nonferrous metals and rubber. Finally, well-informed newspapers throughout the world, studied attentively every day in the Ministry of Security, made continual references to German troop concentration on the Russian frontiers. Yes, Stalin might well have been wrong.

Although Stalin had forbidden that any defensive moves be made along the frontiers, fearing that they might be interpreted by Hitler as acts of defiance, the MGB sent a discreet warning to the Red Army High Command. But the results of the Center's second thoughts could no longer spare the Soviet Union. Hidden in the dense Polish fir forests, under the oaks, beeches and ashes of the Carpathians and amid the cane apples and laurels of Bessarabia, 146 divisions lay, ready to attack. The men were in peak condition and in high morale and dreamed of succeeding where Napoleon had failed. In Berlin, Joachim von Ribbentrop, the German Foreign Minister, was already composing the coded message to send to his ambassador in Moscow, Count Friedrich von der Schulenburg. It was one of the Führer's most cynical declarations of war:

"Information received in the past few days by the government of the Reich leaves no doubt as to the aggressive nature of Soviet troop movements. Moreover, intelligence from a British source has confirmed the existence of negotiations conducted by the British ambassador, Sir Stafford Cripps, to establish close military cooperation between Great Britain and the Soviet Union. The government of the Reich declares that in violation of its solemn engagements the Soviet government has been guilty:

"a—of having continued and intensified its maneuvers with a view to undermining Germany and the rest of Europe.

"b—of having assembled on the German frontier all its armed forces on a war footing.

"c—of making preparations, of an obvious kind, and in violation of the German-Russian nonagression pact, to attack Germany.

"As a result, the Führer has ordered the armed forces of the Reich to meet such a threat with every means at their disposal."

At twilight of the afternoon of June 21, 1941, an embarrassed von der Schulenburg arrived at the Kremlin to present Molotov with Hitler's message. Nine hours later, on a front of more than six hundred miles, a wave of fire swept across Russian territory. The war in the East had begun.

8

O N June 23, 1941, Rudolf Roessler was to discover two of the Center's best qualities: a profound contempt for wounds inflicted on its *amour propre* and a remarkable capacity to adapt itself to changing circumstances. For two and a half months, the Russians had stubbornly refused to listen to Lucy's shouts of alarm. Now, overnight, their attitude was transformed: they offered the despised Lucy more money than had ever been paid a secret agent and begged him to go on with his vital work.

In fact, the very night before, Alexander Foote had tuned his transmitter-receiver to the wavelength usually used by the MGB. It was not his customary day for transmitting, and he was afraid that he would get no reply. But disturbed by the new turn taken by the war, he felt a deep need to be in touch with Moscow.

Suddenly, Foote was startled by an increasingly sharp whistle in his headphones. Someone was on the wavelength. The whistle stopped and was followed by a series of two dashes and two dots: Z,Z,Z,Z. It was the Center. Foote recognized its "signature" at once. A flood of letters and figures arrived as usual. Then silence. Foote made use of the break to translate the dispatch:

"Calling all networks . . . Calling all networks. The fascist beasts have invaded the workers' fatherland. The moment has come to do all in our power to help the USSR in its struggle against Germany. Signed, the Director."

After a short interval, the Center continued its transmission: "NDA . . . NDA . . . NDA . . . Special message."

NDA was Foote.

"NDA . . . The Center has decided that from now on dispatches will be divided into three categories. MSG will designate routine communications, RDO urgent messages and VYRDO will preface messages of the greatest importance. From today all intelligence communicated by Lucy will be classified as VYRDO and be relayed immediately. The Center will be on the alert for communications twenty-four hours a day. NDA alone will transmit Lucy's communications. Edwards and Rosie will be duly informed . . ."

"Edwards" and "Rosie" were, of course, Hamel and Margareta Bolli, Rado's personal wireless operators. Things must be getting very serious, Foote thought. Within a few seconds, he was certain of it. He was ordered by the MGB to contact Lucy at once. Moscow anxiously awaited all his intelligence. He was to be paid a regular salary of 7,000 *Swiss francs a month* (about $1,600), not including additional payments for exceptional intelligence.

In 1941, a monthly salary of 7,000 Swiss francs was something of a fortune. In fact, for a while he used nearly all of it to keep the network going. Sometimes it was not even enough. The regular messengers between Lucerne and Geneva, the code experts and the wireless operators of Rado's network all made personal contributions to the funds of the organization in order that the struggle might continue. Up until June, 1941, things had been relatively easy. The economic service of Vladimir Dekanozov, the Soviet ambassador in Berlin, had been instructed to provide a plentiful flow of money for the network. The only difficulty was in getting the money into Switzerland. Rado solved this problem simply by getting one of his agents to bring the money in secretly. When the Berlin embassy was closed, Moscow ordered the resident-director of its last espionage network in Europe to get its supply of funds from the Swiss Communist Party and these advances would be repaid later. Unfortunately, Léon Nicole's party was itself short of money and said that it would be unable to comply. Rado lost his temper and the Center became increasingly angry. At this point Foote conceived a simple scheme based entirely on trust.

Some of his English acquaintances in Lausanne would introduce him to one of the directors of the Lausanne branch of an important American company. For the benefit of this American, he would play up his role of eccentric and extravagant millionaire and ask help in getting money into Switzerland. He would say that he'd be willing to pay the black-market rate of interest. All that was needed was for the MGB, through someone who could not be suspected of working for the Russians, to credit the bank account of the company in New York with the necessary funds. The company would then credit its Lausanne branch with an equivalent sum in Swiss francs, and it would deliver the money to Foote, after subtracting the agreed commission.

The Center agreed to the idea at once. Nothing could be easier than sending money to the United States. The director of the Lausanne branch also complied, believing he was doing a good turn to a rich English gentleman. The company in New York did not object either, being quite unaware that it was involuntarily helping to finance a Soviet espionage network. Neither the directors of the company in New York, nor the American in Lausanne, expressed the slightest surprise at the size of the sums transferred. None of these transactions took more than ten days to complete—which must have been a record for those troubled times.

Money did nothing to change Roessler's habits. He continued to rise at six-thirty every morning, eat his frugal breakfast of coffee and toast and, at seven-thirty, leave home to catch the trolley, which took him to the center of Lucerne. At eight he opened the Vita Nova bookshop in the Fluhmattstrasse. His mornings were devoted to correspondence and to the day-to-day affairs of the publishing business. At noon he went home to lunch. His tastes in food were extremely simple, not to say ascetic. His wardrobe was limited, and he wore his clothes until they were threadbare—a dark ready-made suit, a long, black overcoat for winter, an outsize trench coat for other seasons and a soft, felt hat that he wore pulled down to his ears.

Roessler did not smoke, as he suffered from frequent and exhausting asthma attacks. He appeared to have only one weakness: coffee; he drank coffee incessantly, at home, at the office and at the Villa Stutz at Kastanienbaum—and well into the night.

Roessler devoted his afternoons to his work for the Swiss secret service, correlating and evaluating all the intelligence they supplied him with for the use of Brigadier Masson. The Brigadier always took Roessler's reports with him when he attended the meetings of the Swiss High Command. After dinner, the German émigré again became an active agent, engaged in the radiotelegraphy that linked him to his friends in the Oberkommando of the Wehrmacht. He often worked until three o'clock in the morning, decoding and writing up the dispatches from *Werther* and *Olga*. In addition, Roessler never ceased to perform his role as Lucy, forever at the disposition of Christian Schneider, his go-between, finding time to transmit news concerning the Soviet Union to the Russians and to carry out the instructions he received from them.

He gave up going to the theater and movies, fearing that he might miss a transmission. He took no time off—no holidays, not even a weekend. The Russians paid him well and he accepted their money. Christian Schneider had insisted that, if he did not, Moscow might again grow suspicious. But even if he had not been paid by the Center he would have worked just as diligently for them. Roessler cared for nothing but the defeat of Nazism.

"Above all, tell Lucy that he must not worry about the payments in the event of delays," the director of the Center declared on June 25, 1941.

Then, again, on June 30 of that year:

"Make it perfectly clear to Lucy that in the event of irregularities in the payment of his salary he must be patient and in no way slacken his efforts at this crucial time in our struggle against Hitler. We will never fail to meet our obligations."

Lucy could not have cared less. For, contrary to the image the MGB had created of him, he was not in the least mercenary.

It might be said that the MGB was the only part of the Soviet war machine to work effectively against Nazi Germany during the first months of the War. Elsewhere, on the fronts, the Russian soldiers, whose job the MGB should normally have made easier, collapsed under the German attack, and the enormous advantage, which the Russians possessed, of knowing the enemy's plans in advance was at first of little use. The intelligence had come too late, and the Russians needed time to recover from the first unexpected blows, before they could benefit fully from their good fortune. This took three months, during which the Germans began to suspect that some deadly parasite had invaded their system and was sapping its strength.

In fact, on July 2, ten days after the beginning of the war in the East, Lucy confirmed to the MGB that the German plan of attack had Moscow as its immediate objective. Most of the German effort would be concentrated on the central front by the tanks of Guderian and Hoth. The troop movements in the north and south would be little more than diversions. This was what the Oberkommando of the Wehrmacht had called "Plan I."

On July 27, 1941, Lucy asked Rado to warn the Center at once that the OKW, sensing that the Russians were building up their resistance on the central front, had suddenly switched to "Plan II." This involved two main thrusts, from the north and south, in a pincer movement, in order to give some respite to the troops of Field Marshal von Bock.

These were obviously two vital pieces of intelligence. If the Red Army was incapable of containing the German advance on all fronts, at least its commander-in-chief, Marshal Boris Mikhailovich Shaposhnikov, was able to communicate at once to the corps commanders at the front those items of Lucy's intelligence that were relevant to them. As a result, there was an important change of tactics, accompanied by an avalanche of details concerning the units that the Soviet troops would find in front of them.

Nevertheless, on August 10, 1941, the fighting post headquarters of the 16th Russian army fell intact into the hands of General Hoth's panzergrenadiers, east of Smolensk. The military security officers blew open the door of a rusty safe and were stunned to discover, among a mass of paper work, exact copies in Russian of the OKW's two plans of campaign, as well as a copy of the sudden decision to adopt the second of the two.

A few days before this discovery, the German military security officers had found another packet of confidential papers, in an office abandoned by the general commanding the 1st Cossack army, at Lomzha. To their amazement, they realized that the Red Army knew of the weak spot in the organization of the German army. The Wehrmacht's Achilles' heel in 1941, which was to remain a vulnerable point despite successive improvements, was supplies. Roessler never ceased to concern himself with this problem throughout the war. The first information on the subject, which he gave to Christian Schneider for transmission to Moscow, was as early as June 27, 1941. It consisted of a complete operations chart and had taken Alexander Foote four hours to transmit.

"Throw everything into the attack" was invariably Hitler's order when drawing up his campaign plans—and the OKW complied. As a result, the Oberkommando of the Wehrmacht was no longer capable of making large-scale plans for retreat when things ceased to go in their favor. The Wehrmacht appeared to have one, universal tactic: concentrate all available troops in a single overwhelming breakthrough and annihilate the enemy in one blow.

The assault plans of the OKW were remarkable and could be studied with profit by military schools even today. The same cannot be said for their support organization, which was far too unwieldy ever to be adapted to shock tactics. Hitler decreed that the German soldier was not to feel weighed down in his lightning attacks. No special supply service would be attached to the fighting units. Food, ammunition, fuel, spare parts, even medical supplies would be brought up as close as possible to the fighting line and placed in clearings where the combatants would come to supply their needs. These depots were obviously enormous, for an infantry division of the Wehrmacht consumed 130 tons of general supplies a day; a panzer division, 300 tons; an army, 5,000 tons; and a group of armies, such as those under von Bock, von Leeb or von Rundstedt, 18,000 tons —18,000 tons a day, the equivalent of 36 trainloads. It was the supply problem that was inevitably to confound the Wehrmacht.

One has only to imagine the long cohorts of vehicles from the fighting units returning to the rear lines to get their food and supplies and the inextricable traffic jams around these monstrous compounds. This is exactly what it was like on the Eastern Front, against a background of dust, mud or snow, according to the season. Moreover, these vast depots provided magnificent objectives for the enemy air force. When the OKW strategists were preparing "Operation Barbarossa," first on a 1/1,000,000th map of Russia, published in 1896, then later on other more modern maps on a 1/500,000th scale, they carefully selected the sites for these huge mobile depots in relation to the advance into Russia, as well as the routes to be followed by the troops to reach them. These were the weak spots that Roessler revealed to Rado, and which the Russians carefully transferred to their own maps.

For the Germans, the dramatic discovery at Lomzha meant only one thing: the enemy seemed to be remarkably well informed. Perhaps they even had spies within the Wehrmacht itself.

This impression soon became a certainty. On August 10, 1941, Roessler informed Rado—as well as the Bureau Ha at Kastanienbaum—that the Wehrmacht High Command had decided to adopt a modified version of Plan I: the group of armies in the center, commanded by Marshal von Bock, would attack again, through Bryansk, in the direction of Moscow.

General Halder, the chief of staff, proposed this modified plan to the Führer only on August 18. The OKW services in the camp at Zossen, near Berlin, worked at top speed on its practical details. Among the technicians involved in the work were Roessler's ten accomplices. Thus Roessler got full details of the plan eight days before its submission to the Führer. Stalin was immediately informed, and he and Marshal Shaposhnikov resolved to make a lightning attack on the Wehrmacht—the first Russian attack since the beginning of the conflict. On August 12, they called in their best tank technician, Eremenko.

"Guderian will attack Moscow in a week's time," Stalin told him. "He will go through Bryansk. I want you to assume command of the defense of this front. I shall even send you as reinforcements the 3rd and 21st armies, which are at present in the Ukraine. We're safe there for the moment. You have a difficult task to accomplish."

It was then that history—and the Führer, whose sudden decisions were always unpredictable and enigmatic—played a dramatic trick on the Russians. On August 18th, as Lucy had said, Halder took his plan to Hitler, who was then in his wartime headquarters, Wolfsschanze, at Rastenburg, in East Prussia, a damp, densely wooded area. The conference lasted five days. Hitler seemed in a particularly gloomy mood, as the generals, whom he terrorized and even insulted, waited submissively for a decision.

The war was dragging too much for his taste. Moscow could wait. He wanted the Ukraine and its rich grain fields. Guderian, who wanted to take the Soviet capital, which he felt was within the grasp of his tanks, could not change Hitler's mind.

"Attack at once in the south," Hitler ordered. "Link up with von Rundstedt's armies. Attack and get me Kiev."

This was the crucial moment that upset Lucy's predictions

and confounded Stalin, who continued to prepare for the Bry-ansk-Moscow operation and had transferred his defenses from the Ukraine for that purpose. Roessler's friends knew nothing of the Führer's latest turnabout—and they were to learn nothing more for the next few days. This was because the OKW had had no hand in drawing up the new plans for Guderian's break-through. Guderian had been left to exercise his own initiative as the occasion arose.

From August 20 to 25, 1941, Guderian's troops moved south-ward exactly parallel to the lines held by Eremenko. A few stiff battles took place on the way when the two armies came into contact, but these were merely the work of Guderian's defensive flank. Eremenko was confused. Did Guderian intend to make a detour to the south and attack Bryansk from the side? Gu-derian was equally bewildered. He could not understand why Eremenko did not attack him from the side and try to break up his columns. What was he going to be met with in the Ukraine? First, by Red Army units weakened by the departure of those armies mobilized by Stalin to defend Bryansk, then by the ad-vance guard of von Rundstedt's armies from the south. At the heart of this magnificent encirclement was Kiev, defended by troops under the famous old Marshal Semën Mikhailovich Bu-dënny, a legendary figure of the Revolution. The Russians fought well, but Kiev capitulated. At one blow, the Wehrmacht wiped out a half dozen Soviet armies, took 660,000 prisoners and destroyed more than 1,000 tanks and 5,000 guns. For Stalin, it was a major disaster. For Hitler, it was a good sign; he now wanted Moscow.

With hardly time for a breathing space, Guderian now moved northward. A month and a half after the original rendezvous with Eremenko, he arrived at Bryansk. Guderian took the So-viet armies from behind and forced open their lines. Like Kiev,

Bryansk fell, then Vyazma. The Wehrmacht now moved straight on to the Soviet capital. They were to get no farther than the city's outlying suburbs, where they halted, exhausted and already handicapped by the approach of winter—a winter for which they had made no preparations. The Germans did not yet know that this was to cost them the war.

However, their confidence was somewhat shaken by what their Military Security service had discovered, in the middle of October, among the ruins of Bryansk—more documents, which explained Eremenko's inertia as Guderian's troops had moved almost under his nose. The Russian general had been expecting an attack on positions he knew to be impregnable if attacked head-on. These documents were a copy of Plan I, as revised by Halder and presented to Hitler on August 18 at Rastenburg.

Military Security then decided to hand over the results of these extraordinary discoveries to the Abwehr, the Wehrmacht's official organization for espionage and counterespionage. But since its head, Admiral Canaris, was already suspected of betraying the cause of the Führer, the SD, then directed by Reinhard Heydrich, was also informed.

Heydrich at once recognized the whole affair's vital importance. Like Hitler, he had always detested the German officer corps, unable to forget that his career in the navy had ended in discharge for gambling debts and dishonorable actions. He was convinced that among that band of officers, in whose hands the salvation of Germany rested, there was a traitor, or perhaps several, who were acting as Soviet informers. The exceptional nature of the discoveries made by Military Security on the Eastern Front confirmed his suspicions. He would have to discover who they were at once.

Heydrich would have liked to have taken over the job personally but hadn't the time; he was too preoccupied with party intrigues. So he decided to entrust the inquiry to his brilliant assistant, young SS-Brigadeführer Walter Schellenberg.

Schellenberg was a Nazi "intellectual," who talked brilliantly of music, literature and painting. He claimed to despise politics —yet at thirty-two he was the youngest of the Nazi leaders, the man whom Himmler affectionately called his "dauphin." Born in the Saar in 1910, the youngest of seven children, Schellenberg was old enough to remember the horrors of the First World War. His father was a piano-maker—not a very prosperous trade back in 1923, when an exhausted, impoverished Germany thought more of appeasing its hunger than of amusing itself. So the family emigrated to Luxembourg. In the summer of 1929, Walter went to Bonn University. For two years he studied medicine, then took up law. The world crises and the desperate economic situation in Germany, exacerbated by the degenerating political atmosphere of the Weimar Republic, did not leave the Schellenbergs unaffected. Walter was forced to ask for a scholarship to complete his studies. The judge who dealt with his case hinted that he would have a better chance of obtaining aid if he joined the Nazi Party and the SS organization. Suddenly, everything appeared to be quite simple.

In 1934, Schellenberg gave a lecture on the development of German law, in the course of which he attacked the Catholic Church. This drew Heydrich's attention, and two of his advisers, both professors at Bonn University, approached Schellenberg and engaged him. His future looked bright indeed. But he owed his extraordinary success to his own gifts and to hard work—not to favoritism, so rampant in Germany since the Nazis had come to power. If Himmler had taken him into his confidence, it was because of his ability as a jurist and because of his sound knowledge of western Europe. Himmler had even ordered his own doctor, a Finn called Karsten, who was utterly devoted to him, to take particular care of Schellenberg's health; he suffered from a bad liver.

He was also on very close terms with Admiral Canaris. Every morning, when they were both in Berlin, they went riding together. In the open air they were able to exchange confidential information without danger of eavesdroppers. The head of the Abwehr was something less than careful in his choice of assistants. He tended to swell the ranks of his organization somewhat indiscriminately, so much so that since early 1941, one of Schellenberg's tasks had been the liquidation of certain unreliable elements in the Abwehr.

Of all Hitler's generals, Schellenberg was the most widely traveled. But he never left his headquarters in the Berkaerstrasse, in Berlin-Schmargendorf, without good reason. It was from there that he ran the "F" bureaus of the SD, that is, all its espionage networks throughout the world.

9

"CONTRARY to the portrait of himself that Schellenberg presented to the British after the fall of the Third Reich, that of a cultured man of Western, not to say Latin, tastes—and which many believed to be true—I was never able to see in him anything other than a faithful copy, a perfect reflection of Reinhard Heydrich. Even to the bearing of the head, the smile, the presence—and the passion for horsemanship. Unfortunately, he also had the same cold cruelty, the same profound amorality and the same aristocratic art of concealing his vices. Heydrich was his intellectual master."

This astonishing portrait was provided by Hans Bernd Gisevius, wartime German Vice-Consul in Switzerland, and one of the organizers of the attempt on Hitler's life of July 20, 1944. It explains the extraordinary similarity between the actions of the two men. In fact, three of Schellenberg's early masterschemes—the framing of two British agents at Venlo, Holland, the manufacture of false pound notes at Oranienburg, and the manipulation of the spy, Cicero—all bore the unmistakable imprint of Heydrich.

The Venlo affair had begun on the evening of November 8,

1939, in a resaurant in Munich, where every year Hitler celebrated the anniversary of his failed putsch of 1923. Suddenly
Hitler had broken off his speech and fled from the table, just before a bomb, clumsily concealed in a pillar, exploded. He was to
recount later how a voice within had urged him to leave. But
everything had led political and technical observers to believe that the entire assassination attempt had been prearranged
by the Nazis themselves in an attempt to increase the Führer's
popularity.

In the early hours of the morning of November 9, Walter
Schellenberg went into action. At Venlo, in Holland, very close
to the German frontier, he led a group of SS that arrested two
British officers, Captain S. Payne Best and Major R. H. Stevens,
agents of the British Intelligence Service. Since October 21,
1939, he had suspected the pair of working for a group of German generals who wished to overthrow Hitler and set up a new
regime with the blessing of Great Britain. In fact, he was holding them in readiness for the right moment.

Captain Best and Major Stevens, accused of having organized
the Munich plot from Venlo, were to spend the rest of the war
in a concentration camp. This accusation was also to serve,
shortly afterward, as a pretext for Germany's invasion of Holland—such an attack being justified on the grounds that "this
country has abused the privileges of neutrality by harboring two
such violent enemies of the Third Reich."

(Hitler was so delighted by the success of this ruse that he
gave Schellenberg the job of devising—and carrying out himself
—a plan to kidnap the Duke and Duchess of Windsor. The Führer was irrational enough to believe that in this way he might
persuade the ex-King of England to collaborate with him and
arrange a peace with Britain. At the end of July, 1940, the royal
couple were in Lisbon. They were to be abducted and given a

residence in Germany, as well as some £40,000 ($160,000), already placed in a bank in Geneva, which would be put at their disposal. If necessary, Hitler would increase the amount. The kidnapping failed by a hair's breadth, when agents of the British Intelligence Service arrived in Portugal one day before the young SS general.)

Schellenberg's counterfeiting scheme—known as the "Bernhard" Operation—involved the production of huge quantities of forged sterling bank notes. These were to be poured into the coffers of the banks of neutral countries, diminishing real British currency in value. Inventive as he was in such matters, this plan was not altogether his own. It had been conceived in November, 1939, by a certain Alfred Helmut Naujocks. Schellenberg had been quite fond of Naujocks, had enlisted his aid in the kidnapping of Best and Stevens at Venlo. And it was Naujocks who had "justified" the invasion of Poland by the Wehrmacht, by carrying out a mock attack on the German radio station at Gleiwitz, on the night of August 31, 1939, with other SS men, disguised like himself as Polish soldiers.

Schellenberg made various improvements on Naujocks' rather crude plan. The paper needed for the false notes was extremely difficult to imitate: it had to be made from pure linen, without cellulose, soiled, then washed in detergents. It was prepared in the Spechthausen factory at Eberswalde, near Berlin. Engraving of the plates and printing of the notes was carried out under the direction of Captain Kruger in a secret hideout, an anonymous shed in the concentration camp at Oranienburg.

The forgery was perfect. Toward the end of 1941, one of Schellenberg's agents changed a large quantity of £5 and £10 notes in Switzerland. He even dared ask that they be verified, saying that he had bought them on the black market. The Bank of England kept only 10 percent of them as suspect and recognized the rest as perfectly genuine. Schellenberg had then proceeded to put the false notes into circulation in Switzerland, through a certain Dr. Willy Grobl, and in Genoa and Trieste, through an engineer called Friedrich Schwerd. Even when these two cities were no longer under the control of the German army, the trafficking continued until the end of the war.

The third scheme was an espionage affair that was to become famous after the war as the "Cicero" affair. SS-Sturmbannführer Ludwig Moyzisch, who was in charge of the SD mission in Ankara, the Turkish capital, informed his chief that he had become very friendly with a certain Eliaza Bazna. Bazna, an Albanian, was the valet to the British ambassador, Sir Hugh Knatchbull-Hugessen. This connection promised a rich harvest. Schellenberg urged him to pursue the contact. But how was Bazna, who was proving very greedy, to be paid? Schellenberg hardly hesitated. They would use the wonderful forged currency made at Oranienburg.

In fact, and as these typical, Machiavellian operations indicate, Reinhard Heydrich and Walter Schellenberg complemented each other so perfectly that one had only to throw out a vague idea for the other to carry it out beyond all the hopes of its originator. Thus, when one evening Heydrich happened to say that the SD ought to set up an establishment in which foreign visitors could come and amuse themselves in agreeable company, and where, involuntarily, they would give away valuable information, Schellenberg began the next day to plan the famous "Kitty Salon." The prettiest German prostitutes as well as ladies of the highest social standing attended its extremly informal gatherings and performed a veritable military service. Many a diplomat lost his self-control in this paradise filled with invisible microphones, tape recorders and cameras. Following indiscreet revelations made in this de luxe brothel, situated in the heart of the fashionable quarter of Berlin of the period, Count Galeazzo Ciano, Mussolini's son-in-law, lost his life.

It was also why, as soon as Heydrich gave him the job of unmasking the traitors who were passing information to the Russians, Schellenberg conceived a scheme that was entirely typical of its instigator.

Toward the end of October, 1941, he drew up his plan of action. He would not attempt to go through the entire officer corps with a fine-tooth comb to find the traitors—at least, not immediately. There were no fewer than 3,000 generals and 320,000 officers of other ranks in the Wehrmacht. Instead, he would concentrate his attention on the weak spot that sooner or later gave most subversive networks away: radio communications.

In fact, it was the unmasking of another spy ring—*Die Rote Kapelle*, a network that had been working for the Russians and had distributed a large number of agents throughout western Europe—that persuaded Schellenberg to begin with communications. The SD had first intercepted, then decoded its messages. Since then, most of the operators had been arrested by means of radiogoniometry, in the act of transmitting their wireless telegrams. It was a simple matter to make these operators denounce their accomplices. One after another, the agents of *Die Rote Kapelle*, which had certainly paid little attention to secrecy measures, fell into the nets of the SD.

Radiogoniometry was as disastrous an invention for secret agents as radiotelegraphy had been for the countries on whom they were spying. It was this technique that helped Colonel Ozaki, the head of Japanese counterespionage, to capture the famous Richard Sorge. A "gonio" set is a simple receiver in which a mobile frame, pivoting on an axis, replaces the usual aerial. Experience and calculation had shown that the reception of a broadcast was always strongest when the frame was directed straight at the transmitting station. The position of the frame, therefore, indicated the geographical line on which the target station lay. One had only to follow this line in order to lay hands on its operators. A "gonio" set could also be used in another way, by orienting it so that the reception became minimal or disappeared altogether. The perpendicular to the frame then gave the required direction. Tripled and operating from three different points, the "gonios" were able to indicate the precise position of an illegal transmitter. It was never long before its operators were seized.

One major motive urged Schellenberg to take an interest in the problem of broadcasts in order to find the traitors that Heydrich sought. He knew that radio alone could be used to pass information to the Russians. It was virtually impossible to imagine a messenger service crossing the Wehrmacht's lines, bearing documents for the Russians.

Meanwhile, at Mayback camp at Zossen, only a few miles away from SD headquarters, Rudolf Roessler's companions had no notion that the most formidable espionage organization in the Reich was about to begin its attempts to localize the intelligence leak. They had little reason to fear, for they took every possible precaution. As soon as a piece of intelligence of sufficient importance reached them, they coded it and awaited a suitable time at night, when the traffic was at its most intense to transmit it. No listening station could distinguish this single transmission among the thousands of coded radiotelegrams crowding the atmosphere. And this message could be decoded only in Lucerne.

In Lucerne, Roessler had not yet learned that Stalin's sudden blind trust in Lucy had caused a strategic catastrophe, the loss of Kiev. The Center made no reproaches. The affair would simply find its way to the profits and losses account. The Germans would pay for it later—with interest. The only urgent requests for intelligence to come from Moscow concerned the German units on the Eastern Front—their manpower, their armament, their destinations. Roessler transmitted these requests to Berlin and the replies came back, usually within forty-eight hours. At the beginning of autumn, 1941, he was even to pass on to the Russians two surprising items of scientific information. The Germans were putting the final touches to a new weapon, which had been called the V-1. They had also begun the construction of a ten-ton rocket. This was one of the last messages Alexander Foote would transmit before an incident occurred that caused considerable concern to Roessler and to his friends in the OKW.

On October 19, 1941, a Sunday night, the operator at the Center in Moscow had been transmitting a dispatch that had lasted about half an hour, involving requests for details on the activities of the Wehrmacht. Suddenly the Morse stopped dead. Foote made two or three calls, but there was no reply. The next day he tried again, and again the day after that, but he was met by silence. He warned Rado, and Schneider telephoned to Roessler. No one knew what was going on.

For the next six weeks, Roessler communicated his information only to his Swiss employers in the Bureau Ha. In Berlin, his friends became angry. The Swiss weren't fighting the Nazis. Some other means of contacting the Russians had to be found.

Every night Foote tuned in his transmitter-receiver to the Center's wavelength in the hope that something would come through.

Seventeen days later, on Wednesday, November 5, 1941, Schellenberg was near Dresden, where the SD had just installed an important new listening station. Germany's best-qualified decoders were engaged on work of vital importance. Not a decimetre of wavelength escaped their attention, twenty-four hours a day. But in that incredibly crowded atmosphere it was often impossible to distinguish those of the enemy among the mass of dots and dashes. Even when an enemy message had been located, it still did not yield up its secrets. It had to be worked on, often unsuccessfully. A "B" never represented a "B," either for the Führer's headquarters, for the transmissions of the OKW or for the enemy. Similarly, a "2" had no meaning in itself in this world of darkness. Sometimes, when the keys to a code did not prove too difficult to break, as was the case of *Die Rote Kapelle,* for example, the experts in Dresden rejoiced. But their work was seldom that easy.

"Persevere!" Schellenberg told them. "One day you will find a series of suspicious signals in the atmosphere."

Chance soon favored his enterprise. For three weeks Schellenberg had been telephoning Dresden, anxiously hoping for news. On November 28, the listening station informed him that on several successive nights they had made out a very brief message, repeated several times on 43 meters. On each occasion it had begun at exactly the same time, 1 A.M. The message was always identical:

"NDA. FRX . . . NDA. FRX . . . NDA. FRX . . ."

"What do you think it is?" Schellenberg asked.

"Difficult to say, though its brevity and the repetition of the signal indicate that it may be a call-signal."

"Where's it coming from?"

"It never lasts long enough for us to find out. We've no sooner got the gonio into position, than the transmission stops."

"Keep trying!"

Paradoxically, perseverance was a quality shared by both Schellenberg and Roessler, as it is by all the best secret agents.

The signal was, of course, that of Alexander Foote vainly calling the Center during the break in contact. That Dresden had heard it was not, in itself, as serious as it might at first seem. For, following a principle practiced by all clandestine operators, neither Rado's network, nor their opposite numbers in Moscow, ever used the same wavelengths for both their messages and their call-signals. Moreover, they used an additional camouflage. Foote called on 43 meters, then tuned onto 39 meters, as previously agreed with the Center. As soon as the Center had replied on 39 meters, Foote stopped using 43 meters. He would then communicate on the same wavelength as his Moscow colleague. These wavelengths were frequently changed to avoid establishing a pattern that could be picked up by a listening station.

Such a ruse could not possibly continue to confuse specialists armed with the latest equipment. Dresden was well aware of the trick. They enlarged the area under observation, using several receivers simultaneously tuned in to a range of neighboring wavelengths. In order to limit the field in this atmospheric cacophony, they eliminated all transmissions whose sources they knew, even if they did not recognize the wavelengths being used. These included, of course, the Oberkommando of the Wehrmacht and Hitler's own headquarters. Meticulously, they noted down thousands of enigmatic fragments, cataloging the incomprehensible, hoping that one day their rigorous classification of similar repetitions of letters and figures would afford a gleam of light.

Meanwhile, as 1941 came to an end, events of the greatest importance were taking place. The United States had entered the war, and Japan had transformed it into a worldwide conflict by making a lightning attack on Pearl Harbor, on December 7,

1941. Britain had stoically survived the Blitz. On the Continent, the German army had just suffered its first setbacks in the East. Under pressure from General Zhukov, at the head of 100 fresh divisions, the Wehrmacht was retreating before Moscow. Field Marshal von Kluge replaced von Bock as commander of the group of armies at the center which had been unable to contain the T34s of Maslennikov and Konev's divisions. Von Rundstedt had lost Rostov and been deprived of his command. A series of dismissals had shaken the Wehrmacht High Command. Hitler had dismissed Guderian and Hoepner on Christmas Day and taken over the supreme command of the German armed forces himself.

The renewal of the radio link between Alexander Foote and the Center was as unexpected as its rupture. Suddenly, on Monday, December 1, 1941, the Center resumed its transmissions. To Foote's great surprise, the Soviet operator continued to send precisely the same message he had been communicating when the interruption had occurred a month and a half earlier—as if those weeks of anxiety had never existed. At the end of the dispatch, Foote asked his unknown colleague the reason for so prolonged a silence.

It was quite simple. Following a German attack on Moscow, the authorities had feared that the Soviet capital might be taken or subjected to a long siege and had decided to evacuate immediately all the administrative services to Kuibyshev, the old city of Samara, now a port on the Volga. There had been no time to contact Switzerland to inform them of the move.

The resumption of contact had calmed Roessler's fears. It was becoming increasingly tense for his friends in the OKW, and they had been getting impatient. The news coming to Berlin from the East showed, in fact, that if the Russians exploited the Wehrmacht's first defeat to the full, Nazism might soon be defeated. Never more than at this moment did this tiny group of resisters have to struggle against their consciences. Every dispatch communicated by them to the Russians would help the Red Army to plunge into the living flesh of the enemy—German flesh.

For the Soviet troops had at last recovered their nerve—on all fronts, from the north to the south. In the Crimea, General Pervushin's troops were attacking those of Count von Sponeck, Colonel von Choltitz and General Himmer. On the Don, Timoshenko, Lopatin and Kharitonov had recaptured Rostov and the "Red Ruhr," which had fallen into the hands of von Rundstedt. In the icebound region before Moscow, the group of armies from the central front were continually being harassed by Zhukov, Kusnezov, Belov and Dovator. At Staraya Russa, on the banks of Lake Ilmen, in the north, the soldiers of Morosov and Eremenko were taking their revenge for the terrible reverses they had previously suffered. A fantastic thrust westward was beginning across a 600-mile front as the Soviet tanks moved in after the retreating Germans.

The Germans were in serious difficulties, still fighting in their threadbare summer uniforms in a temperature of $-40°F$. Snow got into their boots, turned into ice and froze their feet, resulting in amputations. So the Russians now swept down on the retreating Germans—white waves of men against a white background. For the Russians were admirably suited to this kind of warfare; they had been banking on the winter. Wearing white coats and white fur hats, the Siberian troops were ski-borne. Rifles, tanks and guns were painted white. The infantry wore boots that were always two sizes too big, which meant their feet could be wrapped in rags—the famous red socks—and could swell without being painfully chafed. The cold, together with the attacking spirit of the Russian soldier, delivered a blow to the Wehrmacht from which it never fully recovered.

The first complete figures for the German troops in Russia, compiled by General Halder in that winter of 1941, were alarming. A retreat of 60 to 180 miles. Worse, there were 202,500 killed, 725,000 wounded, 46,500 missing, 112,500 frozen to death —a total loss of 1,100,000 men, a third of all the troops engaged at the beginning of the campaign. The Wehrmacht tried vainly to improve its transportation of supplies by organizing a shuttle service between the great supply depots and the front. It launched raids deep into Soviet-held territory. It motorized its troops as much as possible. But it had been irreparably weakened. It was to be finally devoured by the steppes.

At the same time as General Halder, Rudolf Roessler was drawing up his own account. The early work of *Werther* and *Olga* had not borne much fruit. The western Allies had refused to listen to the mass of information that had been offered them with such generosity. But the effects of the Lucy Ring's intervention in the East had been overwhelming. If the West had only listened, Roessler speculated, Hitler could undoubtedly have been beaten in 1940.

The incredulity demonstrated first by Copenhagen and Oslo, then by The Hague and Brussels and, finally, by London and Paris, shows quite clearly that at the beginning of this monstrous war, the state of mind of the military high commands of the western democracies had not really evolved since 1918. For them, spies were still rather shady characters, unworthy of trust, even when they offered their intelligence without hope of reward. As a result, these men had refused to see the signs of the coming Nazi cataclysm, and millions of innocent people were to fall victim to their indifference. Strangely enough, even

Stalin—who was very much more aware of the value of a secret service than were the Western leaders—followed their example until the war had actually reached his frontiers. But the first months of the campaign showed that the Russians were quick to recover from their initial suspicion. In the conduct of their operations,they were to continue to value the intelligence service at its true worth. Roessler, encouraged by the Russians' attitude, continued to work for them without a moment's letup.

The German émigré had another reason for his decision. The Swiss, at least those with whom he dealt, the leading anti-Germans in the Confederation—the Bureau Ha, Brigadier Roger Masson and, ultimately, General Guisan himself—allowed him to continue his collaboration with Moscow and thus acted as silent accomplices. With the entry into the war of the United States, they felt considerably surer of their ground. Their decision at the very beginning of the war to give tacit support to the Allies had been vindicated. By the winter of 1941-2, it had become obvious that Germany, a prisoner to Hitler, would be unable to extricate itself from the situation into which the Führer had plunged it.

Intelligence reaching them through Roessler showed the Swiss how badly things were going inside the Reich: the grave defeats on the Russian front and the series of disgraces that had struck at the entire leadership of the OKW had revived the hopes of the many conspirators who flourished within the Wehrmacht High Command. Hitler, in fact, had dismissed thirty-five generals between December, 1941, and January, 1942—without counting Field Marshals von Brauchitsch, von Rundstedt, von Bock, von Leeb and Field Marshal Walter von Reichenau, who had died of a blood clot, and General Ernst

Udet, of the Luftwaffe, who had committed suicide in November. With the return of these embittered officers to Berlin, the wind of revolt blew up once more.

The abortive attempt on Hitler's life on July 20, 1944, has been given a great deal of attention. In fact, it was merely the culmination of a line of earlier plots—all hatched by the same men, beginning in 1938. Those who, in 1944, ended up shot, or hung up on butchers' hooks in Ploetzensee prison, or strangled with piano cord at Flossenburg, or driven to suicide had previously tried no fewer than fifteen times to eliminate the Führer.

In fact, it was a permanent, but really quite unserious conspiracy. It was destined to fail because it included too many people, and the entire army knew who they were. The Gestapo knew. Even Hitler himself knew. For when he finally lost his temper after the July 20 plot and decided to retaliate, 7,000 people were arrested, 5,000 of whom were summarily executed. In the corridors of the OKW the association of conspirators was irreverently known as "The Barometer of Glory." It went down only when the affairs of the Wehrmacht chiefs were going badly. Similarly, a stroke of good luck in the field, followed by a few judicious promotions by Hitler were enough to send the barometer soaring.

Rudolf Roessler's ten friends kept well away from this vast, shifting mass of plotters, in order to preserve intact their own far more destructive work. Indeed, though unaware of it, these plotters were helping Roessler's friends, for whom they provided a convenient distraction. This explains why the ten men were so invulnerable within the Oberkommando. Alarmed by the evident leaks that were taking place within this permanent nest of intrigue, the SD and the Gestapo made innumerable inquiries into its organization, unfailingly discovering the cur-

Rudolf Roessler

Roger Masson

Reinhard Heydrich

Walter Schellenberg

Villa Stutz, at Kastanienbaum, near Lucerne, the headquarters of the Bureau Ha

TRIBUNE DE LAUSANNE -- Vendredi 6 novembre 1953

PRESSE ANGLAISE

ISANS

UN AUTRE EMPIRE

mise à part), le Conseil fédéral est invité à présenter aux Chambres sans retard un rapport et les comptes ainsi que, le cas échéant, une demande dument motivée de crédits supplémentaires ; 3. l'acquisition ultérieure de chars et, le cas échéant, la demande de nouveaux crédits pour cette acquisition feront l'objet d'un message particulier.

La commission n'a pas vu la possibilité d'adhérer à la décision du Conseil national, attendu que le Conseil fédéral n'a pas présenté de demandes de crédits et qu'il n'est prévu aucune demande immédiate de crédits supplémentaires. D'autre part, la commission, après avoir entendu le chef du Département fédéral des finances, a décidé d'entrer en matière sur le projet du budget de la Confédération et, dans la discussion de débats approuvé ce projet en y apportant une amélioration de 2 millions de francs aux recettes.

La F.A.O.
sera-t-elle dirigée par un Suisse?

(C.P.S.) — Nous croyons savoir que le Conseil fédéral s'occupera dans une de ses prochaines séances de la succession à la direction générale de l'Organisation internationale de l'agriculture (Food and Agricultural Organization F.A.O.) On sait que la Suisse fait partie de cette section technique de l'O.N.U. depuis la création de celle-ci et qu'elle y est représentée par le professeur F.-T. Wahlen, auteur du fameux plan d'extension des cultures pendant la guerre. Depuis trois ans, M. Wahlen fait partie de l'administration de cette organisation en qualité de chef de la division de l'agriculture.

A la suite du départ du directeur général actuel de la F.A.O., l'Américain Norris E. Dudd, atteint par la limite d'âge, l'assemblée générale convoquée pour la fin du mois à Rome aura à régler la succession. En principe chaque gouvernement membre de la F.A.O. est libre de proposer un de ses concitoyens pour l'un des postes d'administration de la F.A.O. M. Wahlen étant un expert en matière agricole et un spécialiste de la F.A.O., quoi de plus naturel que le Conseil fédéral présente sa candidature au poste de directeur de l'organisation. Le Conseil fédéral désignera par la même occasion la délégation suisse à l'assemblée générale.

Le jugement
contre Roessler et Schnieper

(C.P.S.) — La Cour pénale fédérale, siégeant à Lucerne, a rendu jeudi matin son jugement dans l'affaire des espions Roessler et Schnieper. Les deux accusés sont reconnus coupables d'un service de renseignements pour un Etat étranger au préjudice d'un autre Etat étranger et condamnés à une peine d'emprisonnement d'une année pour Roessler et de neuf mois pour Schnieper, sous déduction de la préventive. Comme les deux condamnés ont déjà subi une détention de 242 jours pendant la durée de l'instruction, Roessler devra encore purger quatre mois et Schnieper un mois.

Le tribunal n'a pas donné suite à la demande d'expulsion introduite par le représentant du Ministère public contre Roessler. Dans ses considérants, il relève que ce dernier a effectivement abusé du droit d'asile suisse, mais qu'il faut considérer qu'il est établi depuis vingt ans dans notre pays et qu'il nous a rendu de précieux services durant la guerre. D'autre part, le condamné étant apatride, une peine de bannissement aurait eu pour lui des conséquences très dures.

LAUSANNE, au jour le jour

The "Roessler Affair" of 1953

camouflées à Prague. Lui-même reçut le pseudonyme de Marcel. A la question de savoir pourquoi on le chargea de ce travail.

Le procès intenté pour service de renseignements au profit d'un pays étranger à Rudolf Roessler, éditeur, 58 ans, et Xaver Schnieper, journaliste, 43 ans, a commencé à Lucerne devant le Tribunal pénal fédéral, présidé par Me Corrodi, juge fédéral. Les accusés ont fait de l'espionnage en faveur de la Tchécoslovaquie, contre la République fédérale allemande, les Etats-Unis, l'Angleterre, la France et le Danemark. Notre photo : Schnieper (à gauche) et Roessler arrivent devant la maison lucernoise où a lieu le procès.

The Laufenburg bridge on the German-Swiss frontier

Gasthof Laufen

The Bahnhof Hotel at Waldshut

The embankment of the Rhine at Waldshut. The scene of one of the private talks between Masson and Schellenberg

Wolfsberg, at Ermatingen, where Schellenberg spent his weekend visits to Switzerland

The hotel where the meeting between General Guisan and Schellenberg took place

The beginning of the "Masson affair"

The "end" of the "Masson affair"

A simple plaque in the Swiss cemetery at Kriens marks the grave of the greatest resistance worker of the Second World War

rently suspect elements—but never for a moment suspecting the "technicians," who were well known for their lack of interest in conspiracies. Thus *Werther* and *Olga* always slipped through the nets that had been cast for them. Walter Schellenberg alone got perilously close to them. And if history had granted Nazism a few more months of survival, he might very well have caught them.

10

APRIL, 1942—the mud season on the Eastern Front, a brief time of respite for the troops, from the Crimea to the Baltic. On each side of the front, columns of new men and materials were arriving from the rear to reinforce the combatants. In Lucerne, Geneva and Lausanne, Roessler, Rado and Foote were working at full speed—because *Werther* and *Olga* were doing so too.

Thus on April 14, Lucy transmitted to the Center, now back in Moscow after the crisis of October, 1941, the latest decisions made by the Führer in his headquarters at Rastenburg—a Hitler who was already going gray, suffering from inexplicable fits of giddiness and who seemed tormented by a veritable phobia about cold and snow. Hitler had obviously aged very quickly in the past few months, but his lust for conquest was as insatiable as ever.

Rommel and his Afrika Korps had won a great victory. His "desert foxes" had recaptured Derna and Benghazi in Cyrenaica and were preparing to take Tobruk and enter Egypt. The Führer hoped for even better things in Russia—nothing less than a decisive victory. Or, at least, that is what he declared in his Directive No. 41 to the Wehrmacht. These ten pages of instructions were dispatched to the OKW—orders to be carried out. The December crisis having deprived him permanently of all confidence in his High Command, he left his generals as little room for initiative as possible. He wanted to know everything and direct everything. All orders should go out from Rastenburg, then from Berlin—a marvelous piece of fortune for *Werther, Olga,* and Lucy.

Directive No. 41 was the plan of attack on the Don and the Caucasus. There were to be two simultaneous assaults: the first, in a pincer movement, on the Russian forces concentrated between the Donets and the Don—which must be destroyed; the second, in a direct thrust, toward the Caucasian oil fields. No sooner had the intelligence reached the Center from Switzerland, than Stalin began to get restless—he wanted details, more details. Roessler transmitted the request to Berlin. On April 18 the reply came back.

Setting out from Kursk, Orel and Kharkov, half the group of armies in the south, under Field Marshal von Bock, would reach the Don, then follow its course to its great loop just before Stalingrad. The second half would attack from Stalino and the port of Taganrog, try to recapture Rostov, then link up with the first arm of the pincer movement beyond the Don's convergence with the Donets. Finally, an army corps under Field Marshal List would have as its objectives the Caucasian hills and the Baku oil fields. The date of the opening of the offensive, then of the great attack, would be determined later.

Completing his intelligence, Roessler added that the long front line, which would be conquered across the Don by the Wehrmacht, would then be defended by non-German troops. There would be 52 foreign divisions: 27 Rumanian, 13 Hungarian, 9 Italian, 2 Czechoslovak and 1 Spanish. Field Marshal

Keitel had been sent to the Balkans to raise troops for the "crusade" against Bolshevism. Hitler himself had obtained the Italians and Spaniards. The gaps made during the terrible winter months had to be filled. Because the Rumanians and Hungarians hated each other and were more likely to fight each other than the Russians, they would be separated by the nine Italian divisions and one Spanish division. The German High Command, Lucy added, was not relying too heavily on these reinforcements, being very doubtful of their military value.

The reservations of the German marshals and generals were to prove only too well founded. These "Legions" were to snap, bearing most of the responsibility for the Axis defeat. But in April, 1942, neither the Germans nor the Russians knew this. No more than Foote knew, at that time, that the listening station of the SD, near Dresden, was rapidly tracking down the location of his transmitter.

In mid-April, Schellenberg received a lengthy report from his technicians. They had succeeded in recording a long series of mysterious dispatches—all coming from the same hand, whose "touch" they were now able to recognize. They were, however, still trying to decode them. The use of series of five mixed letters and figures suggested, they felt, the usual Soviet code systems, but it was too early as yet to make a positive decision on the matter.

They were using all the "tracking" techniques at their command. What they needed was time. One important fact had been discovered. The transmitter that sent out these messages almost every night, always at the same time, was situated on a very definite geographical line, passing near Madrid, Saragossa, Toulouse, Lyon, Geneva and Nuremberg. The strength of the broadcast indicated that the transmitter was probably not more than 600 miles away—which would exclude Spain.

Systematically, they had searched all the German territory crossed by this line, entrusting the southern part to the listening post of Captain Frentznik, at Sigmaringen. Though they were aware that the operator using this clandestine post frequently changed wavelengths, moving between 20 and 50 meters, they had managed to draw up a table of his favorite frequencies.

Events were to accelerate during the next two months. In North Africa, Rommel launched his great attack on Tobruk. In the East, von Bock was preparing to begin his offensive. "D" day had been fixed for May 18. But Lucy informed the Russians in time. They had known the date since May 5. At dawn, on May 12, six days before the scheduled German attack, Timoshenko began to cut the ground from under the feet of the Wehrmacht.

The Russian had decided to isolate most of the troops posted in the south by means of a pincer movement from the north with 22 divisions, 6 of them being armored, and from the south, with 60 divisions, including 14 armored divisions. He aimed to get to Kharkov. Opposite him was the German 6th Army under von Paulus which was to bear the brunt of his attack and which was later to be destroyed at Stalingrad. In four days, everything seemed over. Completely cut off, von Paulus was unable to prevent Timoshenko from getting within twelve miles of Kharkov. A last effort and the Russian marshal would seize the town that the Wehrmacht had organized as a depot to supply its troops during the planned offensive.

Timoshenko had been supplied with intelligence that at Kharkov he would find huge compounds of food and ammunition—both of which he needed urgently. His furious breakthrough had used up most of his reserves, and his communication lines had been stretched beyond a reasonable limit. There was one thing that Rudolf Roessler was unable to communicate to the Russians, because it was not a piece of intelligence. In any case, the Russians knew it only too well. This was the German soldier's exceptional tenacity and resilience.

The Red storm had no sooner ended than von Bock launched the Kleist group of armies, on May 18, after Timoshenko's rear lines. On May 21, in a sensational change of fortune, the Soviet attacking force was broken. Half their troops had been encircled and wiped out. The other half were in flight. There were 200,000 prisoners, and 2,000 guns and 1,000 tanks had been captured or destroyed.

In the south, too, things were going badly for the Russians. Sebastopol was about to fall. Manstein and List were to find the roads to Stalingrad and the Caucasus wide open before them. Hitler was feeling triumphant; he had not been able to enter Moscow, but he now had an even more ambitious plan. He imagined Rommel occupying Egypt, then moving further east as far as the Persian Gulf. Rommel and List would link up to give him, at last, the Russian oil fields, as well as those of the Arab world. He would then hold the whole world's fate in his hands. Without oil no one would be able to resist him.

In Berlin, Rudolf Roessler's friends were near despair. The rejoicing that reigned in the German capital, and even within the OKW, because the gods of war were favoring the Nazis once more, disturbed them. Everything seemed lost. They had taken maximum risks to send Roessler a maximum of intelligence for the use of the Russians—plans of attack, details of the composition of the armies, of equipment and of supplies—always well in advance. But all that had not been enough.

The Russians, too, had done their utmost, as demonstrated by the fury of their attacks, amount of equipment destroyed and the number of their dead and of the prisoners left behind. But it had not been enough. The abhorred Nazi power stretched from the Atlantic to the boundaries of Central Asia, from the Arctic to the Nile and the swastika was hoisted over the entire Mediterranean.

The ten conspirators would have been even more despondent if they had known of the intense jubilation then being felt by Walter Schellenberg. He had several reasons for rejoicing. First, Reinhard Heydrich, the only obstacle to his unbounded ambition, was dead. Jan Kubis and Josef Gabeik, two noncommissioned officers of the Free Czech Army, parachuted into Czechoslovakia by the RAF, had hurled a bomb under Heydrich's Mercedes in Prague on May 29, 1942. He died on June 4 from infections in the wounds he had received. But the SD was not long without a leader. On June 6, Heinrich Himmler, the head of the entire SS and No. 3 in the Nazi hierarchy, summoned all the Party departmental chiefs to the palace of the Wilhelmstrasse in Berlin. Standing before the body of Heydrich, laid out in state, Himmler pointed to the young SS-Brigadeführer:

"I place Schellenberg at the head of the Sicherheitsdienst. The man lying there regarded him as worthy of the post and trained him for it. I too consider him to be capable of assuming the tasks that await him. Above all, he is incorruptible. His youth and the fact that he is not a long-standing member of the National Socialist Party should not prevent you too from adopting him.

"He is the youngest among us and for that reason has a right to my special support. I say this clearly, and in his presence, because it was your murdered chief's desire that nothing should stand in the way of this nomination. And I consider Schellenberg to be too intelligent to allow himself to become intoxicated by what I have just said. On the contrary, I hope it will encourage him to carry out all the more carefully and attentively the tasks that will be assigned him."

He was also overjoyed at the progress in the inquiry entrusted
to him by his late chief. It was going remarkably well. Before
long, he might even be able to present Himmler with a valuable
token of his thanks.

The listening station at Sigmaringen had confirmed the research of the Dresden station. The general direction in which
the clandestine transmitter was situated was definitely the Ma-
drid-Nuremberg line. But they still did not know to what point
these regular dispatches were being directed. With the help of
a powerful mobile station based in Strasbourg, a more precise
triangulation had indicated that the transmitter was in Switzerland. It was still impossible to say whether it was in Geneva or
Lausanne, but it was certainly somewhere on the shore of Lake
Leman. This was a discovery of some importance for Schellenberg. The one that followed, a week later, on June 18, 1942, was
an even greater one.

Well before the Second World War, Soviet espionage had begun to base their coding systems on sentences taken from books.
The Germans knew this. Their unmasking of *Die Rote Kapelle*,
for example, had confirmed it. Moreover, their own intelligence
services were now using the same excellent method. It was natural, therefore, for the decoding division of the SD to direct its
researches along these lines when it began to analyze the piles
of dispatches recorded in Dresden since the beginning of 1941.
After three months' extensive work, the mathematical analysis
section had succeeded in isolating a single obscure word among
the mass of hieroglyphics: *Everhard*. A great many specialists
from different fields had been set to work on the mysterious
word, in the hope that it might suggest something to one of
them.

A bibliophile finally resolved the puzzle. *Everhard* might refer
to the name of one of the heroes of Jack London, the American

writer of adventure stories, in particular to the hero of *The Iron
Heel*, a political book written in 1907. At last, a key to a code
had been found—with considerable difficulty, since the book
was banned in Germany. A copy was ultimately unearthed in a
library in Bavaria. Unfortunately, it only served to decipher
a certain number of the messages. The rest remained strictly
incomprehensible, as if the code had been changed in the meantime.

Now the Germans realized how admirably this operator protected himself. Not only did he constantly change the wavelengths on which he transmitted his messages, but just as frequently shifted his codes. An incredible amount of work would
have to be done by the SD decoders before any sense could be
made of all the other transmissions that had been recorded.
However, they had learned enough to know that the broadcasts, dating from January to February, 1942, revealed vital
German defense secrets. Moreover, they had obviously been intended for Moscow, since they provided detailed intelligence
concerning German troop movements on the Eastern Front.

These two discoveries, coming within a few days of one another, both delighted and disturbed Schellenberg. This was
confirmed by his statements to the British after the war.

Reinhard Heydrich had been right. When these messages
had been decoded, they had confirmed Heydrich's initial suspicions when Military Security had first shown him the documents that had been captured from the Russians. The Wehrmacht was obviously being undermined from within.

No one but German officers would be able to communicate intelligence of such extraordinary value to the Russians. They
must have set up an espionage cell among the officer corps—a
cell totally independent of the usual networks that had been
regularly unmasked by the SD since the discovery of the most

important of them, *Die Rote Kapelle*. (This network too had been assisted by two German officers—Becker, a brilliant colonel, and Schulze-Boysen, a lieutenant-colonel in the Luftwaffe—in getting military intelligence.)

Schellenberg had a vague feeling that something was wrong with his analysis of the situation. If this espionage cell in the Wehrmacht existed, why had the Russians concealed its radio operator in Switzerland? He knew only too well how difficult it was to cross Swiss frontiers. New precautions had constantly to be taken to smuggle his own spies into the Confederation. Yet there seemed no other way for the agents of this supposed cell to transmit their news to their technician in Switzerland than by radio. Especially as the transmissions from Switzerland, between January and February, 1942 had been almost daily. But if they possessed a transmitter to send their intelligence to their man in Switzerland, why did they not send it directly to Moscow, as *Die Rote Kapelle* had done?

It struck Schellenberg that there could only be one answer to the torrent of questions nagging him: the Swiss had something to do with this affair. They might even be accomplices. The Swiss might well be performing an incredibly dextrous balancing act, if they were as clever in this field as they had been in organizing their supplies in advance of the war. While Europe was wearing wooden shoes and clothes made of cellulose and staple fiber, Swiss shops were full of articles made from pure wool and pure cotton, not to mention the *Delikatessen* and pure wheat bread. Who could tell what ingenuity they would be capable of to preserve their sacrosanct neutrality.

But the Führer was making plans to put an end to all that— plans that so far had not been given a launching date. He was thinking of incorporating the German-speaking part of Switzerland, the largest and richest part of the country, into his empire.

For a long time Schellenberg had been building up a remarkable espionage organization, which at the right moment would play a considerable part in overthrowing the Confederation. And now this affair had revealed an unsuspected side to that country. Something had to be done. He must find out what was going on in the heads of the Swiss leaders. To do so, he would have to exercise his customary patience and diplomacy to create an atmosphere of trust.

11

BEFORE Schellenberg embarked on his personal mission, the ground had been well prepared. In fact, the coverage of Switzerland by the German espionage services was more concentrated and more active than in any other country in the world. It had begun as early as 1937, as if the Reich had guessed in advance that any internal opposition to Nazism would turn first to Switzerland—a fellow German-speaking state—for refuge.

The German infiltration of Switzerland was entrusted to two organizations: the Abwehr, the Wehrmacht's espionage, counterespionage and sabotage service, under Admiral Canaris; and the SD of Himmler and Schellenberg. Together, the two organizations had established branches in Stuttgart, 75 miles to the north of the Confederation, which would deal specifically with Switzerland.

Lieutenant-Colonel Zeitz had been placed in charge of the Abwehr office. Lieutenant-Colonel Schmidt, specializing in military matters, was kept constantly informed about the Swiss army. His colleague, Major Gayler, had an up-to-date and detailed picture of the Swiss economy. Baron von Stauffenberg, alias "Uncle Frank," was in charge of the espionage network itself. He was to send out more than a thousand agents, who infiltrated Swiss industrial and political circles. Major Heiland armed these spies and supplied them with money, false identities, radios, special inks and cameras. Captain Frentznik, known to his colleagues as "Marconi," was in charge of the transmitter-receiver center at Sigmaringen, which was to be used by the organizations covering Switzerland. Four advance posts—at Lörrach, Säckingen, Constance and Bregenz—directed activities near the Swiss frontier.

The office of the SD in Stuttgart had 20,000 files on Swiss citizens who could be "used." It trained 300 agents every six months, who were then sent into Switzerland to recruit their accomplices. Germans living in the Confederation and naturalized Swiss, or *papierschweizer*, were approached first. Frontiersmen of double nationality were also chosen for indoctrination.

The action of the SD was of a political nature. When a practical operation was required, the SD called in Heinrich Müller's Gestapo or Otto Skorzeny's Jagdkommando. It was the latter that undertook the first hostile action against Switzerland in 1940. Only the perspicacity of a Swiss railway worker, on Sunday, June 16, prevented the attempt from taking place.

He was inspecting tickets on the Romanshorn-Zürich train, when he noticed something that struck him as curious: ten passengers, who had boarded at Weinfelden and taken up seats in two carriages, carried identical brown canvas suitcases. Suspicious of this coincidence, he informed the police at Märstetten, the next stop. Meanwhile, alarmed by the insistence with which he had observed them, the ten men jumped from the train.

A search was set up and two days later nine of them were

captured, seven Germans and two Swiss. Each possessed 500 Swiss francs (about $115), an "infernal machine" loaded with 5½ pounds of TNT, a supply of food, tools, a Luger 9 mm revolver with 40 cartridges and a dagger.

They were assigned to blow up the ammunition depot at Altdorf, in the canton of Uri and sabotage the runways of the military airfields at Lausanne, Payerne, Bienne and Spreitenbach—an operation ordered by Hermann Goering, as reprisal for four German fighters, shot down by antiaircraft guns while flying over Swiss territory. On November 16, 1940, the nine agents were given life sentences. The tenth had succeeded in escaping.

Baron von Stauffenberg, the head of the Action section of the Abwehr in Stuttgart, had greater success in his first assault on Switzerland. At dawn on September 4, 1940, a convoy of cars bearing the emblem of the Red Cross stopped near the Lavillat viaduct, in Haute-Savoie, over which the Annecy-La Roche-sur-Foron railway crossed a ravine. The first car appeared to have stalled. Men were busy under the hood. Meanwhile, another group fixed 176 pounds of melinite under one of the pillars of the bridge. The convoy moved on. Some hours later the bridge collapsed.

This bridge was of great value to Switzerland. Since the destruction of the railway at Pontarlier, the tunnel at Frasne and the fine construction of the Bellegarde-Geneva line, Switzerland had relied on it for the transportation of overseas supplies. For two months, the Swiss had to depend on a shuttle service of trucks between Annecy and Geneva to link them with the free world.

The missions of the Abwehr and the SD against Switzerland ran into thousands. A scale of payment was drawn up: 1,000

Swiss francs for the empty shell of an antitank grenade; 1,500 if full; reports on the national defense program, 1,500; with photographs, 2,000; weapons or new projectiles, up to 50,000. This had already enabled the OKW to publish in 1940 a small volume of 85 pages, entitled *Handbook of the Swiss Army,* intended for the use of German troops in the event of a possible invasion of the country.

To cross Swiss borders, the Germans used two techniques. A few hundred yards away from the chosen crossing-point, they would create a diversion, firing shots as if in pursuit of someone. This would draw the attention of the customs officers and frontier guards and leave the field clear for the spies. Passersby who hid them were paid 1,000 ($225) francs per agent.

The second method was safer, but more expensive: 1,500 francs ($350). The crossing took place in the Basle railway station. The German customs officers would take the spies, disguised as railway workers, across the lines and hand them over to their Swiss accomplices. Basle station, an international junction between Switzerland, Germany and France, was swarming with more spies throughout the war than perhaps any other single place in the world. Colonel Jaquillard, head of Swiss counterespionage, was to count with amazement 350 known German spies on the nights of May 14 and 15, 1940, alone. They were sitting quietly, on the German side of the border, awaiting the best time to slip into Switzerland.

Throughout the war, the SD never ceased its effort to win the Swiss over to Nazism. Its Bureau F in Berne, concealed in the German legation and directed by the Consul-General, Hans Meisner, served as a cell for recruitment and subversion. It included a group of well-trained specialists, who, like Meisner, benefited from their diplomatic immunity.

By the middle of 1942, the number of Germans living in Switzerland had assumed almost the proportions of a state within a state. Brigadier Masson did not underestimate the gravity of this situation. He often exceeded his annual budget of 50 million Swiss francs (about $12 million), without causing too much opposition, but the means at his disposal in terms of men and money were hardly adequate to withstand the Nazi tide. He congratulated himself on having persuaded the local police forces, as early as 1938, to keep a special register of foreign residents in every locality. For each name in this register there was an arrest warrant, made out in advance. At the slightest sign of suspicion, his agents struck. Between 1939 and 1942, they had followed up no fewer than a thousand leads. Of course not all of these turned up German spies, and occasionally an innocent person was incriminated.

By the middle of 1942, however, Masson's service had become so efficient that the best spies began to fall into its nets. The Germans never gave their agents more than three months' activity in Switzerland, which led them to change their tactics. Since their networks seemed to be so short-lived, they resolved to practice the technique of *überschwemmung*, or inundation. If one agent disappeared, he would be replaced by five.

To this, the Swiss replied by increasing the severity of their penalties. Espionage had not previously been treated very harshly by the Federal Courts; they had often been content to expel the "undesirables." Now the courts were ordered by the Federal Council to act ruthlessly. More than 1,500 spies, including 50 women, were charged with activities against the security of the Swiss state; 202 were given sentences of between five and fifteen years—among them were 64 Germans, 16 citizens of Liechtenstein and 164 Swiss. Thirty-three spies were given life sentences and 19 were condemned to death, 16 of these being executed.

This, then, was the situation in Switzerland as Schellenberg struggled to work out a new, more subtle and more profitable way of tackling the Swiss.

12

IN fact, Schellenberg had decided to aim high —at Brigadier Roger Masson himself. A year and a half earlier, on Schellenberg's orders, SS-Stürmbannführer H. W. Eggen, had begun to prepare the ground. Eggen, an executive of the Warenvertrieb G.M.B.H., a large industrial group in Berlin, also had considerable financial interests in Lausanne. When given the job of supplying the Wehrmacht with huts in 1940, Eggen had approached two representatives of the Swiss timber industry—Paul Holzach and P. Meyer (alias Schwertenbach) —and had succeeded in building up close relations with them. His choice of Meyer and Holzach had been deliberate: before meeting them, Eggen knew that both businessmen had been mobilized into the Swiss forces as captains and were among Masson's closest, most trusted colleagues.

At Eggen's repeated request, Meyer decided to introduce him to Roger Masson. They met on Wednesday, December 10, 1941, during one of Eggen's many business visits. They discussed relations between Switzerland and the Third Reich, Masson complaining of the virulence of the attacks on his country in the German press, Eggen assuring him that this problem could certainly be resolved. Eggen suggested that Masson be put into contact with his friend, superior and "spiritual master," SS-Brigadeführer Schellenberg, who had influence in the highest quarters. Masson did not regard such a meeting as very pressing and declined the offer.

Meanwhile, on the Eastern Front, artillery had opened fire once more. For four hours the Russian lines had been shelled, in preparation for the launching of "Operation Blue," which, it was hoped, would be the Wehrmacht's final, victorious onslaught on the Red Army.

Hitler had long been hesitating to give the green light to his troop commanders, Field Marshal von Bock and General Friedrich Paulus. A Fieseler Storch—a small reconnaissance plane—had been shot down eight days before in a sector held by the Russians, east of Kharkov near the banks of the Oskol. In the plane had been an officer of the 23rd tank division, Major Reichel. Reichel's briefcase had contained notes and maps indicating the positions of the divisions and the objectives of the entire 40th tank corps. Field Marshal Keitel had cautiously suggested to the Führer that the offensive be delayed, as the Russians were obviously now in possession of a large part of the Wehrmacht's plans. Von Bock and Paulus protested:

"Even if the Russians do have the plans of the 40th corps, which is not yet certain, they haven't time to arrange their defenses accordingly. Moreover, the 40th corps will only cover part of the front. The rest of the plans remain strictly secret. Delay our enterprise now and it will never have a chance of success. It will be winter before we have attained our objectives."

Despite the lesson of Moscow, Hitler seems to have followed Keitel's advice, in the hope, perhaps, that his scientists, working under Wernher von Braun, would soon provide him with their super-rockets—rockets capable of subjugating the world.

But, of course, the Russians knew not only the plans of the 40th armored corps—though apparently they had found nothing in the wreckage of the Fieseler Storch—they also had full details of "Operation Blue," which was basically the *Directive No. 41* sent out by Hitler in April: Rudolf Roessler had provided them.

Despite his dexterity, achieved by endless practice in the service of the Russians, Alexander Foote had great difficulty in communicating this enormous pile of coded dispatches to the Center. He spent five hours nightly in coding alone, and his difficulties were increased by the frequent shifts in coding ordered by Moscow. Then, from 1 A.M. onward, the silence of his room was broken only by the remorseless tapping of his transmitter. With the windows carefully sealed to prevent any light leakage, he worked steadily until dawn, the air becoming murky from the smoke of his innumerable cigarettes.

Rudolf Roessler had communicated his dedication to Rado's entire network. Foote was no longer able to cope with the sheer quantity of Lucy's messages, and Margareta Bolli and Edmond Hamel were assigned the transmission of WYRDO dispatches, or messages of top priority. There was a particular reason for the sudden increase in their work volume. For the first time since they had begun to use Lucy's exceptional services, the Russians had made radical changes in their strategy.

Until then they had been content, thanks to advance intelligence from Switzerland, to make perfect estimates of the enemy's forces and plans. But when the actual battles took place, they ignored the further use to which Lucy's dispatches could be put and fought according to the academic rules taught them by their instructions in the "black" Reichswehr. Fully aware of the fate that awaited them, they allowed themselves, almost fatalistically, to meet the enemy on the ground and at the times determined by the Germans. An analysis of the tactics used during the first year of the conflict reveals that although the Russians knew exactly what the Germans planned to do, they consistently allowed themselves to be encircled and pinned down. However, from 1942, things were to go differently.

The Red Army began to elude the Wehrmacht. It learned to evade all the pincer movements that had worked so successfully before. It continued to attack and defend from a frontal position, but suddenly adopted tactics involving great mobility, drawing the German troops into terrain unsuited to the broad formations required by armored divisions. Now the Red Army seized the initiative. Now they set the times and places of battles. Moreover, it was the Russians who introduced a new weapon into the conflict—psychological warfare, a barrage of information and threats. The 2nd Hungarian army was its first victim. In the middle of the night, voices amplified by powerful loudspeakers just within the Russian lines announced:

"Hungarians! We know that tomorrow, at dawn, you will cross the Oskol. But we shall not be there to meet you. We shall meet when and where *we* wish. You will then be sorry you ever came to Russia. You will curse your leaders for having given in to Field Marshal Keitel and agreeing to send you here."

The 23rd tank division, which had only just arrived on the Eastern Front from France, was greeted.

"Soldiers of the 23rd. Welcome to the Soviet Union! Your fine Paris days are over now. What awaits you in our country will far surpass anything your comrades, who were frostbitten, may have told you. But you will see for yourselves before long!"

The 24th tank division also received a midnight warning: "Panzergrenadiers of the 24th, we shall not be south of Voronezh the day after tomorrow as your leaders have assured you. You needn't try to encircle us—we won't be there. Save your bread, your ammunition and your gasoline, for we are going to besiege you. The luckiest will be those who have kept a bullet to blow their own brains out."

Here was Lucy's intelligence at its most effective. While, of course, it could never be traced back to its source, its devastating results appear in a great many of the German soldiers' accounts of the campaign. The same anxiety recurs everywhere— an anxiety found in descriptions of the action on no other front. These fighting men got the disastrous impression that the enemy had access to the plans of their chiefs. They were paralyzed by a feeling that the Red terror would engulf them in the middle of the barren steppes. The Russians' first attempt at putting Lucy's vital intelligence to work as ammunition for their psychological warfare was an unqualified success.

Its impact on the ordinary soldiers was particularly devastating, and many suffered complete mental breakdowns. The officers of the Wehrmacht tended to ridicule it, but, in a sense, were even more intensely affected, since they realized that the Russians must possess other, much more valuable intelligence that they did *not* broadcast over their loudspeakers, but which would enable them to subvert completely the usual tactics of the OKW at the front. None of them, however, dared suppose that the source of these terrifying revelations was in Berlin itself.

These mid-months of 1942 also marked a new stage for Roger Masson and the Bureau Ha in their relations with Roessler. They felt that he had changed—and the change was not to their liking. When they had begun to use him in 1939, their attitude was not without a certain condescension. By some extraordinary chance, they thought, this émigré had access to a source of intelligence whose importance he did not himself appear to realize. So they used him—for their own ends, then in the interests of the western Allies, who, they believed, held the same ideals. When Roessler announced that he also wanted to work for the Russians, who had now joined the Allies, they turned a blind eye, fully expecting that it would not amount to very much.

With the first great Russian victories—"his" victories, he had an irritating habit of calling them—Roessler seemed to become a "bigger" person, or simply to reveal his true nature. He may not have been interested in money, but he seemed strangely exalted by a sense of power and pride. This new Roessler, now revealed as the real head of his resistance network, suddenly became dangerous.

However, he continued to fulfill the conditions agreed between them, making no attempt to conceal from the Swiss the intelligence he passed on to the Russians. But Masson and the Bureau Ha now realized that, by means of this intelligence, Roessler would play an overwhelming role in the victory of the Russians in the East. If, by some misfortune, the Germans discovered that it was Switzerland who had made this possible, then the neutrality of the Confederation would be in jeopardy. The very existence of Switzerland as an independent state might be in danger.

From then on, few men were to be as closely guarded as Roessler. Night and day, the Vita Nova Verlag, in the Fluhmattstrasse, in Lucerne, and his home at Wesemlin were watched by shadowy, scrupulously discreet figures. If Roessler was aware of them, he did not reveal it—and he expressed no gratitude for his protection. This irritated the Swiss. They watched over him, but, at the same time, they began to try to discover more about his activities devoted to the Russians.

One particularly warm night, at the end of the summer of 1942, the radio operator at Geneva airport was feeling bored. The Swiss air force that patrolled the skies to intercept over-flights, and thus preserve Swiss neutrality, made no flights after nightfall, but the authorities insisted that someone remain at the radio controls throughout the night. After wandering aimlessly around his office, the operator sat down at his instruments and began to play idly with the knobs. Suddenly, he intercepted a broadcast on a wavelength that was not used by the Swiss armed forces. The letters and figures appeared in groups of five, and the uncertain touch marked the sender an amateur. Failing to decipher the message, the operator informed BUPO, the Swiss counterespionage service. He had carefully noted the wavelength and the time of broadcast. The clandestine transmitter definitely lay quite near the airport, probably in Geneva itself, for throughout the transmission its tone had been extremely sharp and clear. Moreover, its transmission strength meant that the set was using the local electricity supply, not batteries.

The following night, three vans, equipped with gonios, waited near the airport and picked up the same transmission. It was coming from the southeast. Setting out slowly from three different points, and guided by the sound, they gradually converged on a point in the center of Geneva. When the tapping stopped, at almost the same time as it had the previous night, the vans had already crossed the bridges over the Rhône. The next night they got even closer to the clandestine transmitter. One of the gonios was near the university, the second was in the rue Versonnex, beside the Jardin Anglais and the third near the Parc de la Grange.

On the fourth day of the search, they intercepted a new transmitter, in the same area, manipulated by an amateur even clumsier than the first. Then they lost touch with the broadcasts altogether. A week later, the gonio vans were stationed in the route de Florissant, at the gates of the Parc Alfred Bertrand, when the tapping recommenced. This time, it was so strong that the technicians were certain the operator was somewhere in that street.

A single gonio, manned by BUPO agents, did the final work of tracking him down. To pinpoint the house they used a trick invented by the Germans. The electric current of each house was cut in turn, just long enough for an agent to walk from one to the next. If the broadcast continued, then the secret operator was not in the house in front of which they were passing. In this way they eventually focused on number 192, route de Florissant.

The same method located the second transmitter at 8 bis, rue Henri Mussard. It was now child's play for Masson's department to match names to the street numbers. Both were on the lists of suspect persons, because both belonged to the Swiss Communist Party: Edmond Hamel and Margareta Bolli.

A Swiss coding expert, Marc Payot, dutifully set to work to break the cryptic dispatches recorded since the discovery of these transmissions. Masson was less interested in what the Communists might be communicating than in the fact that they had continuous relations with a correspondent outside the Confederation. It seemed obvious that this could only be Moscow—and that Hamel and Bolli must be Roessler's radiotelegraph operators. The couple were carefully watched and the results confirmed the theory. Both Hamel and Bolli often visited a certain Alexander Rado, who also received in his Géo-Presse offices one Christian Schneider, a close friend of Rudolf Roessler. Of course, these discoveries came as a great relief to Masson and the Bureau Ha: if the need arose, they at last had a way of blocking the work of this frighteningly effective agent. They could destroy him as easily as defend him.

The reason for Masson's sudden mistrust of Roessler was due not to any real change in the intelligence that Roessler received, but rather in the use to which it was being put by the Russians. But to understand Swiss fears at that time it is necessary to review events taking place on the Eastern Front.

On July 1, 1942, the Wehrmacht began advancing from its positions won in May. Its first objective was Voronezh, both an economic and industrial center and a road and rail junction. The Germans intended to make Voronezh the fortress that would cover the Wehrmacht's offensive on its north flank. Three German and one Hungarian army would cross the Oskol, with General Hoth's tanks as their spearhead.

Disconcertingly, the six Soviet armies, under Semën Konstantinovich Timoshenko, which the German troops had expected to encircle from the north and the south, had disappeared without engaging battle and it was not certain which direction they had taken. Feeling that their attack had now been inexplicably blunted, the Wehrmacht officers wished to abandon Operation Blue entirely and pursue the Red Army on a wide front in the direction of the Don. Hitler refused: they must first encircle the Russians. Terrified in advance of leaving the initiative to his High Command, the Führer stuck obstinately to his own plans.

On July 3, General Hoth's 4th army and Friedrich Paulus's 6th army rendezvoused as planned. But there was nothing there.

The huge net they had spread was empty. Hitler realized that the Russians had outwitted him. On a lightning visit to von Bock's headquarters, he raged:

"I'm not interested in Voronezh any more! Go south and get Stalingrad."

He did not say that he did not *want* Voronezh. Completely baffled and fearing that he might be reproached later for not following Directive No. 41 to the letter, von Bock temporized. Without knowing it, he was being lured on by Timoshenko, who had allowed the 24th tank division to forge on unopposed to within a few miles of Voronezh. The Germans had no way of knowing how Timoshenko was able to keep fully informed as to their doubts, expectations and troop movements.

In fact, during this period, which lasted for more than a month scarcely *ten hours* elapsed between the making of a decision by the OKW and its reception by Moscow. On one occasion, the interval was even reduced to six hours. Roessler had correctly calculated that speed in the transmission of intelligence was vital. This alone would enable the Kremlin to develop a strategy which, in the course of a decisive battle, could turn the war in their favor. Consequently, he called on the ten agents of *Werther* and *Olga* in Berlin to drive themselves even harder to satisfy his insatiable appetite for information. And the Russians never had occasion to ask Lucy to accelerate the supply of intelligence.

On July 4, von Bock believed that he could take Voronezh in a surprise attack. He remained convinced that Timoshenko's troops could only have escaped from their trap by going south and north, and that they had not yet crossed the Don. After all, he reasoned, the bridges were intact. It did not occur to him for a moment that this might be a trap.

"And what's happening to the attack in the south?" Hitler asked.

"Contingents of the 24th division are already entering the outskirts of the city. The Russians are fleeing," von Bock replied.

This time it was Hitler himself who plunged into the trap. He ordered that the troops be split up. About half, including the 6th Army, would set out for Stalingrad in the south—but they would make no attempt to take the city, their mission being to bypass the Soviet armies. With Voronezh occupied, von Bock was to continue straight on and link up with Paulus. This time the Russians would not escape their net. The second branch of the pincer movement would simply arrive slightly later than the first.

On receiving this news from Lucy, Timoshenko was exultant. The Germans were making a disastrous mistake in dividing their forces. In fact, the full use to which the information from *Werther* and *Olga* was being put enabled the Soviet High Command to work out a system of foolproof tactics: break the strike force of the Wehrmacht, then lure a large body of troops into a cul-de-sac, where they could be wiped out. Meanwhile, the second body of troops was to be engaged in a place suitable for prolonged combat, thus preventing it from rescuing the first column and linking up to form another group of armies that would be difficult to defeat. The cul-de-sac would be Stalingrad and the battlefield, Voronezh.

In answer to Operation Blue, therefore, Timoshenko, like von Bock, divided his forces. But they were more numerous and better supplied with fuel than the Germans, because they held the railways. So the majority of the Soviet troops awaited the advance of Paulus's 6th Army, harassing it constantly without pinning it down, and gradually cutting it off from its rear lines. Meanwhile, the rest of the Russians, under Timoshenko himself, waited in Voronezh, possessing far more artillery than von Bock expected to meet.

When von Bock ordered the city to be taken, the moment of truth for the Third Reich had arrived. In their accounts, his officers were to nickname Voronezh "the cursed city." They fought their way through the suburbs only to come to a standstill in the city's center—but the outcome of the fighting never seemed clear. Withdrawal was impossible—they had advanced too far for their departure not to appear defeat.

But Timoshenko did get out of the city. He left Voronezh at precisely the moment he'd planned and, without leaving a single truck behind, disappeared into the steppe. He withdrew when the mass of troops that he had sent in the direction of Stalingrad to open the way for Paulus's 6th Army had reached the Volga. These troops were eighteen days ahead of the Germans. Realizing one morning that Paulus was no longer following him, the general in command sent word to Moscow asking whether the Germans had changed their plans.

The Center alerted Foote, who passed on the message to Roessler. The incredible reply from Lucy caused much rejoicing among the Russians. Paulus' 6th Army had run out of gasoline and would be immobilized for 430 hours. This unexpected respite allowed the future defenders of Stalingrad to reinforce their lines.

On the Caucasian front, too, the Russians applied the new tactics, and timely warnings from Switzerland enabled them to evade all the numerous attempts at encirclement made by Field Marshal Sigmund Wilhelm List. The commanding officers engaged in Operation Blue were to discover, too late, that what they had interpreted as retreats were, in fact, concerted withdrawals, which were eventually to seal the fate of the Third Reich.

By the beginning of September, these officers were to realize with horror that their scattered armies, separated from each other by sometimes as much as 300 miles, linked by lines of communications stretched to the snapping point, had become terribly vulnerable. Sunk in the sand of the steppe, surrounded by vast, open spaces, the Wehrmacht's formidable strike force no longer existed. The Red Army, aided by the oncoming winter and a continual flow of advance intelligence, would be able to destroy it at leisure. The situation was a brilliant success on the part of the Soviet High Command.

Through his notorious inability to understand, let alone solve, large-scale strategic problems, Hitler was also an involuntary accomplice of the Russians.

"They're finished, they're exhausted," he cried contemptuously to General Halder, his chief of staff, who dared to convey to him the fears of his troops on the Eastern Front. "Can't you see that Russia is finished? Stalin will never be able, as you claim, to mobilize a million and a half fresh men for Stalingrad, not to mention the five hundred thousand he is supposed to be launching on the Caucasus. I forbid you to go on repeating such nonsense."

He even went so far as to withdraw troops from this sector of the Russian front, sending seven precious divisions to France, via Leningrad.

If, then, these were the first tangible results of intelligence conveyed to Stalin by Lucy, it certainly helps explain the anxiety felt by the Swiss secret service. Roessler and his network would have to be watched constantly. Masson would have to make it his business to ensure their protection from discovery by Nazi agents. It was of the utmost importance that Hitler should learn nothing of the part played by the Confederation in this affair. Switzerland's destiny depended on it.

Apparently one man had already considered such a possibility. In Berlin, Walter Schellenberg had coldly analyzed the development of the summer's events on the Eastern Front. He alone among the leading Nazis understood the vital role of the resistance network he was trying to unmask. By September, 1942, the meeting which Roger Masson had so far obstinately avoided had, from Schellenberg's point of view, become most urgent. He would have to strike before this leak did any further damage to the Reich. Reinhard Heydrich had been convinced that the traitors who were informing the Russians were to be found among the officers of the Wehrmacht, and Schellenberg still believed that they were being aided by the traditional opposition to Hitler. He had thought immediately of Admiral Canaris, then of Vice-Consul Hans Bernd Gisevius, the head of the Abwehr's network in Switzerland.

Only one person could help Schellenberg prove his theory that conspirators in the OKW headquarters in Berlin were also involved in the affair—Masson. This was why he had to meet him. He did not, of course, hope to find an ally. Rather, he intended to strangle Switzerland in a tight net of obligations. And he did not lack the proper bait. Only when he felt that Masson had been securely hooked, would he reveal his true intentions. If the Swiss really were unaware of this affair —which was still conceivable—then Schellenberg would quite simply ask for their help in destroying these enemies of Nazism.

However, Schellenberg lacked one thing. He would have liked to have entered this power struggle with an ace up his sleeve. Unwittingly, Masson was to present him with just such a card.

Among the dispatches concerning Switzerland that reached

him twice a week from the office of the SD in Stuttgart, Schellenberg found a piece of information which, although apparently innocent enough, immediately set him scheming. A young Swiss officer, Lieutenant Möergeli, had just arrived in Stuttgart: a new clerk in the chancellery of the Swiss consulate. It was his first post. Having him watched would be ridiculously easy. For it was well known that employees of embassies and consulates were often used to carry out "information" missions.

An hour later, Schellenberg telephoned SS-Sturmbannführer Hügel, the head of the Stuttgart office, and ordered him to mount a *Herausforderung,* or provocation, intended for young Möergeli. He was to be arrested as a spy and given the full treatment. A tribunal was to hand down the maximum penalty for espionage. Möergeli's consul and the Swiss authorities would certainly intervene, which was just what Schellenberg wanted. In this way he would force Roger Masson to come to Germany.

The ruse worked perfectly for, as Schellenberg had suspected, Möergeli had been carrying out a minor secret assignment: he supplied certain information concerning the Wehrmacht's movements in areas adjoining the Swiss frontier. One evening in a brasserie in Stuttgart, Möergeli made the acquaintance of a German civilian, who confided that he was a staunch anti-Nazi. Möergeli was impudent enough to say he shared his views, thus falling for a trick of infantile simplicity. He was arrested on the spot and condemend to death. The terrified consul immediately informed Berne, which passed the message on to Masson in Lucerne, asking him if he could intervene. Masson had immediately agreed. On September 8, 1942, Schellenberg and Masson would meet at last.

13

$\mathbf{M}$ASSON had laid down one condition to his accepting the meeting. It would have to take place in a town on the German-Swiss border—Laufenburg would do. Schellenberg had agreed but had secretly determined that it would be far easier to beat an opponent on home ground. In order to justify changing the meeting place to somewhere farther inside Germany, Schellenberg needed a serious delay. Moreover, the delay should last long enough for a Gestapo agent to intensify Masson's sense of insecurity at being suddenly plunged into hostile surroundings—to "condition" Masson a little before actually confronting him. So Schellenberg invented an auto accident.

When at 8:15 A.M. of a clear, late-summer Thursday, Brigadier Masson, wearing civilian clothes and sucking on an old pipe, crossed the international bridge over the Rhine, linking the Swiss and German halves of the ancient city of Laufenburg, he was distressed to discover that arrangements had been drastically altered. Instead of being immediately conducted to the Gasthof Laufen, where he was to have been met by Eggen and Schellenberg, Masson found himself being led by a silent

German customs officer straight to the guard post at the German side of the bridge, where he was confronted by a stranger in a green trench coat who looked very much like the Gestapo.

Though Masson cautiously declined to identify himself, the Gestapo officer did not hesitate to let Masson know he was aware of his destination:

"You were expecting General Schellenberg, I believe? The General won't be coming to Laufenburg. He's had a car accident. Oh, nothing serious. Nothing to worry about."

Masson was far from reassured to learn that Eggen would "come to collect him within a couple of hours."

The minutes seemed to creep as the Gestapo officer fired a barrage of questions at Masson. What did the Swiss think of the way the war was going? Did they have any doubts as to the ultimate victory of National Socialism? It was a difficult situation. Masson grew increasingly anxious. What was happening? This car accident could so easily compromise everything. There he was, the head of Swiss Intelligence, trapped in Germany, in the hands of the worst elements of the Nazi regime. Masson was perfectly well aware of the Nazi leaders' attitude toward him. SS-Reichsführer Heinrich Himmler, for example, had been known to shout, during one of his infamous fits of anger, when he would fire off pistol shots in his office:

"I pay whoever gives me service; he who gives me disservice pays. I have no enemies. If I do make any, then I liquidate them. The scum of the earth will be liquidated, including Churchill and Roosevelt—and Masson, that Swiss who has sided with them ever since war broke out!"

At 10:30, a relaxed, affable Eggen arrived. Yes, on the road from Berlin to Laufenburg, General Schellenberg's Mercedes had indeed crashed into a ditch. They were saved by a miracle. The general sent his apologies for the delay. They had been forced to come by train. But the meeting could still take place, though not at Laufenburg. They would go to Waldshut, nine miles up the Rhine, to the Bahnhof Hotel.

Nine winding, twisting miles along the banks of the river. Masson had reason to feel apprehensive. Should he believe Eggen? After all, Schellenberg could easily have come to Laufenburg—with Eggen or by train. Why had he chosen Waldshut? Had he been trying to sap his morale by subjecting him to that agonizing wait with the Gestapo officer? The thirty-two-year-old SS-Brigadeführer was quite capable of such a trick; he had a reputation for just that sort of thing. Masson was deeply disturbed, recognizing that he was quite possibly caught in one of Schellenberg's Machiavellian traps. If he were not careful, he could end up in his triumphant grasp, like Best and Stevens—or worse, perhaps. Masson had, of course, already realized that there was some significance in the disproportion between Lieutenant Möergeli's error and his threatened punishment. Clearly, the SD, who had provoked the whole episode, wanted to contact him. Moreover, they intended to put him in a precarious position at the outset. Masson would be forced to ask for a favor. But what would Schellenberg want in return?

The car driven by Eggen entered Waldshut—an old tourist town of 10,000 inhabitants, built on a hill overlooking the Rhine. Just before the railway station, they turned right down the Poststrasse. The Bahnhof Hotel was a gray, gloomy, three-story building. Major Eggen led Masson into its small, dark oak-paneled lounge.

Shortly afterward a man pushed open the door. He was tall and slim, wearing a superbly cut gray tweed suit. His thick, brown hair was combed straight back and parted on the left. He had a wide, sensual mouth, gentle, deep-set eyes and an attractive smile. Masson immediately recognized Walter Schellenberg. He was exactly like the photographs that his Lucerne office had supplied him before his departure. His voice, too, was gentle, though lightly ironical.

"I imagine you think that this hotel is filled with cameras and microphones, Monsieur Masson. After all, it's what you'd expect in wartime. I suggest then, that we go outside. We can sit on whichever bench you choose along the embankment by the Rhine."

The two men walked through the winding streets to the embankment. Here they sat beneath alders that overhung the river. On the other side, in the distance, lay Switzerland, veiled by light mist.

Schellenberg attacked at once. "I must warn you immediately, Monsieur Masson, that I came here only after a great deal of hesitation. I have proof that your intelligence service is in the pay of the Americans."

Schellenberg held out a paper. Masson recognized it as a copy of a cable sent by the American military attaché in Berne to Washington in 1940.

In June of that year, Masson had called a meeting of foreign military attachés. Rumor had it that Switzerland was about to be invaded. Panic was sweeping through northern Switzerland, emptying its towns and villages; every room, every bed along the banks of Lake Geneva was taken. The American military attaché asked if it was true that there were twenty-five German divisions stationed between Basle and Lake Constance. Masson had just received secret reports on the subject. Between Basle and Karlsruhe there were no more than four divisions: the 554th, the 555th, the 556th and the 557th, and under cover in the Black Forest, south of Ulm and Rastatt, were five more, fully equipped—a total force far from adequate for invasion.

Careful to observe the strictest neutrality, Masson replied, quite simply, that "there was some troop concentration" to the north of Switzerland.

Impressed by the importance of this information and anxious to emphasize his own part in the affair, the young American immediately cabled Washington: "Extraordinary meeting with Masson. He confirmed to me that there are twenty-five German divisions near the Swiss frontier. He added that they are ready to attack."

He then sent the cable by courier to the experts for coding. The courier was a German agent. On his way to the embassy, he copied the text of the message and dispatched it to Berlin. It was this copy that, two years later, Schellenberg now showed Masson.

The Brigadier returned it to the general.

"This does not prove that Washington finances my services, and you know it, Brigadeführer. Perhaps you wanted to demonstrate the efficiency of your espionage service?"

Schellenberg immediately parried.

"What do you want from *me*, Monsieur Masson."

The conversation was proceeding exactly as Masson had anticipated. It would inevitably lead up to an offer of a deal.

"You know that, too. I asked for this meeting with the agreement of my superior, General Guisan. Only he and Colonel Barbey, his private chief of staff, know I am here. I am advised to inform you, as the General's official representative, that our position is frequently misunderstood in Germany, and that we are determined to defend ourselves against any aggressor. I have also come to ask you to abandon the espionage system you are now building up against us."

Masson paused for a moment, then, carefully choosing his words, went on:

"I would also like you to know that I am no fool. I admit I have been forced to come here to ask for the pardon and safe return of Lieutenant Möergeli, one of my officers in Stuttgart, who was arrested by your services."

Schellenberg showed no hesitation:

"Agreed."

The brevity of the reply and Schellenberg's apparent nonchalance surprised Masson. Now, what would he want in exchange?

"Have you no other request, Monsieur Masson?"

Masson was disconcerted. What *did* Schellenberg want? At any rate, he resolved to take him up on his offer. In 1941, two Swiss Nazis, Ernst Leonhardt and Franz Burri, had settled in Vienna and set up an agency, the International Press Agentur. They had since conducted an all-out campaign against the Confederation, attacking Guisan and the principles of Swiss neutrality. Many of their publications were getting into Switzerland via Lörrach and Basle. Masson requested the suppression of the agency and was again astonished when Schellenberg immediately agreed.

Then, rising, he confronted Masson:

"I speak for the Reich when I say that we should not like the relations between our two countries to be disturbed in any way. Switzerland is a neutral country and should remain so. A world at war needs somewhere where it can breathe freely. That place could be Switzerland. Within a month, you will have Möergeli back, and the agency run by Burri and Leonhardt will be shut down. But I must warn you that in Berlin, in Ribbentrop's office in the Ministry of Foreign Affairs there is a very incriminating 'Masson file,' containing a great deal of information supplied by Burri and Leonhardt. I shall try and get hold of it. There's a lot I can do, you know. By the way, thanks to me, Rothmund, the chief of your police division, will—within twenty-four hours—receive his visa to go to Berlin to settle some business about secret frontier crossings . . . Now let us go back to the Bahnhof for a little refreshment. Then Sturmbannführer Eggen will take you to the bridge at Koblentz. I dare say you would like to get back to Switzerland as soon as possible."

Round one of the secret struggle between Germany and Switzerland seemed to have gone entirely to Masson's advantage. Without argument and without in the least committing himself, he had obtained everything he wanted. And Schellenberg had asked for nothing.

In fact, Schellenberg's amazing reasonableness on the occasion of that first meeting was only one more example of his diabolical cunning, and he was deeply satisfied with its outcome. While secretly forcing his hand, he had left it to Masson to make the initial contact. Should that meeting at Waldshut, and the others that were to follow, one day become known, the head of Swiss Intelligence alone would be held responsible. If the Allies learned of these meetings, Switzerland would be suspected of a tendency to *rapprochement* that was contrary to her own intentions and interests. One may well wonder if, apart from the many qualities that made Schellenberg one of the most remarkable secret agents of the last war, he did not also have to an unusual degree the ability to anticipate the future.

The foresight that he showed on that occasion was even more far-reaching. By granting a pardon to Möergeli and by promising to close down the International Press Agentur, he had quite simply put the Swiss in his debt—and without revealing earlier than he wished his motives for doing so. Schellenberg now knew that entry to the last island of free territory, encircled in a Europe that was going up in flames, would not be entirely denied him. More important, he had seized the initiative to put Masson very much off balance, and then taken advantage of the situation to disconcert him even further by making one concession after another. Now Masson could hardly refuse him additional interviews. He must be enticed further into the net and suffocated by progressively greater obligations before Schellenberg could ask the crucial question—the answer to which held the key to the very survival of the Third Reich. Did Masson know who was betraying the Wehrmacht? If, in the end, Masson still refused to cooperate, he could then be destroyed.

14

SCHELLENBERG'S plan had one very serious defect—it needed time. And time was Germany's most precious commodity, for things were happening with disturbing swiftness on the Eastern Front. This convinced him that the Russians were still receiving vital intelligence in abundance—intelligence that enabled them, always with sufficient warning, to evade whatever traps the Wehrmacht might lay for them.

On September 2, 1942, for example: at a distance of about 25 miles from Stalingrad lay an imposing belt of fortifications that blocked any access to the city. Defense of this line, should it be attacked head-on, would require a great many men as well as a vast amount of material and ammunition. To the west, flowed the Don; to the east, the Volga; to the south, the Karpovka. Parallel to the Don, hills overlooked the Rossochka, a mere stream compared with the other great rivers. The summits of these natural strongholds were heavily fortified—with guns and men.

At their foot, Paulus and his 6th Army waited, hesitant. Hoth was advancing from the Caucasus in the south, with the 48th tank division, a number of infantry divisions and the

Rumanians of the 6th corps. On that side, too, hills preceded the steppe of the Kalmuks, broken by a few ravines that led to Stalingrad. However, there was one weak spot in this defense system—the little town of Gavrilovka. It was there that Hoth intended his breakthrough. If he succeeded, he would take the Russians from behind. Paulus could then attack, trapping the Russians in the classic encirclement so dear to the Wehrmacht strategists. The OKW agreed to the maneuver and the troops went into action.

On September 2, 1942, in the early hours of the morning, German reconnaissance patrols signaled that the Russians had abandoned the positions in which they should have been annihilated. They had vanished—as if two days before they had been reading, over the shoulders of Hoth and Paulus, the telegram approving the plan from the OKW. Nonetheless, Paulus gave orders for the advance to continue. Unknown to him, Eremenko and Zhukov lay in wait for him, on the outskirts of Stalingrad, in a place that made encirclement impossible.

For Schellenberg, this and many similar episodes since the beginning of Operation Blue confirmed any remaining doubts. His listening post at Dresden had reported that clandestine broadcasts coming from Switzerland were continuing uninterrupted—from Switzerland, where the members of the opposition to the Führer plotted together and kept up innumerable contacts with the enemies of the Reich, particularly with the western Allies. One such contact had only just been uncovered.

At the beginning of autumn, 1942, the Gestapo arrested a Munich businessman named Schmidthuber. He was suspected of smuggling foreign currency into Switzerland. Pressured remorselessly by the SD, he suddenly revealed that he worked for the Abwehr, and that he was carrying the money on Ad-

miral Canaris' orders. Investigation revealed that Schmidthuber had not been lying. Schellenberg's Bureau F, in Berne,
also undertook a lightning investigation in Switzerland.

The currency Schmidthuber had been smuggling was intended for a group of Jewish refugees. The Abwehr supporting
Jews—this was just about the worst crime a Nazi could
imagine. Realizing that Canaris would never escape *this* trap,
Schmidthuber talked, hoping at least to save himself. He
denounced Canaris, accusing him of trying to negotiate a peace
with the British. Canaris' first attempt had been negotiated
through the Vatican as early as December, 1939. Schmidthuber also revealed the names of the accomplices: Colonel
Hans Oster, Judge Hans von Dohnanyi, Oberleutnant Josef
Mueller and others, who were later executed by the SS. However, even Schellenberg had connections of this kind with the
British, through one of his adjutants named Jahnke. But he
hoped he would never need them—they were merely one more
escape hatch in the unthinkable event of Hitler's being deserted by fortune.

If the opponents of the Führer were capable of betraying
Germany to the West, they could just as easily do so to the
East. This is what strengthened Schellenberg's original conviction that the traitors he was looking for were to be found among
the traditional opposition. After the Schmidthuber affair,
Schellenberg left Wilhelm Canaris no freedom. Even afterwards, when he had become certain that the admiral had no
part in the extraordinary case he was now studying, he continued to hound him, goaded perhaps by a sadistic desire to
hasten the admiral's fall. He spied on him constantly, even following him on his riding excursions in the Berlin suburbs. It
was Schellenberg himself who arrested Canaris in 1944, and
who drove him in his own black Mercedes convertible to

Fürstenberg, where he handed him over to a colleague, SS-Brigadeführer Trummler. He then took over the Abwehr, incorporating it into his own 4th and 6th counterespionage bureaus. However, Schellenberg was not convinced that Canaris and his co-conspirators in Switzerland were innocent of the steady flow of military intelligence to the Russians until November, 1942, a month after his second meeting with Brigadier Masson, at Wolfsberg, Captain Meyer's house at Ermatingen.

Ermatingen is a big village on the edge of Lake Constance. To the right of its square is an inn at which, it is said, Napoleon spent a night during his conquest of Europe. A narrow road, leading to Sonterswil, winds its way up the hillside into the thick forest. But before it reaches Sonterswil, at a distance of about a mile from Ermatingen, it emerges onto a plateau where there stands a large sixteenth-century building, known rather pompously as a *schloss*. In fact, it is more like a manor house than a castle.

This was Wolfsberg, where on the morning of Friday, October 16, 1942, Schellenberg and Masson met for the second time. It was arranged, as in September, on the initiative of the SS officer. A few days before, Schellenberg's protégé, Eggen, had remarked to Meyer that "it would be a pity not to take advantage of the growing mutual understanding between the heads of the secret services of the Reich and the Swiss Confederation . . . Schellenberg would very much like to come to Switzerland . . ."

So, with the approval of General Guisan, Masson agreed to invite him. A secluded place had to be found for the meeting, for it was essential that Schellenberg should pass unnoticed. Swiss public opinion was now violently anti-German, largely due to the activities of Gauleiter Böhle, director of all Nazi organizations outside Germany. On October 4, 1942, Böhle left Germany to preside at a harvest festival meeting in the Hallenstadion in Zürich. The "festival" turned out to be a large-scale Nazi ceremony, complete with propaganda and military songs, attended by a considerable number of Germans who happened, at that time, to be in Switzerland. This was a tactical error on the part of the Germans. The Swiss were furious, and there were street demonstrations. So dangerous was the situation that the Federal Council had to forbid all meetings of foreigners on its territory.

What is more, Ermatingen was in the German-speaking part of the country—and the German-speaking Swiss were the fiercest opponents of Nazism. For them, it was a betrayal, the very negation of the German culture that many of them had absorbed in German universities. In the event of invasion, they too would be in the front lines—and they were well aware that the Brown Shirts would like to take over their country. Maps distributed by Nazi propagandists left no doubt as to the Führer's intentions. These maps, showing the Europe of the future and the frontiers of the Great Reich, destined to endure for a thousand years, quite clearly enclosed German-speaking Switzerland. If any doubt remained, one only had to read the German press, which was filled with attacks on the Confederation. The Swiss responded so violently in their own newspapers, that Masson began to fear the worst.

He learned that Ribbentrop's services were compiling dossiers on hostile German-speaking Swiss journalists; messages had already been received from Berlin demanding that the editors of the three most important papers in the Confederation should be removed, and that the head of the Agence Télégraphique Suisse be severely reprimanded for the partiality of his radio communiqués. When these suggestions were not taken up, the head of the press section in the Foreign Ministry in Berlin publicly threatened the journalists with exile, or worse, after the occupation of Switzerland. This tactic came to be known as the *Blutschuldthese*—the thesis that if blood flowed in Switzerland, it would be completely the fault of the Swiss press.

Brigadier Masson, favoring more subtle action, through diplomatic channels, had tried vainly to soft pedal such overt hatred of the Germans. At last, he burst out angrily:

"If they really want to let themselves go, why don't they come out openly on the side of the Allies?"

Thus, with no desire to exacerbate an already explosive situation, Masson arranged for his meeting with Schellenberg to take place in the greatest secrecy. At dawn on Friday, October 16, Masson's chauffeur picked up Schellenberg and Eggen at the frontier—wearing civilian clothes, of course—without anyone suspecting their identity. At Wolfsberg, along with Masson and Meyer, was Captain Paul Holzach. They welcomed the SS officers warmly. The Germans were to stay until Sunday evening, October 18. Despite the warm, sunny autumn weather, they would not leave the house. No risks would be taken, and no expense spared to make things as pleasant for the guests as possible. Masson hoped for a great deal from this second meeting.

During the long weekend that followed, Schellenberg surpassed himself. He was at his most calculatedly charming, amusing his hosts with juggling, card tricks and sleight-of-hand, and regaling them with the edited version of his life story. Indeed, to hear Schellenberg talk, it seemed that the only thing that really mattered to him was Irene, his second wife since 1940, who was of Polish descent, and his five children from a first marriage. Overwhelmed with work as he was, Schellenberg counted it a great pleasure to be able to escape for a few days to come to Switzerland among friends. He insisted that he would never forget that weekend.

For he needed rest. In Berlin, in the Führer's entourage, he was known as a *Märzveilchen,* March violet, a term used to denote those who had rallied to Nazism after the party came to power in March, 1933. And many were jealous and made things dfficult for him. It was an exhausting business being continually on the defensive. The envious could soon be turned into enemies. Nothing was impossible in that slightly mad, plot-infested Reich of theirs.

"So my office has to be a fortress," he continued. "It is a large room, with a thick carpet. In it there is a very beautiful, old cupboard—I call it my poison-cupboard—in which I keep my personal files, a habit I picked up from Heydrich. It was he who gave me the most confidential file of all, establishing that Adolf Hitler is of Jewish descent, incredible as that may sound . . . Poor Heydrich. He was obsessed by it—he tried to find Jewish ancestors for everyone around him. . . .

"I had to set up a system of photoelectric cells that give the alarm as soon as anyone approaches the chests or my cupboard in my absence. When I'm there, two machine guns concealed in my desk are trained on whoever is talking to me. In an emergency, I simply press a button . . .

"When I go abroad on a mission, I have an artificial tooth prepared, containing a lethal dose of poison to prevent my falling into Allied hands."

To prove his point, Schellenberg opened his mouth and showed Masson the tooth. Then, with a slight smile, he removed the large blue stone from the ring he was wearing. Its bezel held a small transparent capsule containing cyanide.

Had Schellenberg come to Switzerland simply to talk about himself, then? Or for a rest? He had not mentioned his previous meeting with Masson. Yet he had kept his word—the International Press Agentur had suddenly stopped the flood into Switzerland of its inflammatory publications; and Möergeli had been freed. A plane had taken him from Stuttgart to the military airfield at Dübendorf, near Zürich, where his fiancée awaited him.

Masson and Schellenberg spoke of the war, and of the miseries it entailed. Schellenberg indulged in one of his favorite sins, attributing the aims of others—in this case those of Admiral Canaris and his group—to himself. He implied that he was concerned about the way the war was going, that he would be willing to serve as an intermediary between Germany and the western Allies, with a view to negotiating a compromise peace. He also hinted at the possibility of forming a united front, after such a peace, against Bolshevism in the East. Britain was still too weak to open a second front and was awaiting the arrival of strategic materials from America, materials that were slow in coming. When the United States threw in their full strength, the balance would be destroyed, he admitted, to the detriment of Germany.

Schellenberg told Masson that he had discussed this problem with Himmler two months earlier, in August, 1942, at Zhitomir, on the Russian front. He had even suggested to Himmler that the constitution of the new Europe that could be created should be based on that of Switzerland, which was a perfect model. Himmler had agreed that he should try to make approaches to the West. And he undertook, himself, to convince Hitler before Christmas, 1942—and at the same time to eliminate Ribbentrop, who was implacably opposed to any idea of a separate peace. Schellenberg ridiculed Ribbentrop —a lamentably poor figure as a foreign minister.

He had hoped to get some reaction to his expansiveness out of Masson. But Masson remained noncommittal—and far more difficult to manipulate than Schellenberg had thought at first.

On his part, Masson was interested, but also infuriated by this small talk. For Schellenberg had said nothing about the real problem, nor thrown any light on why he had come to Switzerland. When the night of October 18 arrived, and Schellenberg still had not revealed his intentions, Masson realized he must broach a subject that had long been bothering him. In the most casual manner possible he mentioned the existence of a document that could be terribly compromising for Switzerland . . .

It was the Guisan-Gamelin military convention signed long before the outbreak of the war—a document that could have severe consequences for the future of the entire Confederation. For it could partly justify the accusation leveled repeatedly against Switzerland by Germany, that it could no longer be regarded as a neutral country. It was an explosive document that should never have fallen into German hands.

However, as Masson had known for some time, it was in their possession. Proof of this had appeared shortly before Masson's first meeting with Schellenberg at Waldshut—and in a very curious way.

The Gamelin affair had begun in 1940. After the appointment of General Maxime Weygand as chief of the French army, General Maurice Gamelin, fearing the war was lost, abandoned a train, carrying the archives of General Headquarters, at Charité-sur-Loire. On June 19, German troops discovered the train and alerted Major-General Ulrich Liss, head of the 3rd section of the G.Ic, one of the secret services of the Wehrmacht.

Liss had the convoy thoroughly searched. The booty was of astonishing proportions—whole cases filled with confidential documents: the text of an agreement of cooperation between the French and Belgian armies, dated November 9, 1939; the plan of action and the identities of the French special agents in Rumania, whose mission was the destruction of the petroleum plants supplying the Reich; the codes used by the Allies, and a top-secret note concerning the conduct of the war and, in particular, the attitude to be observed toward neutrals aiding Germany, meaning, at that stage, Sweden.

Major-General Liss studied all the documents and found the information to be of little more than historical value . . . Except, that is, for an interesting French military convention with Switzerland.

And Liss underlined two passages in the treaty:

"On 14 April 1940, General George, commander of the northern front, asked General Gamelin to form a group of nine divisions, which would cooperate with Switzerland."

"On 20 May 1940, General Prételat referred to the task force formed by the 13th and 27th infantry divisions, and the 2nd brigade of Spahis of the 7th corps of the 8th Army, ordered to make contact with the left flank of the Swiss army, near Basle, in the Gempen Gap."

If Hitler were to learn of these papers, he would certainly denounce Switzerland officially for violating its neutrality and immediately launch an invasion. He had invaded Holland for less. He had attacked Poland on a slender pretext forged by his own secret service.

Having had full knowledge of the Gamelin treaty since 1940, Masson's worst fears concerning its whereabouts had only just been realized, when he was told by a friend at the German Embassy in Berne that the deeply incriminating document was indeed in the hands of the SD in Berlin and could be brandished at any time. The Confederation was obviously in grave danger.

Masson had sought in vain for a means of disarming this mine that jeopardized his country's freedom. Now, with the enigmatic Schellenberg so mysteriously accommodating, Masson resolved to ask him what he planned to do with the military convention: "You claim to be a friend of Switzerland. Then show it. What do you hope to do with that old treaty now?"

Schellenberg showed no trace of surprise. He knew all about this "interesting" military convention; it lay in his "Switzerland" file. He could well understand the Swiss general's uneasiness about it. So to convince Masson that he was indeed a friend of Switzerland, he would promise to destroy the papers on his return to Berlin. Berne would never hear of them again.

And again he gave Masson no sign of what he wanted in exchange.

As he took leave of his host, Schellenberg said simply:

"I am very concerned for the safety of the Führer."

Only then did Masson realize that Schellenberg had repeated these few words several times during the weekend—words that were to haunt him later on.

15

DURING the weeks that followed, Masson grew more apprehensive about the larger significance of these curious encounters and shared his forebodings with his superior. Guisan had received detailed reports of the two meetings Masson had had with Schellenberg; he had written them up himself, so that no one else would know of their contents.

This Schellenberg was, he warned, entirely too elusive. His cautious, catlike manner of approach revealed that he set great store by whatever he hoped to find in Switzerland. He had tried to entangle Masson in an inextricable net of obligations—he had obviously decided to ask for what he wanted only when he felt that Masson could refuse him nothing. There was still time to get out, and Masson told General Guisan quite categorically that he ought to do so. But, while recommending the greatest caution, Guisan insisted on the importance of preserving so valuable a contact.

As the year 1942 was coming to an end, Switzerland could not neglect anything that would increase her chances of survival. In general, the situation was not very promising. Switzerland had shown many signs of Allied sympathy. Its antiaircraft defense, even its fighters, which had been so effective in preventing the Luftwaffe from flying over its territory in 1940, somehow never managed to intercept the thick waves of British bombers that violated Swiss air space on their way to sow destruction in Germany and northern Italy. It was also a common occurrence, despite blackout orders from the Army High Command, for Swiss towns to light up "accidentally" when Allied planes were passing overhead, thus "unwittingly" acting as guidelights.

Moreover, Switzerland had long been secretly banking on an ultimate Allied victory. Despite the surveillance of Germany, which had the country completely encircled, Switzerland had continued to mail to London large quantities of parcels, weighing about four pounds each, that contained spare parts for watches, which could also be used as explosive mechanisms.

But these gestures did not satisfy the Allies. The British blockade of Switzerland continued. For some months they had allowed through a small number of shipments essential to Switzerland's survival; then, even this tiny artery was stopped. The Allies criticized the Confederation for continuing to trade with Germany, refusing to admit that she had no alternative. She obtained the coal, iron, mineral oil, gasoline, sugar and alcohol that she needed, and in exchange, she supplied Germany with Gruyère, Emmenthal, butter and meat, as well as certain industrial products, such as machine tools and, sometimes, weapons parts and munitions. (These last were purchased by Walter Krüger, the assistant of the German military attaché in Berne and a man highly trusted by the German Army High Command.) Every day, in every railway station, secret British supervisors took careful note of everything that left Switzerland and of its destination; others visited factories and made the most "intolerable" investigations. Masson's assistants had tracked them down, but done nothing to stop them.

A British blockade would not really embarrass the Confederation. If there were shortages, the government would ask its farmers to make greater efforts. This was nothing new. In March, 1938, an unknown agronomist, F. T. Wahlen, was asked to make an official estimate of the potential production of the country's agriculture, and two years later, he had come up with a detailed plan of action. As a result, stony ground was cleared, marshes drained and barren land made fertile. Woods were cut down and parks and gardens cleared; every available piece of ground was sown with seed. This enormous enterprise, based on an exact calculation of calories and vitamins, was a complete success. The area of cultivated land rose from 467,500 to 915,000 acres; and even more could still be done.

No, Guisan was worried on another account. What were the real reasons for the Allies' irritation? The transit across Switzerland of German trains destined for Italy? That, and the loans granted by the Swiss to Germany. But Guisan was helpless to do anything about the secret activities of Swiss banks.

At the end of the war, the Allies were to claim that the gold stolen by the Germans in Europe and transferred to Switzerland was worth about 800 million French francs—1945 francs. On January 5, 1943, through the press, the Allies had urged all neutral countries, including Switzerland, not to accept this stolen gold, which at the time totaled something like $585,000,-000. This appeal was repeated by the Americans on February 23, 1944. But the Swiss bankers do not appear to have paid any attention.

So, already suspecting, in 1942, that the end of the war could present his country with a number of awkward problems and very probably fearing that Switzerland might be unable to assuage the bitterness bound to be shown her, Guisan preferred not to lose contact with this German, who stated that he wished to negotiate with the Allies. If Schellenberg succeeded, the Confederation would benefit—such a success might even redound in part to his own credit. The Swiss frontiers would be open for Schellenberg whenever he wanted to come; all that was necessary was for him to be watched closely.

On October 18, 1942, when Schellenberg arrived back in Berlin, the war was raging on all fronts and no one could predict its outcome. The Americans had just involved themselves in an uncertain battle at Guadalcanal in the Pacific. Violent, but uncertain battles were being waged in the industrial districts of Stalingrad. For his part, Schellenberg knew that more than ever before Switzerland had to act with the greatest prudence and dare not antagonize Germany. Moreover, he was convinced that he fully understood the way the Swiss reasoned. Switzerland, he believed, was a timid country, so apprehensive that whenever it thought fit to concede something to one side, it always felt obliged to follow it at once by a concession to the other.

It was true that certain Swiss industrialists were unwilling to deliver arms to the Wehrmacht. But the Swiss banks, preserving their customary discretion, placed their numbered safes at the disposal of anonymous customers, which was extremely useful when one wanted to hide stolen wealth.

Switzerland also showed an irritating tolerance toward French and British spies and a no less marked hostility toward German secret agents. But it did allow the Reich 300 million Swiss francs per year, as trade between the two countries slightly favored the Confederation, which was something of a consolation.

But what really convinced him that the Swiss were anxious to remain on the Germans' good side was the utter callousness —in complete contradiction to Switzerland's professed humanitarianism—that the Federal Council displayed toward Jews who asked for asylum. Ever since 1939 the Confederation had been playing an incredibly dangerous game. Colonel Victor Henry, the Swiss Commissioner for internment, rendered innumerable services to members of the French resistance, but remained absolutely intransigent toward these refugees— a fact Schellenberg could not help feeling was another example of their usual balancing act, and would be used to counter the suspected treason he was investigating.

In his talks with the British secret service in 1945, he made the following statement that startlingly illuminates one of the most disturbing episodes in Switzerland's conduct during the war:

"In exchange for their participation in your victory, the Swiss, or at least some of the Swiss leaders, sacrificed thousands of human lives to Hitler's madness. Not, of course, Swiss lives, but those of the desperate men and women who came and asked for asylum—Jews. Perhaps 100,000 . . . They were turned away, thrown back into the hands of my countrymen, who sent them off to concentration camps."

Coming from an SS general, this statement is somewhat surprising. But it must not be forgotten that in 1945 Schellenberg, too, tried to buy his life in exchange for his disclosures to the British. In writing this chapter, the authors checked Schellenberg's statements against an official document, written in 1953 at the request of the Federal Council by Carl Ludwig, a professor from Basle. It was a private report intended only for the Swiss deputies, but some of them, moved by threats from Jewish international organizations to cause a public scandal, brought the affair out into the open.

It was only on October 10, 1942, that Schellenberg learned of the extent of the measures taken by the Swiss against the Jewish refugees. He was astonished to hear that the day before, General Guisan had ordered the 1st and 4th army corps to reinforce the frontiers in the sectors of Geneva and the Bas-Valais. In fact, on October 10, the 1st army corps began sealing these zones off with barbed wire, forming a no-man's-land between Switzerland and France.

"An operation intended only to prevent the Jews from entering the country," the Bureau F in Berne explained to Schellenberg.

"Open a dossier on the problem," he replied.

The inquiry, conducted by German agents in Switzerland, went back to 1939, to the first day of the war.

The Confederation had long calculated that the twenty-five cantons of the country would not be economically capable of supporting more than 7,000 aliens. And 7,100 refugees had already been granted asylum since 1933. Even before the thousands of refugees began beating against its walls, Switzerland had declared it had reached its limit and was unable to take more.

It was not with indignation—he would have tended rather to approve—but with curiosity, that Schellenberg wondered how Switzerland had managed to accept no more than 308 refugees, almost entirely Jews, between September 1939 and January 1942. Switzerland had shown mercy to these 308 refugees—mainly German and Dutch Jews—as a sop to the consciences of a number of national councillors, including Maag and Rittmeyer, who had begun to voice their disquiet.

After January, 1942, the numbers of Jews who appeared every day at the Swiss frontier and who were sent back, after being caught trying to crowd their way through the police posts, increased markedly. Between January and April, 1942, eighty-two had succeeded in being admitted. At the end of July there were 850 in all, of whom 335 were Dutch.

Then came the massive deportations organized by the Germans throughout Europe, and the danger became acute for all Jews. They rushed toward Switzerland, but were turned back. Two methods were used to expel the unwanted refugees. One, they could be smuggled back across the frontier, where they had a one in ten chance of escaping recapture, but at least had some chance of survival. The second method was nothing less than simple condemnation. The refugee was handed over to the police of the country from which he had come. This method, used more frequently, gave rise to some very embarrassing scenes.

To escape this fate many refugees preferred to kill themselves at the frontiers. Professor Ludwig's Federal report on the Swiss policy toward refugees contains this brief accusatory note: "They often committed suicide at the feet of the Swiss soldiers in order not to fall into the hands of the Germans."

Not this dramatic fact, but the sharp increase in the numbers of refugees at the Swiss frontiers since July 30, 1942, alarmed Herr Rothmund, head of the Federal police. Jews were still getting through from the French side of the Jura mountains, and Rothmund asked for motorized formations to patrol the frontiers. The Federal Council granted his request.

On August 4, he ordered that the rejection of refugees

should continue to be strictly observed, "even if it results in serious risks for these persons, that is injury or death." He followed this up by decreeing—in the face of all the information that reached him—that the Jews were in no serious danger in Europe at that time.

Swiss Jewish organizations protested, but Rothmund dismissed their pleas: "We must be content to look after the Jews we have already saved. In any case, German officials have assured me that the detainees in these camps are only made to work. They are not harshly treated. There can be no question of rescinding our decrees. Switzerland will remain closed to the Jews."

The agitation reached the Federal Council, where a serious internal crisis was predicted if the decisions of the Council were retained. The Socialist Party and the Federation of Protestant churches added ther protests. Finally the frontiers were ordered opened to pregnant women, young children and the very old. But fourteen days later, Herr Rothmund terrified the authorities by revealing that in less than a month a thousand new refugees had been arrested for entering the country illegally.

The Federal Council was not alone in its intransigent attitude; the vast majority of cantons were just as severe toward the refugees. The sole exception was the canton of the City of Basle. Although it had taken in a great many refugees before the war, it declared it was willing to accept more. When their humane attitude became known, other cantons did not hesitate to get rid of their own refugees by leaving them in Basle's marketplace.

Others acted even more cynically. They warned the unwanted refugees that if they were found on the canton's territory after nightfall, they would be sent into Germany that night—thus saving the price of transport. The refugees had no alternative but to try and seek refuge in Basle.

Herr Rothmund had no difficulty, therefore, getting the Confederation's support; and on October 9, the Federal Council asked General Guisan to take over responsibility for patroling the frontiers—as Walter Schellenberg was duly informed by his agents.

From October, 1942, onward Schellenberg never ceased to keep account of Switzerland's behavior toward the refugees. In the "debit" column he wrote the number of refugees accepted by Switzerland; in the "credit" column those it had turned away and who had been caught by his SS colleagues. The Swiss Federal authorities, of course, simply reversed the headings, placing to their "credit" those they had saved from the Nazis.

Between September, 1939, and October, 1942, 4,700 refugees had been granted asylum by the Confederation. On December 31, 1942, there were 9,100. At the end of the war, adding together civilian refugees, the military internees and the German and Allied deserters, Switzerland reached a total of 100,-000. But approximately an equal number of refugees were turned away at the frontiers—given the alternative either of suicide or arrest by the SS.

Another fact confirmed Schellenberg in his hypothesis: the surprising silence of the Swiss authorities concerning their knowledge of the atrocities in the concentration camps. Paradoxical as it may seem, until 1944, when the fate of Germany had been finally sealed, the Swiss appeared to know nothing of the genocide being practiced by the Nazis. However, Walter Schellenberg knew that this was not so.

In October, 1942, Herr Rothmund visited the concentration camp at Oranienburg. It was with "a certain curiosity"—the

words are his own—that Schellenberg awaited the reactions
of the head of the Federal Police. He was not disappointed. In
a statement to the Federal Council, Herr Rothmund said:

"I must admit that the Jews are not treated with much consideration in this camp. But nothing led me to believe that
they were being executed en masse there."

However, seven months prior to Rothmund's visit, Switzerland had officially been informed by reliable witnesses that
the Germans organized mass executions in their concentration
camps. After one such report the informant was ordered to remain silent and never to repeat what he had just said. But he
talked and was later reproached for having violated profes-
sional secrecy.

The Swiss knew. There were other informers. In vain the
Federal authorities tried to muzzle their newspapers. Schellenberg was absolutely certain that their callous treatment of
the Jewish refugees was something the Swiss could cast into
the scales as a counterbalance should the Germans ever discover the role they were playing with the Allies. Yes, he had
every reason to feel satisfied. Schellenberg knew that the contact with Switzerland could not be broken, that the Swiss were
well aware of the strength of the Reich and the need to maintain relations with Germany.

16

A MONTH after Schellenberg's return to Berlin, a new complication arose: the sudden appearance of Allen Dulles.

The grandson of an American missionary in India, Dulles had attended the École Alsacienne, in Paris, before going on to Princeton. He then became a schoolteacher, first in India, then in China. In 1916, he joined the diplomatic service, and as early as 1917 he was spying on Austria and Germany from Berne. When President Roosevelt appointed Major-General William J. Donovan head of the Office of Strategic Service in December, 1941, it was quite natural for Donovan to ask Dulles to work with him.

Dulles apparently began work in Switzerland shortly after the Allied landing in Morocco and Algeria, although only the Swiss authorities knew exactly when he had crossed the frontiers of the Confederation. In any case, he did so at some time before November, since he entered Switzerland from the "free zone" of France. Unofficial sources have suggested that he had been in the country since the spring of 1942.

No one suspected that a special envoy from Roosevelt—one

who enjoyed the President's full confidence—had been operating all this time incognito in Switzerland. Anonymity had enabled Dulles to get a more exact idea of the people who might be able to help him. First, he could depend on complete, unconditional support from the Swiss themselves. General Guisan, Brigadier Masson and the entire Swiss secret service agreed to cooperate with him and the American government. He had also approached a number of French resistance workers, who had agreed to act as "sources." But Dulles wanted more than that. He also wanted to gain the cooperation of Germans—not just any Germans, but representatives of a true, sincere opposition to Nazism. When Dulles discovered that the Swiss were working with such a group, he attempted to bypass them and contact them himself. This was the only thing the Swiss refused him. However, in the end, they did reveal that they knew and dealt with only one member of the network, the leader himself, who had been living in Switzerland for a long time. They knew nothing, of course, about *Werther* and *Olga*.

It was then that Allen Dulles decided to announce his intentions to the world. Almost immediately his house in the Herrengasse in Zürich, his flat in the Schweizerhof in Lucerne, and his flat in the Jubiläumsstrasse, in Berne, became very popular places.

Dulles had failed to contact the opposition to Hitler by secret means; he now hoped that they would contact him. Strangely enough, some of them, the less serious, did—as if the Gestapo or the SD did not exist in Switzerland. The first to reveal himself was Hans Bernd Gisevius, the enormous German Vice-consul in Zürich, an ex-police administrator from the early days of Nazism, the permanent special envoy of Canaris and the Abwehr to the Confederation.

H. B. Gisevius and Allen Dulles met frequently, almost daily at critical periods. Gisevius' mission was to communicate to the Americans messages from General Ludwig Beck and Carl Goerdeler, the moving spirits behind the conspiracy that organized the July plot, and to keep the United States informed about attempts against the Führer.

At first, Gisevius tried to conceal his visits. One evening, as they were dining together in Berne, Dulles' cook, who did not yet know the vice-consul, noticed that the two men were speaking in German. She examined the guest's hat and found his initials: H.B.G. That night, she informed the German embassy. Two days later, when Gisevius went to his embassy on routine business, he was accused of treason by two senior officials. Gisevius rebuked them soundly. Of course, he visited Dulles—and he had an excellent reason for doing so. Dulles was quite simply his best espionage source among the Allies. He added that if the two officials wished to keep their jobs, they had better forget what they had just heard. Dulles thus learned that his cook was a Nazi spy, and Gisevius realized that a secret agent never displayed his initials on his hat band.

This is an excellent illustration of the extraordinary atmosphere in Switzerland at the time. Almost everyone appeared to be working for some secret service or other. Ironically, this provided an admirable smoke screen for the few really important agents.

If the game he played with Gisevius seems somewhat naive, Dulles himself was not. He had a difficult task in persuading the plotting generals around Beck and Canaris—all of whom wanted a separate peace and sometimes suggested the most bizarre plans for disposing of Hitler—that Britain and the United States would never turn on the Soviet Union, so long as the war continued. For example, Beck suggested the following plan, which he had communicated to Dulles through Gisevius:

"The British and Americans land in western Europe. The German generals then send all their troops west to meet the attack. The western Allies then send three divisions of para-troopers to land on Berlin, to help the plotters hold the capital. Meanwhile, dependable anti-Nazi troops are sent to seize Hitler in his mountain hideout on the Obersalzberg. The war then continues against the Russians."

Dulles had the greatest difficulty in bringing the con-spirators down to earth.

However, his sudden emergence in November, 1942, had one result that he could not have foreseen. As soon as Walter Schellenberg learned, from his agents in Berne and Zürich, that Gisevius, one of his favorite suspects, was flirting with the Americans, he abandoned his earlier theory; he felt his quarry would be most unlikely to work for both the Russians and the Americans. For despite the fact that they were now allies, the Americans made no secret of their violent anti-Communism. Schellenberg had to reconsider his problem. Since the men he sought no longer appeared to be among the usual plotters, he would turn to the Swiss.

Anything now seemed possible. The Confederation might be totally unaware that the Russians were using its territory as a radiotelegraphic relay station. But it was equally possible that this tiny nation might be running an espionage network that had its roots at the heart of the Reich, in Berlin. There was only one way to find out: a trap had to be laid—a trap such as Schellenberg excelled at elaborating.

Meanwhile, in Stalingrad, the myth of the invincibility of

the Wehrmacht was collapsing. Since November 23, Batov, Zhukov, Eremenko and Rokossovski had surrounded Paulus and his 6th Army, and the Germans had already lost 140,000 men out of 400,000 in front of Stalingrad.

As Lucy had predicted, both to the Russians and to the Bureau Ha, the Italian, Hungarian and Rumanian legions spread out over the 340 miles from Voronezh to Stalingrad had not held their ground. Their lines had been broken and their defenses had crumbled. It was there, west of Paulus's troops, that the Russian grip had inexorably tightened. One last, slender hope remained: the 6th, 17th and 23rd tank divisions under Hoth, which had gone south to the Caucasus, were speeding back to attempt to break the formidable pressure from the Red Army; Paulus was to be alerted to make a breakthrough. Only an element of surprise could win the day.

But, of course, Moscow was kept informed, through intelligence supplied by Lucy, of the advance of Hoth's three divisions, on their degree of freshness and on the morale among the troops. They were beginning to show signs of exhaustion. They made a stop at Vasilyevka, hardly thirty miles from their goal—gasoline was running short and new supplies had been held up sixty miles away. The Russians chose this moment, this pause before the planned German attack: the 51st and 67th armies and the full contingent of Group 2 hurled themselves on the German tanks, decimating them. Hoth retreated, thoroughly beaten. There was no more hope for Paulus. Hitler abandoned him, conferring on him the rank of Field Marshal. He was not told this, of course. On the contrary, he was informed that a rescue force, formed at Kharkov, was on its way from the west. Paulus was to grit his teeth, wait and stand up to the Russians as best he could.

From the west came nothing but death, administered by the Red Army. Once more, information reaching Moscow via Lucy uncovered the Germans' bluff.

Rokossovski sent an ultimatum to Paulus, who rejected it, believing perhaps in the reinforcements that were supposed to be coming from Kharkov. As at the beginning of this campaign of 1942, Russian loudspeakers announced the truth to the Wehrmacht troops, stripping away their last illusions. Then, knowing that they would meet with little resistance, seven Soviet armies, sixty shock divisions, went to work. The cold weather, eternal ally of the Russians, made matters worse for the Germans. Very little Wehrmacht blood flowed that day: it froze in the bodies of the dead.

On December 25, 1942, General Guisan celebrated Christmas with the 2nd light infantry regiment in the public square at Aarberg. Neither he nor his compatriots knew of the plans that Walter Schellenberg was meanwhile presenting to Heinrich Himmler for approval.

Schellenberg could not have failed to notice the profound change that had come over his superior in the past months. Himmler's shoulders seemed to droop and his eyes, hidden behind thick lenses, protruded more than ever. His upper lip twitched intermittently. Nervously, he turned and twisted the famous green pencil which he used to annotate all the reports that passed through his pudgy fingers—and with which he so often signed orders for the extermination of Jews.

"Are you sure the plan will be a success, Schellenberg?"

"I'll take responsibility for it."

"And you're sure Canaris, Beck and their gang are not behind it?"

"I'm convinced of it, Reichsführer. We can go on playing with them."

It was one of the strangest, most surprising facts about this period that Himmler and Schellenberg always knew, in advance, every detail of the plots to assassinate Hitler. What was more, once Himmler realized that, with his SS, he was virtually in command of the situation in Germany, he sometimes went even so far as to lend them his passive support. Indeed, the opposition sought such support and actually offered Himmler the Führer's place; the Wehrmacht refused to act without him. But Himmler equivocated, hoping for a more favorable opportunity, and in the end, he missed his chance.

Himmler was delighted with Schellenberg's plan; the trick his subordinate intended to play on the Swiss was very much to his taste. How amply Schellenberg had justified his encouragement! He had proved a most able successor to Reinhard Heydrich.

A week later, Himmler entered the Führer's headquarters. Goering, Goebbels, Rosenberg and Bormann, whom he detested, were all there. He requested that the OKW swiftly draw up a plan to invade Switzerland.

Hitler observed Himmler intently. What, he undoubtedly wondered, lay behind this latest plan? Was it part of some vast scheme directed against his personal enemies? Why Switzerland? The 6th Army was dying in Russia and it was even possible that the entire Wehrmacht in the East would collapse. Hitler had too much on his mind to concern himself with a pigmy like Switzerland. However, Himmler must have his reasons for proposing invasion, and the Führer gave the desired approval.

The next morning, the order arrived at Zossen, the permanent headquarters of the Oberkommando of the Wehr-macht. For two weeks nothing was done about it; then, when a command direct from the Führer arrived, the commissions immediately set to work.

On Saturday, January 30, at 9 A.M., Rudolf Roessler arrived at the Villa Stutz. He seemed preoccupied. The night before *Werther* had informed him that the OKW was preparing plans for an invasion of Switzerland under General Dietl, a specialist in winter and mountain operations. The same report specified that Dietl's force, consisting of armored units, para-troops and *Gebirgsjägers*, or Alpine troops, was training near Munich. This was certainly a bombshell for Masson and Guisan. Yet, curiously enough, Roessler felt there was some-thing wrong with this information; it failed to jibe with what he was certain must be the concerns of the Nazi leaders at that time. He confided his doubts to Christian Schneider.

Six hundred miles away, in Berlin, Walter Schellenberg waited anxiously for the results of the trap he and Himmler had set. He expected the Swiss to lie low, at least for a while. But if they were involved in this extraordinary affair, as he be-lieved they were, they would come out of hiding soon enough. Throughout the Confederation his spies redoubled their ef-forts, ordered to observe all Swiss movements particularly closely. At the slightest sign of any unusual activity on the other side of the Rhine, Schellenberg would have his proof that one or several spies were to be found within the OKW, and that they were passing information to the Swiss, who in turn informed the Allies.

17

BACK in Switzerland, General Guisan had just returned from a disillusioning tour of the frontiers. The border defenses had suffered from serious delays, particularly in the Glarus Alps. Moreover, the outposts were inadequately defended, owing to insufficient manpower. In May, 1940, Switzerland had 450,000 men mobilized; in August, 1940, 145,000; in October, 1941, 130,000; in June, 1942, after a new attack of the Wehrmacht against the Soviet Union, only 70,-000; by October, 1942, little more than 100,000. This was because the Federal Council regarded mobilization as very costly. In one month, the troops consumed as much as in a full year in peacetime. If he listened to his strategists, Guisan would nonetheless demand and maintain general mobilization until the end of the war. But, of course, there were the civil authorities.

M. Pilet-Golaz, head of the Political Department, who had given public receptions for such notorious National Socialists as the German writer Jacob Schaffner, who wanted to form a Nazi movement in Switzerland and who had granted the German legation the unusual privilege of having a direct telephone line to Berlin, maintained that since Switzerland was not directly threatened, it would be imprudent to display her total military potential. Such an action could be interpreted as a hostile move against Germany and provoke the Nazis into attacking the Confederation. So Guisan had to be content with accelerating the final defense of his fortresses. The light brigades would guard the airfields, leaving the infantry regiments free to reinforce the guards on the transalpine highways. Guisan also decided to advance the blackout time to 8 P.M., instead of 10 P.M. Finally, he urgently requested the Military Department to supply his mountain troops with white camouflage material.

The Swiss people themselves knew nothing of their general's anxieties. The main topic of interest appeared to be the new American film, Wyler's *Mrs. Miniver*, with Walter Pidgeon and Greer Garson. It was the first film to deal with the Battle of Britain, and the censors had cut only one scene: the conversation between the heroine and a German fighter pilot in a garden. Schellenberg himself had decided to see the film on his next visit to Switzerland, but it was not to see *Mrs. Miniver* that he again planned to leave his lair.

That Saturday morning, when Roessler reported the preparation and execution of Dietl's invasion plan, Guisan and Masson reacted in exactly the same way. They did not for a moment doubt the source of the information; it was its value and veracity that were so surprising. The latest intelligence concerning the movements of German troops in Austria and Bavaria had arrived the day before. Their agents in Germany had been quite categorical: the total number of land forces available to the Germans were three armored divisions and six divisions of mountain troops; no more than a third of the Luftwaffe was available for all of western Europe. The rest of the Wehrmacht was engaged on the Russian front. Then was this sizable army of Dietl's a bluff?

The winter of 1942 was not a happy time for the Third Reich. With half its plumage lost at Tripoli and badly mangled at Stalingrad, the German eagle no longer soared proudly over the world. It was binding its wounds. In Russia, reverses had forced it to contract its front. And according to General Adolf Heusinger, chief of the Operations section of the OKW, serious psychological errors were beginning to undermine the morale of the Wehrmacht.

"New units are formed," he reported, "while seasoned combat divisions are driven beyond the point of exhaustion. They fill out green units, untried in battle, with convalescents and soldiers on leave, and they employ reinforcements inadequate in both numbers and courage. In an incredibly inept way, the medal for service on the Eastern Front has been awarded indiscriminately both to men in the rearguard services and men who have been fighting for a year in snow and ice.

"The entire infantry has been renamed the 'Grenadiers,' when this name should be reserved for only a few units who have given outstanding service. The German Cross, made of gold, looks extremely ugly with its enormous swastika. Finally, the callous manner in which families of men killed on active service are informed by the Party has caused a lot of ill-feeling. The Party has nothing to gain by this."

In short, as Winston Churchill had declared on November 10, 1942, on the BBC:

"This is not the beginning of the end, but it is already the end of the beginning."

Moreover, Germany knew, through her spies, that the Swiss "porcupine" could hold out for another two years behind its defenses against any army. Masson's organization had "over-heard" this opinion, expressed by Herr Köcher, the German ambassador in Berne, when it was being radiotelegraphed to Berlin.

Köcher had added that even before planes carrying para-troops could reach the Swiss frontier, the great tunnels of the Saint Gotthard, Lötschberg and Simplon would be blown up by the Swiss themselves. Switzerland would then no longer provide the invaluable passage through the Alps so coveted by the Wehrmacht, but would become instead a fortress de-prived of strategic importance. Nor would it offer any economic advantage: more than a thousand of the country's factories could be demolished at once on orders from Berne. In each of these factories, the machine parts had already been painted different colors, according to whether they were to be blown up, smashed or simply detached and taken to a redoubt. Fi-nally, and an important point for Germany at a time when Allied pressure was beginning to be felt on the frontiers of Europe, it would not be reasonable to immobilize an army to settle the Swiss "problem," even if this war was not to last two more years.

"No," Köcher concluded, "such an operation was definitely not to be recommended."

Was the announcement by Dietl of a future invasion of the Confederation no more than another of Schellenberg's elaborate schemes? A new means of applying pressure? For a long time, General Guisan and Masson weighed their chances, trying to foresee a possible trap. To ask the Federal Council to declare a general mobilization would be an admission of fear. No, the only safe and wise solution was to wait. If it was another of Schellenberg's maneuvers, the SS general would appear on the scene soon enough, when he realized that his plan had not succeeded. So Guisan simply told Herr Kobelt, the head of the Military Department, of his decision and Masson took due note and did nothing.

It was a judicious decision, as it turned out. In the weeks that followed that anxious January 30, 1943, no further reports reached Lucerne of the preparation of any army under Dietl. And at the end of February, Schellenberg's assistant, SS-Sturmbannführer Eggen, reappeared. His chief would like to come to Switzerland. Masson had asked for a great deal from him and he had refused him nothing; now it was Schellenberg's turn to make a request: he would like to meet General Guisan. He had only one condition to make regarding the journey—he must absolutely come by plane.

Masson had some difficulty in locating Guisan, who was still touring his troops. On Tuesday, March 2, they met in Berne. Would he agree to see Schellenberg? This must be the great day. Surely, he would at last show his hand. Guisan agreed. Masson set the meeting for the following day, March 3, at 8 P.M., at the Hôtel Bären, at Biglen.

The Hôtel Bären, a heavy rectangular structure, looked down over the village of Biglen, 10 miles from Berne on the Zürich road that passed through Burgdorf and Lengenthal.

Brigadier Masson arrived first, driven there by Renaud, his favorite chauffeur. Shortly afterward, Guisan's Buick arrived, driven by his adjutant Burnens. Schellenberg arrived rather late, accompanied by Captains Meyer and Holzach, who had gone to Berne to meet him. Eggen was also there, as well as two civilians, both security agents of the SD.

Very much at ease, Schellenberg apologized for being late. "I understand your surprise only too well, gentlemen. You know me to be a friend of the Confederation. I would never of my own accord have taken the liberty of visiting you with an escort. It was entirely at Hitler's insistence. He has become very suspicious lately. In fact, the Führer had strange misgivings about my coming to Switzerland at all. He was afraid the British Intelligence Service might kidnap me and send me to England, rather like Rudolf Hess. I told him, of course, that I had nothing to fear in Switzerland. But he insisted that I should be accompanied by these two guardian angels."

Bending over toward Guisan and Masson, he went on, in a serious, confidential tone:

"Hitler is also afraid that the Italians know of this visit. If they found out that I had been in Switzerland, they might think that it was leading up to an abandonment of the common struggle at a time when Rommel is making a final, hopeless attempt to defend Tunisia and when, in any case, his recall is seriously being discussed. If the Italians discover my presence here, they might—in the Führer's opinion—conclude that after the loss of North Africa we were going to abandon the Italian peninsula and make the Alps our line of defense. The Alps would then become the southern boundary of the new Fortress Europa, which I would have to force upon you."

Schellenberg paused, attentive to the effect of his threat. Neither Guisan nor Masson said a word, but simply exchanged a furtive look. They were both stunned by Schellenberg's latest maneuver.

"So," he went on, "despite my protestations and to quiet Hitler's fears I had to accept this bodyguard and come by plane."

The hotel dinner was an exceptionally good one. The landlord, recognizing the commander-in-chief of the Swiss army, excelled himself. Throughout the meal, Schellenberg was amusing, witty and full of gossip.

"Each month," he told them, "Hitler meets all his SS generals for dinner. In the course of the last one, the Führer raised his glass of mineral water and, pointing at me, laughed, saying, 'Let us drink to our young Swissified general.'"

At the end of the meal, Guisan, Masson and Schellenberg retired into one of the lounges. Suddenly, Schellenberg grew serious and turned to Masson.

"You have asked me for a certain number of favors. I believe I have always given you what you asked." Then he confronted Guisan.

"General, you must now do something for me."

Concealing their anxiety, Guisan and Masson waited.

"I have been sent by the Führer to make a request. He believes that our recent reverses in Tunisia will be followed by an invasion of Italy. Once again the war will be fought out in Europe. Because of its geographical position, your country could be of great importance for the Allies. The Führer fears that Switzerland may not in *all* circumstances, defend its neutrality. He would like your assurance that in no case would you allow our enemies' troops to cross your frontiers."

"I find such a suggestion highly offensive," Guisan interrupted. "Our army will fulfill its mission in *all* circumstances. It will fight whoever violates our territory. Switzerland will remain neutral."

"And yet," Schellenberg objected, "Swiss public opinion is violently anti-German. One only has to read your newspapers."

"A perfectly normal reaction," Guisan replied. "Your own newspapers are constantly attacking us. I repeat, no one will be allowed to cross our territory."

"Could you give me written assurance?"

Guisan replied that he could give no such guarantee without the permission of the Federal Council. Nevertheless, he could reassure Schellenberg and Hitler. A week before he had been interviewed by a Swedish woman journalist who had asked the same questions. Guisan had given her identical replies and would be willing to sign a copy of the article, if that would be enough.

Schellenberg agreed. He was sure that this would allay the fears of Marshal Keitel and the strategists in the Oberkommando of the Wehrmacht. Guisan, too, seemed satisfied. Only Masson remained apprehensive. Schellenberg could not possibly have created such a buildup for so little. Hitler's request was trifling. The nearest Allied troops, the Americans and British, were still six hundred miles away in North Africa. As for the Russians, they were fifteen hundred miles away.

Masson suddenly realized that Schellenberg was staring at him. Only the nature of the trap remained hidden. For Masson was now sure that there was one. Schellenberg was obviously trying to undermine the Swiss leaders' suspicions. To prove this, Masson decided to make a further request. After the escape of General Henri Giraud, the Gestapo had arrested the French general's family. Could Schellenberg do something to improve the conditions of these hostages until they could be freed? In which case Switzerland would be quite ready to give them asylum.

"Certainly," Schellenberg replied.

Then, after a moment's pause:

"Is that really all you have to ask me, Brigadier?"

Masson said that it was. For a moment Schellenberg looked disappointed. But they sat up late that evening laughing and joking. Then Schellenberg, Eggen and their two guards returned to Berne to the rooms they had booked at the Hôtel Bellevue. This was certainly a curious decision on his part—to choose to stay in one of the biggest hotels in Switzerland, when Schellenberg did not want the Allies or the Italians to know that he was there.

Masson then allowed an incident to occur that shattered the secrecy of this "historic" meeting at Biglen. In other circumstances, his guard would not have dropped, but Schellenberg's strange behavior obsessed him. Just as they were about to leave the hotel, the landlord innocently passed around his distinguished visitors' book. Flattered by the presence of General Guisan, he persuaded him to sign. Masson did the same. And Eggen. Only Captain Meyer realized, shortly afterward, that these signatures could someday be compromising and returned to tear out the page.

The landlord was furious and called in the military police. They, in turn, called in the Federal police. Discreet inquiries were made. In this way Herr Kobelt, head of the Military Department, learned, on March 24, that the commander-in-chief of the Swiss army had dined with a leading Nazi, a few miles from the Swiss capital, in the middle of a world war. This event did nothing to improve the already cool relations that had existed between Guisan and Switzerland's civil authorities since the opening of hostilities.

Masson had been decidedly careless. But he was to make a second, much more serious mistake at that sinister March 3 meeting. Anxious above all for the safety of his country, he asked Schellenberg, just before the latter departed for Berne, whether it was true that General Dietl was training an army in the Munich region with a view to attacking Switzerland. Masson failed to notice the gleam of triumph in Schellenberg's eye. He had wanted proof, and Masson had presented him with it!

Just as he thought, the fact that the head of Swiss Intelligence possessed this piece of information proved the existence of a "leak" in the highest echelons of the Oberkommando of the Wehrmacht, in the very shadow of the Führer himself, and that vital intelligence was finding its way to Switzerland. Masson's knowledge of the plan indicated that there must be one or more traitors at work in army headquarters at the Maybach camp. Schellenberg's next task would be to find out who they were.

Concealing his delight, Schellenberg promised Masson to do everything in his power to dissuade Hitler from attacking Switzerland. However, he asked to meet him once again.

18

FROM the middle of January to Wednesday, March 3, 1943, Schellenberg had been living on his nerves, tensely awaiting proof that the Confederation was directly linked to an informer within the Oberkommando of the Wehrmacht. Fear that his trap had not worked was beginning to grip him until that Wednesday evening at Biglen. Brigadier Masson had at last decided to put his head in the noose. Still, it was not long before Schellenberg's pleasure at this victory began to pall. It was one thing to know there was a leak: it was quite another to locate it.

A quiet meeting was arranged by Masson and Schellenberg for March 12 in Zürich, at the Hôtel Baur au lac. This time there was no direct witness to what passed between the two secret service chiefs. Nevertheless, there is no reason to doubt the version of the meeting Schellenberg gave to the British after the war.

Two facts reveal that the relaxed atmosphere that Schellenberg had tried to promote between the Reich and Switzerland had vanished. Schellenberg arrived after an unbroken journey from Berlin, looking tired and anxious. He seemed to suspect enemies everywhere and was deeply apprehensive about the meeting. He feared that Masson, realizing that he had made a serious blunder a few days before at Biglen, might have him seized or even executed. Schellenberg himself would have done as much in Masson's position. So he took the greatest possible precautions. He was followed by a host of agents supplied from the espionage centers of the SD in Switzerland. They escorted him at a distance, fingers on their triggers, throughout his walk with Masson along the left bank of the Limmat. At the first sign of violence from the Swiss, Masson would have been killed on the spot.

No one knows what the two men said to each other on that Friday in Zürich. All that is known is that Masson's expression suddenly altered. His usually mobile features seemed to have frozen; the sharp brightness of his blue eyes, often so warm and lively, dulled. Those who knew him were aware that this transformation always occurred when things were not going his way. There was no doubt that Schellenberg had asked him for something that Masson had had to refuse.

At his trial at Nuremberg, in 1949, where he was sentenced to no more than four years' imprisonment, Schellenberg was content simply to say of this meeting: "It was my intention to arrange a kind of regular exchange of information. However, the idea was abandoned, as Masson was unable to agree to it."

He had earlier proved more communicative in London. During those three years when the British "treated" him after Schellenberg had been handed over to them in 1945, he had given abundant information concerning his relations with the Swiss to the British Intelligence Service agents.

Faithfully describing his series of meetings with Masson, he was to dwell particularly on the one in Zürich. He told of warning Masson that the Führer still persisted in his determination to invade Switzerland. However, he had not yet given up hope of persuading Hitler to abandon his plan. The salvation of the Confederation was of incalculable value to him. But he needed psychological support. As someone who had already given innumerable proofs of his friendship, he advised Masson to cooperate.

Schellenberg then broached the real problem—the problem that had never, in all their previous meetings, been mentioned —revealing himself at last as a master blackmailer.

This was Schellenberg's trump card. As he had often repeated during his visit to Meyer's house at Wolfsberg, he was deeply concerned about the safety of the Führer. He felt torn between his personal feelings and his sense of duty. For he knew that there were generals within the Oberkommando of the Wehrmacht who formed a constant nest of intrigue and who would even go so far as to plot against Hitler's life. Moreover, he was well aware that Masson was using these same men for his own intelligence service. But their days were numbered. The Gestapo had already built up a convincing body of evidence against them. They would soon be unmasked. He alone, with all the power of his own organization and his influential friends, could intervene while there was still time. In a few more weeks, it would be too late. By helping these officers, he would be helping Switzerland. But in order to aid them, Schellenberg would have to have their names at once—Masson would have to reveal them.

To what extent, if at all, did Masson succumb to Schellenberg's magnetism? No one can possibly say. But one fact remains. The chief of Swiss Intelligence never gave him the names of the men who had been working for his organization —and for others—since the beginning of the war.

No, Masson would never present Schellenberg with such a

prize—for one very good reason. Those names—the identities of those German resisters who had refused to bend before Hitler, who were to have such a dramatic effect on the fate of Nazi Germany and who were steadily draining it of life—those names were entirely unknown to Roger Masson.

Schellenberg was not the kind of man to be disheartened by Masson's refusal. Failure had no meaning for him. If one plan miscarried, he would immediately set about elaborating another. Tirelessly, he continued his assault on Switzerland, willing, as ever, to grant requests. On the surface nothing had changed. On March 23, eleven days after the Zürich meeting, Masson was able to inform Guisan through Colonel Barbey, that the OKW had dropped its plans to invade Switzerland and that he had learned this through his extremely "valuable" contact, Walter Schellenberg. Their relations would seem, therefore, to have been as strong as ever.

In fact, things were very different. The second indication that the mask had been taken off was the change of tactics adopted by Schellenberg. This time he did not dupe Masson. For Masson had realized that what Schellenberg had been unable to get by charm, he now wanted by force. And if Masson had not taken certain precautions, Schellenberg might well have ultimately gotten his hands on Rudolf Roessler and probably on *Werther* and *Olga*, as well. Perhaps, too, the OKW would have revived its plans to invade the Confederation.

On Schellenberg's orders, almost every German agent in Switzerland was brought into the chase. They were to concentrate entirely on Geneva and Lausanne, which, Schellenberg now knew, were the key cities. He intended to home in on his target by utilizing its one weak spot—its radio communications.

For more than a month, goniometry had been used simultaneously from the German, Italian and French frontiers. At least one transmitter, it had been discovered, sent occasional dispatches to Moscow from Geneva, while at Lausanne another —probably the main transmitter—sent out long, regular broadcasts.

Schellenberg's spies were not left to their own devices, but followed a systematic plan to penetrate a precisely defined area. The idea was his own. He knew the Swiss and their congenital caution. He did not imagine that their secret service, whatever its convictions, would officially communicate information to the western Allies, let alone the Russians. Although he did not understand exactly how they sent their information to London, on the other hand he felt sure that he knew how it went to Moscow. The work was almost certainly done by Swiss Communists, of whom there were more than was generally realized. Since Stalingrad, they had gained many sympathizers among the Socialists, and it was on these left-wing circles that his spies would focus.

Schellenberg's reasoning was flawless. It proved, if proof was needed, that there was little he did not know about his Swiss neighbors. In the Swiss elections on October 31, 1943, there was a marked improvement in the Socialists' performance. They gained nine seats in the National Council and five in the Council of the States. This was undeniably the result of Russian military successes.

The BUPO, or Swiss counterespionage service, was not immediately disturbed by this new wave of German espionage activity. As the cafés, clubs and cinemas frequented by the left-wing citizens of Geneva and Lausanne became inundated with these outsiders, the Swiss simply responded by arresting one leading German spy after another.

Rudolf Roessler had also sensed a change in the atmosphere. The shadowy figures whose job it was to protect him swiftly multiplied. He could no longer be unaware of them as he traveled from Wesemlin to the Vita Nova Verlag or visited the Villa Stutz at Kastanienbaum. However, he went on with his work, as imperturbable as ever. In the East, the Russians had embarked on a series of victories; it was not the time for Lucy to relax. Moscow was constantly asking for information.

April, May and June, marked during the previous year by intensive military preparation for the offensives, were calm in 1943. The Wehrmacht was binding its wounds. Opposite, the Red Army waited. This strategic method was to serve it well in the last six months of the year. The "wearing-down" tactics it had so far used had been profitable. Moreover, the Russians knew that the Wehrmacht was preparing to launch a new attack.

Lucy had kept the Kremlin completely up-to-date on the plans of the OKW. New heavy tanks, called "Tigers," had been sent to the front, enough to equip seventeen panzer divisions. The Führer was depending on them. Five hundred thousand men would be thrown into the battle—"the flower of the German armies" as William L. Shirer described them in *The Rise and Fall of the Third Reich*. Field Marshal Guenther Hans von Kluge had personally worked out the overall plan of what was to become the second large-scale German defeat in Russia—the offensive that Hitler had named "Operation Citadel."

It was planned to surround—still the same tactics—1,000,-000 Russian troops forming a huge salient in the Wehrmacht lines west of Kursk, a town situated at the mouth of the Tuskor. Kursk was an important railway junction, an industrial center planted in the heart of a district of orchards, grain fields and grazing land. These million Russians were the victors of Stalingrad, who had shattered the German dream of world conquest. Nothing could boost German morale more than annihilating these men.

Von Kluge had three armies spread out over a distance of seventy-five miles, between Kharkov and Orel. The 9th, seven of whose twenty divisions were armored, would operate from the south to the north. The 4th, comprising seventeen divisions, plus an SS armored division, would attack from Kharkov, from the north to the south. Finally, the 2nd Army—six armored divisions and two infantry divisions—would meet the Russians head on. A classic pincer movement, which, if the enemy was not expecting it, could prove one of the major victories of the campaign.

But unfortunately for von Kluge and for the Reich, the enemy knew the plan, down to its last detail. Rudolf Roessler had sent them abundant information in his dispatches. Once again, *Werther* had brought off a masterpiece of military intelligence. Everything was there: the sectors to be attacked, the numbers of men and material to be used, the positions of the supply posts and of the command posts, the proximity of possible reinforcements, "D" day and "H" hour. Meanwhile, the Russians waited, sure of victory.

On July 5, 1943, there were large-scale infantry preparations on the German front. Von Kluge's troops moved into the attack. Then came the deafening reply. The Russians had filled their salient with guns and tanks.

On July 10, as the western Allies were landing in Sicily, and as the Swiss were considering a general mobilization in case of a sudden advance in Italy, the Wehrmacht gained about six miles at Kursk. The Russians had let all the famous heavy Tiger tanks enter the net. They would then be blown up. The Russians had full knowledge of the Tigers' capability and had been able to put in precisely the right guns to meet them. On July 22, seventeen days after the beginning of the offensive, the Tigers were no more. And the Wehrmacht retreated, thoroughly beaten.

Sure of their own forces and knowing, through Roessler, the state of the German troops along the rest of the front, the Russians did not wait for the end of the massacre at Kursk to launch an attack themselves—on the German salient at Orel. From the middle of July, 1943, to the taking of Berlin in 1945, they were never to lose the initiative.

On August 4, 1943, the Red Army drove the Wehrmacht out of Orel. The next day, they took Belgorod. On August 23, Kharkov went back to the Russians. At Kursk, everything had long been over, when, on September 20, Bryansk was recaptured. Smolensk followed on the 25th. Then the entire industrial basin of the Donets. Then the Dnieper. On November 6, Kiev fell to the Russians. By the end of this fatal year for the Reich, the Russian armies in the south had penetrated the frontiers of Rumania and Poland, practically completing the liberation of their own country.

Meanwhile, in Switzerland, a battle of another kind had broken out between General Guisan and the political authorities. Sensing a possible danger in the first Allied landings on Italian territory—namely, a "preventive occupation" of Switzerland by Germany—Guisan considered it reasonable to plan a possible general mobilization. However, Monsieur Pilet-Golaz, the head of the Political Department, refused—wishing, above all, not to anger the Germans.

It was also at this time that the new tactics adopted by Schellenberg in his dealings with Switzerland began to pay off. At Geneva, his agents, who had set up a provisional base near the Gare de Cornavin in a hotel run by a Swiss Nazi, had completed lists of left-wing suspects and were now compiling dossiers on them. There was one name on the Geneva list that would have shocked Alexander Rado had he known it: Margareta Bolli.

In Lausanne, the Nazis had been even more successful. They had succeeded in placing two double-agents in Rado's network—again on Schellenberg's own initiative. In order to be absolutely sure of success, Schellenberg had decided to use the best Soviet agents, captured by the SD in Europe. These Russians had agreed to work for the Germans in exchange for life and security.

This was why Georg and Johanna Wilmer, known in the espionage world as "Lorenz" and "Laura," suddenly turned up in Switzerland. The Wilmers were well known to the Center, which had been using them since 1926. They had lived and worked in Japan until 1935, when they were sent for a brief training period to the Soviet spy school at Sekhjodnya. It was there that they met and became friendly with Alexander Rado. When the MGB decided to dispatch 300 of its best agents into and around Germany in 1936, the Wilmers were among them, for they were both gifted photographers and microphotographers.

At the outbreak of the war in Europe in 1939, the Center lost all trace of "Lorenz" and "Laura." They had been caught by the SD and sent to the Ploetzensee, the huge prison in Berlin where the members of the July 20 plot were later to be hanged. The Wilmers knew that the Germans were always willing to use specialists—so they were saved by their ability to reduce a message the size of a normal sheet of paper to the size of a period.

Schellenberg soon discovered Georg Wilmer's Achilles' heel.

He liked money. For some time, Georg and Johanna worked in the archives of the SD, helping the Germans to capture a large number of their former colleagues. When the German spies in Geneva told Schellenberg that they had drawn up an interesting list of suspects, belonging to or close to Léon Nicole's Swiss Communist Party, Schellenberg immediately enlisted the Wilmers.

He allowed the couple to roam freely around Geneva. Within two weeks they had met Rado. The reunion had appeared to be a congenial one, but in fact Rado had found their explanations unconvincing. The Wilmers claimed that they had escaped from Germany shortly after the war broke out and had taken refuge in German-speaking Switzerland, where they had done everything possible to remain unnoticed. Then, wishing to resume their espionage work and to help the Center in its fight against Nazism—for they still had valuable contacts in Germany—they had decided to attend activities of the Swiss Communist Party in the hope of meeting up with former colleagues. Could Rado inform the MGB that they were once more available?

Rado's first decision was to double his precautions to preserve the secret of where he lived. He even went so far as to rent a luxury flat in Berne, where he sent his wife, Helene, and their two sons. For he, like Roessler and Masson, had noticed that there was a lot going on in Switzerland at that time, especially in Geneva.

His second decision was motivated solely by egotism. He had somewhat resented the independence the Center accorded Alexander Foote. This Englishman, who should really be working as a wireless operator under his direction, had been promoted—undoubtedly owing to the value of the information communicated to him by Lucy. The MGB, he felt, had almost begun to regard Foote as his equal. He was still suspicious of the Wilmers—so he would send them to Foote. If anything went wrong, he would serve as scapegoat.

So when Rado next met the couple he advised them to go to Lausanne and get in touch with him again when they had found lodgings. He would then introduce them to one of his top agents, who communicated regularly with the Center and would be able to use them. In any case, they were not to come back to Geneva: he did not feel safe there at the moment and did not wish to endanger them, too.

So Georg and Johanna Wilmer went to Lausanne, where they rented a luxurious villa overlooking the city. There they made a great show of spending Schellenberg's money, which quickly impressed their neighbors. Their lines were cast; it would not be long before the big fish began to bite.

This surpassed all Schellenberg's hopes. Until then nothing had led him to suppose that the Russians operated a network in Switzerland—and what a network. How could it have escaped his agents for so long? He would not now be surprised to learn that the Swiss used this channel to communicate their information to Moscow. For he knew Masson too well to imagine that he did not know of its existence.

Switzerland never ceased to astonish him. This bourgeois nation that regarded Communism as the scourge of God, that had even sent doctors to the Eastern Front to give medical aid to German troops in the name of the crusade against Bolshevism—this same nation was capable of helping the Soviet Union, in the most effective way possible, through espionage.

Schellenberg considered that he had been given a good lesson in duplicity. He would have to do everything possible to make up for lost time. First, he must leave the Wilmers to catch their big fish, for his agents in Geneva to do their work. Then, they would all be taken at once. Schellenberg knew how to make people talk. He would soon get to the top of this network that was draining Germany's life-blood away through the Oberkommando of the Wehrmacht.

19

ALEXANDER Foote did not hide his dislike of the Wilmers. Georg struck him as being altogether too glib, too vain, too self-satisfied. Johanna, on the other hand, seemed too silent and withdrawn; her eyes had a hunted look. He could not imagine how they were able to rent such a magnificent house. With the law concerning the residence of foreigners in Switzerland so strict, such permission was virtually unobtainable. Where did they get the money they spent so freely? Although he waxed eloquent on his prewar days, "Lorenz" kept strangely silent about his activities since 1939. No, Foote neither liked nor trusted Georg and Johanna Wilmer.

Anxious to receive Foote in a manner fitting the importance Rado had attributed to him, the Wilmers spared no expense —excellent food and wine, followed by the best cigars. Johanna took little part in the conversation, but watched attentively over their guest's needs, never allowing his glass to become empty. Over coffee, Wilmer talked at length and emphatically of the importance of his contacts. They continued to supply him regularly with information—from France, where he had friends in the Maquis, and even from Germany, where he knew valuable anti-Nazis. It would be a pity, he added, not to put such information to use.

After these obviously pressing offers of collaboration came a flood of questions—on Foote's activities, on how often he was in radio contact with the Center, on his changes of codes and wavelengths. Wilmer sounded just like a friend talking shop, but Foote sensed beneath the camaraderie a formidable and insidious technique of investigation.

Foote evaded their questions and followed Rado's example that night by making innumerable detours and doublings back to get to his home at 20 chemin de Longeraie. He definitely did not like people who threw themselves at him and talked excessively—and tried to get him to talk. Rado, whom he consulted by telephone, was not at all reassuring and simply advised him to inform the Center—something he hardly needed to be told.

However, he had an unpleasant surprise. Moscow refused to share his doubts. The Wilmers were reliable agents who had spent years serving the workers' cause. Their way of life did not matter: excess was a well-known habit of theirs, picked up in the course of mingling with the rich and powerful in the capitalist world. Foote could work with them without fear.

But later visits to the Wilmers only increased his anxiety. One evening, on his way home, he realized that his trench coat had been searched, probably during dinner. He was in the habit of leaving pieces of paper everywhere—but only those that had nothing to do with his work. Several unimportant papers had disappeared from his pockets.

Next time, his jacket was rifled. Wilmer had insisted he take it off in order to feel more comfortable in the stuffy room. Johanna then took it away to a coat rack in the hall. She found nothing. Foote had concealed his wallet in his underwear.

Later, he went through his jacket himself and saw that it had been searched. The fine thread he had sewn across one of his inside pockets as a precaution had been snapped.

His hosts plied him continually with questions about his work, even though he had implied that they were contravening the strict injunctions to secrecy, imposed by the Center on members of the same network. Each time he left their house he made ever greater detours to get home.

In the end, Alexander Foote became certain that the Wilmers were agents who had gone over to the enemy. The final confirmation of his suspicion occurred on a Sunday early in the autumn of 1943.

It was a warm sunny day. After lunch and coffee, his host had taken him out into the garden in front of the villa. They were talking with their backs to the house. As he told a story, Wilmer had put his arm around the Englishman's shoulder. Suddenly, Foote realized that Wilmer had spun him around. He raised his head with pretended nonchalance—and noticed, out of the corner of his eye, a camera lens pointing at him from a first-floor window.

Foote gave no indication of what he had seen. He invented an urgent meeting that he had forgotten, and said he must leave at once. Johanna Wilmer, who only a few moments before had been behind the camera, was too embarrassed to look Foote directly in the eyes. Georg Wilmer, on the other hand, was studying his face intently, as if trying to make up his mind whether he should suddenly change his tactics. Foote did not give him time, but pushed past him and hurried away.

That evening, he told the Center that no matter what orders they gave him, he would not see the Wilmers again; he was convinced that they were now working for the Germans. Their reply came back the following night:

"If you have convincing proof, break off relations. Move house."

As if a foreigner in wartime Switzerland, who was lucky not to be interned, could move whenever he wished. Convinced that the Wilmers, or those they were working for, would turn Lausanne upside down to find him, Foote shut himself up in his flat, supplied with food by his cleaning woman. However, he was not to stay there for long. From then on, events came to a rapid head.

Brigadier Masson, too, felt that Walter Schellenberg, or rather his agents, were beginning to get very hot in this game of hide and seek. He could not allow the fate of Switzerland to be exposed to such danger any longer. He was under no illusion. If, as he suspected, the Nazis would soon get their hands on living proof that the Soviet Union had agents in Switzerland, who worked there with impunity, not to say with the complicity of the Federal authorities, a major scandal would erupt. Moreover, if, by means of this living proof, the SD reached Rudolf Roessler and thus implicated the Swiss secret service in a serious espionage affair, nothing more could save the country. One could not reasonably depend on the Swiss army, however devoted it might be, to stop the advance of the Wehrmacht and SS for long.

There was only one thing to do: cut the ground from under Schellenberg's feet.

At 9 A.M. on October 8, 1943, two black cars filled with men in plain clothes, drew up before the tree-lined drive leading to 192 route de Florissant. The Hamels understood at once what was happening: the BUPO, or Swiss counterespionage, had arrived. While Edmond received the police, Olga ran upstairs and hung a dustcloth out of the windowsill of her room.

Alexander Rado would be arriving soon—he came every day. A cloth in the window was the alarm signal.

The BUPO had no difficulty in finding Hamel's transmitter —it was concealed in the basement under a workbench. They then collected a pile of documents, which would be sorted out and analyzed later.

At just that moment, Alexander Rado arrived in the route de Florissant. He had turned into the drive leading to the villa, when he noticed the two cars and the cloth in the window. Without showing the slightest surprise or curiosity, Rado returned to the road. He walked on and then turned right into the long avenue Krieg, which curves northward. He walked on for five hundred yards, then turned left again, into the route de Malagnou. Another hundred yards and he took the first turn on the right, the rue Henri Mussard.

Rado looked calm, but he was panic-stricken. At the end of September, on the 20th or 21st, he couldn't remember which, fearful for his own safety after the appearance of the Wilmers, he had taken all his papers to the Hamels. These included financial reports, copies of the messages for Moscow, the transmission codes and the list of agents, with their addresses. All this was now in the hands of the BUPO. However, he must try to save Margareta Bolli.

He arrived at 8 bis rue Mussard too late. The counterespionage service had got there first. There were two cars there, too—but no alarm signal—she obviously hadn't had time. However, it wasn't necessary. Margareta Bolli emerged from the building flanked by two detectives, who led her to one of the cars. She did not look up. Then, to Rado's astonishment, two more guards appeared with a handsome young man, wearing handcuffs. This arrogant, fair-haired athlete was named

Hans Peters, a German spy working for the SD and Margareta's lover for the past week. The BUPO had found them in bed. Yes, it really was time Brigadier Masson intervened, to save Rudolf Roessler, to save *Werther* and *Olga* and to save Switzerland.

Alexander Rado did not return to his apartment. He abandoned the Géo-Presse, dropped everything and took the train for Berne, where he joined his wife, Helene, and their two sons in his secret lodgings. On October 10, he telephoned Foote's flat from a public telephone. He did not expect an answer. Foote, he felt sure, would already have been arrested.

"Hello? Foote?"

The Englishman recognized the voice at once. Rado telephoned him only when something had gone wrong.

"Yes. What's the matter?"

"Edmond is very ill. The doctors decided he must be taken to the hospital. I must see you. Come over to Berne. I'll meet you in the Botanical Gardens, near the Lorrainebrücke, the bridge near the station. Don't look for me, I'll find you."

Throughout the journey, Foote puzzled over the call. He had understood perfectly that Hamel had been arrested. He wondered what Rado would decide to do. He must have been terrified to have set such a vague rendezvous. However, Rado found Foote easily enough.

"Don't let's hang around. I'm sure the taxi driver who drove me to the station recognized me. Just as I was walking away, I saw him look at a photograph and drive off at top speed. A Swiss technique. The police issue photographs of suspects to all the public services. I must disappear. I'm handing everything over to you." Rado seemed terribly apprehensive.

"You don't think they'll arrest me."

"Warn the Center. For some reason, the BUPO don't seem

to suspect you yet. But they've got your name. It was in my papers, which were seized at Hamel's. Go on transmitting to the end. I have given your address and telephone number to all the survivors of the network, warning them to be vigilant. These include my two go-betweens with Lucy, Christian Schneider and Rachel Duebendorfer. Good luck!"

October went by. November began. Each day, Rachel Duebendorfer, alias "Sissi," or Christian Schneider, alias "Taylor," passed Roessler's information directly to Foote, now the head of the network. Otto Pünter, alias "Pakbo," also provided all the information collected by his group, *Rot,* in south Germany, and which had formerly been transmitted by Hamel and Bolli. The Center confirmed Rado's decision and accepted Foote as its new resident-director, though wondering anxiously how much longer Foote would remain free.

Not much longer. The SD were getting very near his flat in the chemin de Longeraie. Foote did not realize it, but Masson's service knew. They arrested two or three Germans; then the next day others took over the search. When these, too, were captured, they were immediately replaced. Foote remained Roessler's last link with Moscow, which was why Masson was protecting him, leaving him free for as long as possible. But this immunity could not continue without incurring tragic consequences for Switzerland.

Kiev had just been recaptured by the Russians. Lucy contributed much to this victory—as he had done for Kursk, Kharkov, Orel and Smolensk. The Red Army's summer campaign seemed to have come to an end. Foote had just sent the Kremlin the latest figures of the Wehrmacht's strength drawn up by the OKW. One hundred seventy-six German divisions remained on the Russian front, grouped into 11 armies, 3 of which were armored. Forty-five Rumanian, Hungarian and

Finnish divisions were still fighting beside them. On the Western Front there were 72 divisions, 18 in the Balkans, 22 in Italy, 11 in Norway and 12 in Germany. The Reich was obviously finished.

On November 18, 1943, Foote received the latest dispatches from Roessler and coded them for transmission. They concerned the newest German weapons: the night-fighters of the Luftwaffe, rocket-propelled for more rapid take-off, and the *Volksjäger*, the first jet-propelled aircraft, on which the German engineers were working furiously. Foote transmitted most of these documents to the Center on the nights of November 18 and 19. He said he would send the rest the following night.

At 1:15 A.M., on November 20, 1943, Foote heard a stampede on the stairs, followed by banging at his door. He immediately thought of Wilmer and the Germans. He transmitted his last word, "Adieu," and broke off his dispatch.

He could not escape, but he would destroy everything. He poured some gasoline into a large bowl, put in his codes and set them alight.

On the landing, his door was beginning to give. It wouldn't be easy—it was very strong. And when it had finally given, they would find another, equally strong, at the end of his hall.

The codes had now been destroyed. He took a hammer and smashed the marvelous mechanism that had enabled him to correspond so long and so effectively with the Center—and which had enabled him to participate, in his own way, in the triumph of Stalingrad and all the other victories of the summer of 1943, that brought about the destruction of Nazism.

When the last obstacle separating him from his assailants had collapsed, Foote was calm. Only a pile of twisted metal remained of what had been a secret radio station. But when he saw his "aggressors" his calm turned into relief. It was not the SD, as he had feared, but Inspectors Pasche and Knecht of the BUPO, accompanied by Marc Payot, their chief code specialist.

Here, too, they were only just in time. Among the projects in the SD archives was a plan to seize Foote—on November 23! It was to be done quite simply by sending in a number of agents after the cleaning woman, who had been in their pay for the past few days.

With these arrests over—arrests that were so vital to Switzerland—Brigadier Masson could relax. At the Bureau Ha, Rudolf Roessler was reassured concerning the fate of his colleagues. However, he was now deprived of all means of communicating with Moscow and did not conceal his displeasure. The Russians would win easily now without his help. The Germans could never check their advance. In any case, he could be more useful to the West, now that the war had started moving again.

The intelligence that he carried daily to the Villa Stutz did not, unfortunately, receive the same welcome from the western Allies as it had from the Russians. These innumerable reports must have found their way to some bureaucratic dead end in London. Yet Roessler took great care in sorting out the intelligence he received. To the British, he sent any details concerning the V-1 and V-2 rockets. He continued to supply the Swiss with an ever increasing number of analyses of the general war situation.

Schellenberg had not abandoned his search. His listening post in Dresden had informed him that there were no more transmissions on the wavelengths they had been observing and which until November had been so frequently used. In stopping the transmissions to Moscow, Masson had pulled off a major coup. And he still had two more cards up his sleeve.

His agents had located Christian Schneider and Rachel Duebendorfer when they appeared at Foote's flat with Lucy's messages. They continued to watch the couple closely and noticed that they sometimes met a Lucerne bookseller. A quick check revealed that the bookseller was a German émigré. Where did he come from? Why hadn't he presented himself to the National Socialist organization set up by the Party in Switzerland? Only one answer was possible: he was an enemy of the Reich. Perhaps he too was one of the gang passing intelligence to the Russians. The search began again.

This time, Roger Masson decided to end it once and for all. On May 9, 1944, Rudolf Roessler was escorted under heavy guard to Bois-Mermet, the prison of Lausanne. Christian Schneider, Rachel Duebendorfer, her daughter Tamara and Paul Boetcher were taken to Sainte-Antoine, the Geneva prison.

A prison was just about the only place in Switzerland that was inaccessible to the SD. Schellenberg knew this—as he also knew that he had no other means left of fulfilling his mission. He had underestimated the Swiss brigadier: Masson had beaten him hands down. He tried to stifle his intense bitterness over this failure by turning his full attention to an important event that was being "secretly" planned in Berlin. The usual plotters intended to assassinate the Führer during the summer—probably in July.

Roger Masson was now completely reassured. The Nazis could no longer get their hands on the least known, but greatest and most effective secret agent of the Second World War. At the same time, he was placed in an embarrassing predicament.

In fact, at the end of May and the beginning of June, 1944, the Swiss government was in a state of terror. German troops were massing in Alsace, accompanied by transport planes. It was said that about twenty divisions had been observed within an area of 125 miles around the Swiss frontier. Herr Jaeger, the Swiss minister in Hungary, reported a rumor that had been circulating in Budapest: Switzerland was about to be invaded, as Hungary had been three months before.

On June 5 an apprehensive General Guisan called a meeting of his high command "working committee": Huber, Gonard, Bracher and Masson. Masson wondered whether the whole thing might be an act of revenge engineered by Schellenberg, but kept his suspicions to himself. It was now estimated, unofficially, that the German divisions in the 125-mile area numbered thirty-five. What was the significance of these groupings? Masson, supported by Gonard, was in favor of a full mobilization. Huber, however, did not think that the situation was comparable to that of May and June, 1940. The Wehrmacht was then intact and victorious, hardly the case in June, 1944. Colonel Barbey, who followed Guisan wherever he went, made the following revealing remarks in his wartime diary:

"5 June—Struck, during this meeting, by the fidelity with which the Chief [General Guisan] sticks to his idea of a general mobilization. Struck too by what was *not* said: no one, not even Masson, explained why the *Viking Line,* which until then had been so remarkably productive, could not be of any use in these circumstances . . ."

The reason, of course, was obvious. Brigadier Masson could hardly let the whole world know that to save Switzerland he had been forced to imprison the head of this unique intelligence network.

The next day, June 6, 1944, all Switzerland's fears disappeared. The Allies had landed in Normandy. At Bois-Mermet, the detainees spent their days quietly. They had all been brought to the same prison—Roessler, Schneider, Duebendorfer, Foote, Hamel and Bolli—and put in separate, comfortable cells. On September 8, 1944, when they were completely out of danger, they were released.

On his return to Wesemlin, where he found that nothing, not even his transmitter, had been disturbed, Rudolf Roessler wasted no time in sending out a call to his ten friends in the OKW. He feared for their safety. While in prison he had had all the newspapers at his disposal and had followed closely the details of the July 20 attempt on Hitler's life and the savage reprisals taken against the Wehrmacht High Command. He was deeply apprehensive of what might have happened to *Werther* and *Olga* in all the turmoil. He stayed all night at his set, listening. No answer came. Every day he repeated the attempt.

Finally, on September 15, he received a reply. They were happy to know that he was safe and free. They had come through the July tumult unscathed. Ten times they had slipped through the net of purges, free of suspicion. Better still, when Heinz Guderian was appointed chief of staff of the Oberkommando of the Wehrmacht, the day after the assassination attempt, he had fired all his colleagues except one, their friend G. *Werther* could therefore continue its work. The Nazi beast was mortally wounded, but it was not yet dead.

From September 16 onward, Rudolf Roessler began visiting his Swiss colleagues in the Bureau Ha once again. Unfortunately, his extremely valuable dispatches remained unused in a safe, together with the copies of his reports that had bled Germany to death. To whom could they be given? And why? In any case, the fate of Nazism was sealed.

For Switzerland, the war was already over. It had ended on

September 5, 1944, when General Jean de Lattre de Tassigny's Moroccan troops marched along its frontiers on their way to Germany. On that date, the Confederation lifted its blackout regulations. It was already making preparations for its peace celebrations.

After a long stay in a Lausanne hotel, Alexander Foote decided to try and get in touch with his colleagues. With careful searching, he located Rachel Duebendorfer at the end of November, thanks to Pierre Nicole, the son of the Swiss Communist leader. From her, Foote learned that Rado, who had remained in hiding in Berne, had left for Paris in order to renew contact with the Russians, who had already opened an embassy there.

"What are you going to do?" she asked.

"Go and join him."

"Then, before you go, you must see Lucy. He will give you some documents for the Russians."

A meeting—the first meeting between these two men who had worked so closely together—was arranged for December 15, at the Bolognese restaurant, in the Kazernenstrasse in Zürich. Foote arrived first, with "Sissi." At exactly midday, he saw a smallish man winding his way among the tables toward them. An unobtrusive man in his fifties, with an emaciated face and feverish eyes blinking behind spectacles. At first sight Roessler appeared a colorless enough figure, but Foote was fascinated by the subtle impression of power he emanated. Roessler nibbled at his food without interest, but he talked a great deal—in a quick, nervous, rather jerky way. He spoke of the war and of Nazism, which he said must be entirely purged from Germany. He handed Foote a bulging briefcase:

"Sissi tells me you're leaving for Paris. I want you to do something for me. Here are the latest plans of the Wehrmacht. Give them to the Russians. Tell them to work out a system which will enable me to continue to send them all the intelligence I receive from Germany. My network was not affected by the reprisals that followed July 20. This Germany must be crushed once and for all."

As they were leaving the restaurant, Roessler repeated his request for a means of corresponding with Moscow.

"Do you think it is still worth it?" Foote asked.

"I don't see what you mean," Roessler answered.

"Well," Foote explained, "as things are at the moment, the war can't go on much longer. I have a feeling that the Center no longer needs us, because the Red Army no longer needs the Center. Our work is finished, Lucy, and we've got to realize it. I'll take these documents to Paris, but I think I know what they'll say. They'll say that it's all over."

A sudden transformation seemed to come over Rudolf Roessler. He seemed to have aged. Without a word of goodbye to either "Sissi" or Alexander Foote, Roessler turned on his heels and walked off, muttering incredulously to himself:

"All over?"

CONCLUSION

VERY often the existence of people who are revealed to the public by some dramatic event seems to end with the event itself. Yet they go on living, though usually deeply affected, sometimes even traumatized, by the events they have experienced.

It seemed only right, therefore, that this book should not end as abruptly as the activities of the Lucy ring. So we pursued our investigations beyond the war's end to discover what had become of the principal actors in this extraordinary drama. Some seem to have vanished without a trace—returning to the shadow world from which they had come. Others, like Rachel Duebendorfer and Paul Boetcher, set off for the USSR in 1945. No sooner had they arrived than they were quietly removed to work camps in Siberia, where they remained for twelve years—until their release in 1956 under Khrushchev's liberalizing measures. Stalin had determined to get rid of any witnesses that might tarnish his reputation as a strategist of genius—by revealing to the Russians, for example, that German resisters had helped them to defeat Hitler.

Rudolf Roessler did not leave Switzerland in 1945. He continued to work in his publishing house, the Vita Nova Verlag,* in Lucerne, and to live in his modest home at Wesemlin. He still had his transmitter-receiver, but it lay unused and useless, because there was no longer anyone on the other end, neither the Russians nor *Werther* nor *Olga*. As Foote had predicted, the Russians no longer needed him, even when, after the war, he went to their fine new embassy in Berne and offered his services. Roessler found it even more inconceivable that when the war was over his friends in the former OKW would leave him without news—no messages, no letters, no visits, nothing but silence. It was inexplicable. Later, Roessler and his wife Olga worked out a psychological hypothesis:

In their desire to free their country from Nazism, his ten companions had not realized that the death of the Third Reich would bring about the death of Germany altogether. They would never be able to return to the pre-1933 Germany which they loved. They must have realized this when they saw the Red Army in Berlin itself and the division of their country into two blocs. Seeing at last the full results of their actions—a resistance in continuous operation since 1939—they made the terrible decision not to meet again, to ignore each other's existence.

If this had indeed been his friends' state of mind, it was certainly not Roessler's. He had no regrets. What he had done, he had done in full awareness of the outcome. He knew that if Nazism had triumphed, the world would have known considerably more than 36 million dead—not to mention the dark night into which it would have been plunged.

Roessler also realized that the end of Hitler and the defeat of

* A curious detail: after the appearance of our book, the Vita Nova Verlag changed both its name and its location. It is now called the Büchlandung Stocker, at 5 Kapelgasse, Lucerne.

Germany did not mean that all the Nazis had been exterminated. Many who were lying low would emerge later. Some had escaped punishment, while others, like the mysterious Gehlen, had "changed sides" and were working for the western Allies, until they could show their true colors. No, Foote had been wrong when he had said that it was "all over." His ten friends might retire into their ivory towers, but Roessler would not give up.

In the spring of 1947, an officer in civilian dress, Captain Wolf of the Czech legation in Switzerland, called on Roessler at his office in the Vita Nova Verlag and asked him to draw up analyses of the military and strategic situation in Europe. Roessler agreed, convinced that by doing so he would be continuing to work for peace.

In 1939, it was his friend Xavier Schnieper who had initiated him into active espionage work, when he had introduced him to Major Hausamann, of the Bureau Ha. Roessler now called on Schnieper's services—an increasingly left-wing Schnieper. In 1945 he had become chief librarian of the canton of Lucerne. He then worked for the Caritas organization as literary director, which involved frequent visits to Prague. Schnieper joined the Swiss socialist party and became a journalist on *Volksrecht*, which sent him to Bonne as its regular correspondent. In fact, it was there that Schnieper became Roessler's agent. He also met the Czech Captain Wolf. When this officer returned home in 1951, Roessler and Schnieper corresponded with two other Czechs, known only by their nicknames, "Conrad 1" and "Conrad 2."

In January, 1953, Roessler went to West Germany, to Düsseldorf, to write a thirteen-page report on military power in Europe. This report was intended for Czechoslovakia. First, however, it had to be sent to Zürich, to an agent whose sole function was to receive the mail and dispatch it to its real addressees.

The report did not contain any major secrets. It had been based on official publications circulating in NATO circles. However, Roessler thought fit to conceal it—in a pot of honey! —for mailing. An "anonymous person," who occupied a high post in West Germany and who had been following Roessler's activities for some time, alerted the Swiss police. The parcel was intercepted. On March, 1953, Otto Maurer, a police officer of Lucerne, arrested Rudolf Roessler and Xavier Schnieper.

They were given 242 days of preventative detention before being brought to trial on Monday, November 2, 1953. This was the time it had taken for the Swiss police to build up their case —or to "make up" their case, as some people suggested. The trial lasted for three days. The Federal judge, Corrodi, presided over the penal tribunal of Lucerne, assisted by Judges Pometta, Rais, Albrecht and Schwarz. The prosecution was led by the assistant public prosecutor, Haenni. Roessler was defended by Schuerch, of Berne, and Schnieper by Eckert, of Basle.

Roessler and Schnieper were charged with spying on the West German Federal Republic for Czechoslovakia—of sending 160 reports to Prague, in exchange for 33,000 Swiss francs (about $8,000). The defense proved that these reports were based on publications that could be bought by anyone in any bookshop. Yet Roessler was condemned to one year's imprisonment and Schnieper to nine months.

Roessler realized that the Confederation had changed. This was no longer the Switzerland that had been so accommodating toward his activities, that from 1939 had accepted the secrets of the OKW, that had allowed the transmission of so much intelligence to the Soviet Union and which, in 1945, had presented him with an expression of its gratitude for his conduct during the war. Disillusioned, indifferent and exhausted, Rudolf Roessler died in October, 1958. Few people attended his funeral at Kriens—his colleagues and Xavier Schnieper. None of his wartime comrades were there. He went, as spies always do, even the greatest of them, discreetly. A small marble plaque bears the simple statement:

"Rudolf Roessler. 1897-1958."

Xavier Schnieper still lives in Lucerne, where he worked as a journalist and writer. He often meets Roessler's former partners, who still run the Vita Nova Verlag. But he rarely sees Major Hans Hausamann, now a photographer in Zurich, the former head of the Bureau Ha, to whom he introduced the German émigré in 1939. Although Hausamann was reluctant to receive us and to answer questions regarding Roessler or the Lucy ring, in the course of a television broadcast in Zürich, on May 17, 1966, he confirmed that his office, the Bureau Ha, had financed Roessler throughout the conflict, knowing perfectly well that he was working for the Russians.

In 1945, as the Third Reich was drawing to its agonized end, Walter Schellenberg arrived at the Swedish frontier with a party of Scandinavian internees whom he had freed from concentration camps for the occasion, with the agreement of Heinrich Himmler. Schellenberg knew that one never arrives empty-handed when one wants something. What he wanted was asylum. Count Bernadotte agreed to let him stay temporarily in Stockholm.

Bernadotte also helped him get to Britain. On June 16, 1945, a transport plane took him secretly to London. In exchange, Schellenberg had promised to reveal everything he knew concerning matters that interested the British government. Such a proposition, coming from the head of the SD, who must have sensational information on the events that had taken place in the world since 1933 and on the men who had directed them was too valuable to spurn.

For three years Schellenberg revealed enough to satisfy the curiosity of the British agents. The result was an impressive harvest of intelligence, though, of course, the experts of the Intelligence Service had to evaluate it with exemplary care. For Schellenberg often lied or twisted the facts to his own advantage. But the truth that emerged more than justified the time and energy spent in obtaining it.

On January 4, 1946, Schellenberg gave evidence against the Nazi leaders at Nuremberg. No one was surprised when he returned to London flanked by two nurses. Schellenberg was a sick man—stones were forming in his bladder. Back in London he was given treatment. When he had fully recovered, the interrogation continued.

In 1948, squeezed dry of intelligence by the British, he was called up before the international court that was still in session in Nuremberg. Schellenberg appeared before the judges toward the end of spring, 1949. The British and Americans agreed to an acquittal, but the Soviet delegate protested strongly. Naturally, the Russians found it incredible that the western Allies should want to acquit the former head of the SD. As a result, Schellenberg was given four years.

In 1952, three years after his condemnation, the British had him released—on health grounds. He knew where to go. He got in touch with his old enemy, Roger Masson. Moved somewhat by Schellenberg's obvious physical and mental deterioration, Masson did what he could—secretly—for the Swiss might not take kindly to such help. He entrusted Schellenberg to one of his friends, a surgeon called Lang, who hid him near

Romont, halfway between Lausanne and Freiburg. After a few months' respite, the Federal authorities learned of his presence and ordered his immediate expulsion.

It was little more than an invalid that left for the shores of Lake Como—where he was supported by money from the British government. He began writing his memoirs, but they were finished by a German journalist. Great was the relief among a number of people when they finally appeared, to see that Schellenberg had, in fact, revealed very little. He died in the autumn of 1954.

One of the most intimate witnesses to this extraordinary affair, Alexander Foote, also wrote a book—a small, deliberately incomplete work, on the "advice" no doubt of the British counterespionage service. For Foote had left the Communist Party and lived respectably in Britain until his death in 1958.

In December, 1944, after his first and only meeting with Rudolf Roessler in the Bolognese in Zürich, Foote went to Paris, with the documents given him by Lucy. This mass of intelligence provided an entrée to the Soviet Embassy where, at first, he was thought to be an *agent provocateur*. The expert who examined the papers immediately got in touch with the Center, which said that Foote was to go to Moscow. He was to travel with Alexander Rado, who had been in Paris for some weeks.

Rado and Foote celebrated their reunion with caviar and vodka. Under the effects of the alcohol Rado lost some of his caution. He admitted he was frightened. First, because he had abandoned his post at a dangerous moment and, second, because he had never been able to distinguish between the money he had been sent for the running of his network and his own salary. He knew he had "embezzled" something like $50,000. What could he do? If he went into hiding, he would be condemned just as surely as if he had admitted to working for the Nazis. If the MGB really wanted to rid itself of an agent, they would find him.

On January 6, 1945, at 9 A.M., the first Soviet plane to leave Paris since 1939 took off from Le Bourget. On board was a cargo of Russian officers and two civilians, Foote and Rado. The pilot was to make a vast detour. There was no point in exposing oneself to possible danger by flying over Germany— the war was not quite over yet. They would reach Moscow via Egypt and Turkey and break the journey for forty-eight hours in Cairo.

When the DC-3 took off again at dawn on January 9, one of the civilian passengers was no longer there. Rado had disappeared into the Egyptian night.

On January 11, Foote was in Moscow. He was warmly welcomed and even given a charming female interpreter who took care of him until he was called before a commission that examined his conduct during the war. He had no difficulty in proving that he had been unable to escape arrest in November, 1943, which had deprived the Red Army of Lucy's valuable information. He was questioned lengthily about Lucy and about the functioning of the network. Then, freed from any trace of suspicion, he was sent to the famous spy school at Sekhjodnya—after which, no doubt, he was ready once more to serve. Foote proved a brilliant pupil and was even given the rank of Major of the Red Army, which brought with it a more than adequate salary. In the course of the summer of 1945, he learned by chance at Sekhjodnya that Rado had finally been extradited from Cairo, where he was discovered by agents of the MGB, judged at once and executed.

The news of the treatment meted out to the former head of his network, proof enough that one could never trifle with the

Center, did nothing to deepen Foote's conviction that Communism was still the best possible social system at man's disposal. Gradually, as his experience as a secret agent grew, he began to lose his illusions.

At the beginning of March, 1947, Foote's masters considered that he was ready to confront the capitalist world once more and he was flown to East Berlin. Foote decided that he would get out at the first good opportunity. He had a new identity—that of Albert Mueller, a German. At the end of July, he was to be posted to Mexico, where he was to work as the resident-director of a network spying on the United States.

The time had come, he thought, to change sides. On August 2, 1947, he escaped and presented himself to the authorities of the British sector of Berlin.

For the next eleven years Alexander Foote worked for the British government. But he might never have gone back to Britain had he known that Alexander Rado was not dead, and that he had been told so only as a warning. Rado is now professor of geography at the University of Budapest, old but still useful, despite twelve years spent, like Rachel Duebendorfer, in a Siberian work camp.

And what of the other characters in this drama? Many of them are dead—like General Guisan, who was accompanied to the Pully cemetery, in Lausanne, on April 12, 1960, by more than 200,000 Swiss soldiers, who came down spontaneously from their mountains to pay their last respects to the man who had realized that "total neutrality" would not have saved the Confederation between 1939 and 1945 and who had preferred an "active neutrality."

But one of the most tormented actors in this tragedy, along with Rudolf Roessler and Walter Schellenberg, was Roger Masson. Long ago, France could have given him the Legion of Honor, Britain its Distinguished Service Order, America its Distinguished Service Cross and the Soviet Union its Red Star. Like Guisan, he, too, served the Allies' cause—in the interests of Switzerland. One might even be permitted to wonder why postwar Switzerland, which condemned Rudolf Roessler to prison, did not also deal with its former secret service chief.

As Walter Schellenberg had foreseen when he planned his scheme to force Masson to visit him in September, 1942, it was Masson who had to take the blame when, after the war, the facts were exposed. It had happened in a particularly cruel way.

On September 28, 1945, the Swiss press announced that on the 21st of the month, Roger Masson had disclosed, in an interview with the Chicago *Daily News*, that during the war he had met Walter Schellenberg, the head of the SD, on several occasions—the first in Germany, then subsequently in Switzerland.

Two Federal deputies, Herr Dietchi, a Radical from Basle, and Herr Bringolf, a Socialist from Schaffhouse, immediately attacked Masson. They expressed astonishment that such contacts could have taken place, inferred that the head of the Swiss secret service had been duped by Schellenberg and declared that, in any case, Masson had considerably exceeded the brief that had been entrusted to him. They demanded that an inquiry into the whole "affair" be opened at once.

To suppose from what is known of the facts that Masson was the victim of Schellenberg's stronger personality is to judge too hastily the very delicate situation in which he found himself. It is also to ignore the advantages for the Confederation, of maintaining a contact with the Nazis. Although in June, 1943, the Federal Council had had to threaten Masson with

severe sanctions to prevent him from going to Berlin to meet
Schellenberg, and although in October, 1943, Masson received
the German once again for a long weekend at Wolfsberg, and
despite the fact that over numerous protests and an expulsion
order drawn up by the Federal Council, Masson continued
to receive Schellenberg's adjutant, Eggen, on Swiss territory,
right up until 1945, only on one other occasion after Masson
had refused him the identities of the members of Lucy Ring
did Schellenberg, who on countless occasions had granted
Switzerland's requests, himself ask Masson for something. And
on that occasion—April 11, 1944—Masson showed how cool,
even severe, he could be toward the SS general.

Two days before, a German fighter plane landed at the
Swiss military airfield at Dübendorf, near Zürich. The plane
was intact. The pilot told the head of the Swiss base that he
had landed there intentionally. He had had enough of the war.
His was no ordinary fighter plane, but a Messerschmitt 110,
specially equipped for night fighting—a prototype that was
still secret. Apart from the traditional equipment, it was armed
with two vertical-firing 30mm guns. A formidable machine.
On hearing of this catastrophe, Goering flew into furious rage.
He sent for Schellenberg and ordered him to dispatch the head
of his commandos of Section VI F, the famous Otto Skorzeny,
to Switzerland at once. With thirty men, Skorzeny was to go to
Dübendorf and blow up the plane before the Allies discovered
it. This would be easy enough, since 10,000 people a day were
flocking to admire, from the edge of the airfield, all the
American and British bombers which had been forced by antiaircraft fire to make forced landings on Swiss territory.

Schellenberg got in touch not with Skorzeny but with Masson. He knew that an intervention by the excitable Skorzeny
at Dübendorf would constitute a veritable *casus belli*. He

simply got Masson to have the Messerschmitt 110 destroyed in the presence of the German military attaché in Berne. In exchange for her cooperation, Switzerland was at last allowed to acquire twelve Messerschmitt 109s, which she had coveted for some years. Twelve Messerschmitt 109s, in April, 1944, when the Luftwaffe was being bled on all fronts, two months before the Normandy landing, during which only two German fighters took the air, was a high price to pay for two 30 mm guns, even if they could fire vertically.

Nonetheless, Dietchi and Bringolf had their way. Judge Couchepin opened a government inquiry on October 23, 1945. On January 28, 1946, he published his conclusions: Masson was entirely exonerated of any suspicion.

Entirely? Such attacks always leave their scars. Even today there are pro-Masson and anti-Masson parties in Switzerland —the same people as those in 1945—those who believed Judge Couchepin and those who did not. Roger Masson has never really recovered from the accusations made against him—because he has never been able to tell the truth. He has never been able to defend himself in broad daylight, because of the oath of secrecy that prevents him from revealing the slightest details about this still recent, still controversial period. His military career was cut short that September 28, 1945. From that, too, he has never recovered.

We met him several times in the Hôtel de Lausanne, in the center of that city. Masson feels at home there. When he was head of the Swiss secret service he often used this large, discreet hotel for appointments; with its numerous exits and its proximity to the station, it was particularly suitable for meetings that should go unnoticed. Today, twenty years later, it was there that he arranged to meet us.

He received us cordially and talked freely of his meetings

with Schellenberg. But when, one day, we asked him certain embarrassing questions concerning Rudolf Roessler, Brigadier Masson rose to his feet, looked straight at us and, without a word, walked away. We did not see him again.

The day before, he had said to us:

"A few days ago it was my seventieth birthday. I spent it quietly at home on Mont Pélerin, the hill overlooking Vevey. To my great surprise, the postman arrived that morning with hundreds of letters. Hundreds of men had remembered—former colleagues of mine. It was my best birthday in twenty years."

As for Switzerland itself, the country that formed the background to this extraordinary chapter in history—was it, too, marked by events?

The Swiss do not like it to be said, but the Confederation did not suffer from the war.

Switzerland was bombed on a few occasions, accidentally: Bürglen in October, 1941, Basle and Zürich in December of the same year. These were mistakes made by the RAF. There were a small number of victims. In autumn, 1944, the American air force also accidentally bombed the railway station at Delémont, the Solothurn-Moutiers train and the Basle-Zürich express, near Pratteln. Mougins was bombed. On February 22, 1945, eleven raids on Stein am Rhein and Ruf killed eighteen Swiss and wounded fifty. On March 4 it was Zürich's turn. These were all the result of aerial attacks on objectives situated near the frontier—their calculations were a few miles off.

Contrary to what has sometimes been claimed, Switzerland was never seriously short of food—far from it. The most it ever suffered was a temporary rationing of various foodstuffs.

During the war Switzerland performed a number of services

that supported its popular image. Parcels sent from the Confederation did much to alleviate the distress of prisoners of war. Between November, 1940, and December, 1942, Switzerland gave a three-month holiday to 21,365 children from France, Belgium and Yugoslavia.

But one cannot forget that the same Switzerland turned away thousands of Jewish children, who ended their lives in gas chambers.

"We took in a hundred thousand of them," it is often said. It should be explained that out of the 100,000 refugees accepted by the Confederation between 1933 and 1945, there were exactly 21,944 Jews. To conclude this painful chapter in Switzerland's history, we feel we cannot do better than borrow the words of the Dutch government. In 1952, in a report on the attitude of Switzerland toward the Netherlands, it wrote:

"We should both thank Switzerland and refrain from doing so . . ."

It should not be forgotten either that Switzerland gave invaluable help to the enemies of Nazism. Was the role of Switzerland an indispensable one in the defeat of Hitler?

If it is true that the secret services contribute more to victory on the battlefield than do the generals, then, without doubt, Switzerland had a rightful share in the victory of 1945. Without Switzerland and the hospitality her government gave to Rudolf Roessler's anti-Nazi resistance network, the war might well have ended differently.

This affair was undoubtedly also responsible for the final collapse of the myth of Swiss neutrality. In its place a new image of the Confederation had emerged, that of a country sharing, like every other country, in the glory and the horror of the world's great upheavals. Contrary to what has often been said, history has not deserted Switzerland.

BIBLIOGRAPHY

Abshagen, K. H.: *Canaris.*
Anet, Daniel: *Carnets d'un soldat en campagne.*
Andree, Georges: *L'Armée allemande.*
Barbey, Bernard: *P.C. du Général.*
Béguin, Pierre: *Le Balcon sur l'Europe.*
Carell, Paul: *Opération Barbarossa.*
Delhorbe, Florian: *La Raison d'être de la Suisse.*
Diesbach, Maximilien Francois de: *Vérité sur la Suisse.*
Dulles, Allen: *The Craft of Intelligence.*
Feldmann, Marius: *La Suisse face à la 4e année de guerre.*
Feuille fédérale: *Rapport sur les activités anti-démocratiques exercées par des Suisses et des étrangers durant la guerre.*
——— *Réponse au rapport du général Guisan sur le service actif.*
Foote, Alexander: *Handbook for Spies.*
Gafner, Capt. Raymond: *Le général Guisan et la guerre.*
Groussard, Georges: *Service secret 1939-1945.*
Guderian, Heinz: *Errinerungen eines Soldaten.*
Guisan, Henri: *Rapport à l'Assemblée Fédérale sur le service actif.*
Hagen, Walter: *Die geheime Front.*
Hermes, R. A.: *Die Kriegshauptplütze.*
Heusinger, Adolf: *Befehl im Widerstreit.*
Hossbach, Friedrich: *Zwischen Wehrmacht und Hitler.*
Jaquillard, Col.: *La Chasse aux espions en Suisse.*
Kimche, Jon: *Un général suisse contre Hitler.*
Lederrey, Ernest: "Importance stratégique de la Suisse," *Revue Militaire Suisse.*

Ludwig, Carl: *Rapport sur la politique pratiquée par la Suisse à l'égard des Réfugiés pendant la guerre.*

Martelli, George: *Agent Extraordinary.*

Mourin, Maxime: *Les Complots contre Hitler.*

Petitfrere, Ray: *La Mystique de la croix gammée.*

Rougemont, Denis (de): *Mission ou démission de la Suisse.*

Sayers, Michael, and Kahn, A. E.: *The Great Conspiracy: The Secret War against Soviet Russia.*

Schellenberg, Walter: *The Labyrinth.*

Shirer, William L.: *The Rise and Fall of the Third Reich.*

Starcky, Georges: *L'Alsacien.*